A Great Place to Visit

A GREAT PLACE TO VISIT

a political novel of the 70s by
IRVING SCHIFFER

ARLINGTON HOUSE   *New Rochelle, N.Y.*

Library of Congress Catalog Card Number 72-77643

ISBN 0-87000-168-X

MANUFACTURED IN THE UNITED STATES OF AMERICA

To *Roslyn,*
the beautiful girl from Chester Avenue

LIST OF CHARACTERS

Progressive Party
    Lou Rabin, Chairman
    Max Pizensky, Vice-Chairman
    Addison Blum, Executive Secretary
    Russ Pryor, Assistant to the Executive Secretary
    Shelley Greenfield, City Assemblyman
    Earl Eaton, City Assemblyman
    Tom Valente, City Assemblyman
    Barbara Williams, District Leader
    Milt Holloway, Public Relations Director

Republican Party
    Casey Bohland, Mayor
    Warren Wilkerson, Governor
    Ron Corbett, candidate for reelection as United States Senator
    Mike Eberly, Corbett's Campaign Manager
    Walter Johnson, candidate for reelection as State Attorney-General

Democratic Party
    David Ornstein, candidate for Governor
    Fred O'Brian, Ornstein's Campaign Manager
    Ezekiel Carter, candidate for Lieutenant-Governor
    Henry Simmons, candidate for United States Senator
    Ted Michaelowitz, candidate for State Attorney-General
    Sylvia Lazarus, candidate for Congress
    Sam Waldman, incumbent Congressman
    Randy Payton Jones, incumbent Congressman
    Luella North, incumbent Congresswoman
    Kevin Cameron, Senator from New England
    Tony Giachetti, defeated Mayoral candidate

Other
    Buzz Taylor, Freedom Party candidate for United States Senator
    Bernardo Rodriguez, Leader of Young People's Army
    Bill Sokolov, reporter for *The Ledger*
    Naida Slaughter, Commissioner of Human Affairs

A Great Place to Visit

ONE

THE big city was stunned that night to learn that the Progressive Party had incredibly, single-handedly, elected a mayor. Reelected him, actually, inasmuch as he was an incumbent who had been beaten in the Republican primary, rejected by his own. It was like a fable—what the Progressives had done—a lesson in giant killing. The party had only ninety thousand enrollees in the entire state, about sixty thousand of them in the counties of the big city. Yet on the jubilant second floor of the Carling Hotel, where the Mayor had his campaign headquarters, the newscasters of different channels, seen on a handful of television sets blaring simultaneously, were now excitedly predicting that the vote on Column D for Casey Bohland would exceed seven-hundred-thousand, scoring a sweeping victory over the candidates of both major parties.

Alice, the Mayor's patrician wife, was clapping her hands, half crying in her happiness. As he embraced her and the children while cameramen crowded about, the youthful Mayor remarked to himself that all of this had been far more difficult for her than for any of them. There were many moments when he was low in spirit, sometimes in despair, but it had been a deeper wound for her. She had walked the streets with him once and heard the people revile him, and certainly seen the same on television many times, and it had done something to her. "Nigger lover," they had cried and "You bum." Actually she'd heard and seen very little of what had happened. But it had been enough. As for his own reaction, he'd learned to take it, even the moments of violence; he'd developed the technique of walking among them like Jesus (or so he thought), tall and cheek-turning. But Alice had been traumatized in a way that only those who loved her and loved her generosity of spirit could understand.

The stinging in his own eyes as he held her was not so much the knowledge of personal vindication as it was a surge of gratitude that the vote of the people had vindicated *them* in Alice's eyes, that she would learn again to trust them. It was true that for such a vindication victory had been necessary; and for victory the Progressives were the prime ingredients—they and their extraordinary leader, Lou Rabin.

Now, where was Lou? How like him to be seated in a corner of one of the rooms, quietly analyzing the neighborhood and the ethnic breakdown of the votes, while everybody else was leaping about. The handsome Mayor left his family and strode through the rooms of the floor-wide hotel suite that had served as campaign headquarters for the past many months. The reporters scurried after him. "Rabin," they cried, picking up the Mayor's query. "Has anybody seen Lou Rabin?"

They found the bespectacled man seated before a portable television set, a highball glass on the small table before him. legs crossed, pencil and scratch pad in hand. Seeing the Mayor enter, he stood up to shake his hand as the reporters respectfully hung back.

Those who had heard of Lou Rabin as a soft-spoken man of seventy-four, said to equate politics with chess, those who were inclined therefore to envision him as a wizened old Jew hunched over a copy of the Talmud, were sometimes shocked and thrilled when they first encountered his soldierlike glare from on high. He was a tall man, as near to the ceiling as the Mayor, straight and imperious, haughty in the backward tilt of his head. When he turned stiffly to gaze through his thick eyeglasses, one had the feeling of being surveyed by a two-headed periscope. His appearance was so disconcerting and commanding, in fact, that it was difficult for those who did not know him well to understand that beneath his political fierceness and wily intelligence, and beneath his haughty mien, he was a sentimentalist —and a typical 1930 unionist in so many ways, one of a breed that was almost extinct.

The reporters watched the two men standing there, shaking hands, the chairman of the Progressive Party and the Mayor. The two men said not a word, just looked at each other and smiled. They stood, hands clasped, for so long in this wordless state that the others in the room who had not risen at first started to get up from their seats as though drawn by the emotion in the air. Then the two men were nodding, each knowing what the other was thinking, and Rabin said it: "Next year Jerusalem." The Mayor threw back his head with laughter. The reporters joined in. Rabin was enjoying himself. He held up his hands.

"All right, Casey, so you're in for a second term. Now I ask you, who's going to be credited with this miracle, you or me?"

Mayor Bohland grinned. "You, Lou. It's your miracle."

"Ah, then the press will say I'm a political genius."

The press and media men were all smiles and ears. Casey played to them good-humoredly, with the artistry of long practice. "They already say that, Lou. Don't you, boys? No, we'll have to think up some new appellations."

"Master tactician?" asked the old man. "Supreme strategist?"

"No, that's been said too often."

"How about mayor-maker?"

Casey made a face. "No, they used that long ago, after you showed Venable how to win by fighting the machine. He got the Democratic nomination because of you, everybody knows that. And they used it when you stood beside me the first time I ran. No, it'll have to be something else," he teased.

One of the reporters leaned forward. "Mr. Mayor, how about president-maker?"

Lou pointed his finger appreciatively at the young man from A.P.

"That's not bad, Tim. I kind of like the sound of that." He tilted his head and became more serious. "All right, Casey, I'll take a little piece of the credit for the miracle, that we beat both major parties. But you've got to promise me that you'll never cease to be the stuff that miracles are made of. They said you made mistakes in your first administration, and you had the bigness to admit it publicly, but no one can ever say you had your heart in the wrong place. No strategist or mayor-maker would ever desert a man whose heart was truly in the right place."

Bohland bowed his head slightly. "Thank you, Lou."

There was more to thank this old man for than the reporters could ever understand or would ever bother to remember, thought the Mayor. Four years ago, when he had first run for the big job, an unknown, a Republican Congressman, the backing of Lou Rabin had given him the stamp of liberal approval he'd needed, but it had also caused an intraparty battle that almost resulted in the wrecking of the Progressive Party. Running against Casey was a Democrat who had all the right credentials of liberalism. It was this man that the president of the party's most important member union insisted on backing. After all, the argument went, the party had traditionally endorsed Democrats; why change now? The union chief warned Rabin that if they switched their allegiance to a Republican, no matter how progressive and promising he was, he would quit the organization, take his union membership and other unions with him, and virtually leave the party bankrupt. For in all truth, contributions from his union and those unions allied with him were all that kept the party solvent.

But Lou Rabin refused to bend. He pressed for his party's endorsement of the young Ivy League Republican, prevailed, and regretfully watched several of the big unions walk out, never to return.

Indeed it looked like the end of the Progressives. Lou had barely managed to hold it together with glue and matchsticks since that time. If it weren't for the man's fund-raising talents and Casey's help once he took office, the party might have been too impoverished to continue. Casey had helped by giving patronage, big and small city jobs, to members of the party who could then trickle in occasional contributions. Apparently it wasn't much but it paid the rent and the staff and enabled the gallant party four years later to make history, to beat the Republicans and the Democrats, and, for the first time, to elect a mayor on its own line. It accomplished this at a time, moreover, when the state, the city and the country—having already chosen a Republican president—were going into a period of bitterness, racism and conservatism. This year the Progressives' counterpart, the Freedom Party, had supported the Republican, a decidedly conservative type who had bested Casey in the primary. The Democrats, in turn, after a wild primary featuring some reasonably good men and some publicity-hungry writers who split up the liberal vote, threw their nomination to their most conservative member, an Italian who relied on the law-and-order motif. As Lou Rabin was saying now, "There simply was no one for the decent progressive people to vote for except our candidate . . ."

"And that," said the Mayor, smiling at the reporters, "sounds like my cue to move on. Why don't you boys talk to Lou awhile. Let me go shake a few hands and we'll get together in about half an hour."

They turned in a body towards Lou Rabin, who held up a finger to silence them as he listened to the election analyst on television.

"Three of our assemblymen," he said contentedly. "It looks definitely as if three of our city assemblymen have come in on Casey's coattails."

"Do you mind if we quote you on that expression?" asked the A.P. man.

Lou shrugged. "Why should I mind? It's the truth. You don't imagine Casey got in on *their* coattails. No, let's put it this way—it's been a reciprocal blessing. His own party repudiated him and only we stood beside him when he was down on his knees. We didn't just give him a line for the people to vote on, we gave him an organization, we gave him workers with spirit. But I have to admit that he gave us something far more precious: his youth, his sincerity, his faith, a new reason for believing in old principles, and, yes, his coattails.

"You know," the old man continued, "in Casey's first administration he was certainly honest and concerned, eager to do the decent thing, especially for the poor in our city. But in my opinion he was still a boy. Now he's no longer a boy, he's a mensh. That doesn't mean he's merely become more political and pragmatic, although I hope he has, but what I really mean is that his human qualities have deepened. I think now he's going to be a very darling and innovative Mayor."

"And make more enemies?" someone suggested.

Lou smiled. "Yes. I may have to call him up sometimes and say, 'Casey, be nice, be nice.' I hope he'll listen to me."

"Is it true, Mr. Rabin, that the Mayor consults you on all important appointments?"

"Yes, we consult," said Lou. "If you're really asking whether there's patronage, whether the Progressives are given city jobs, the answer is why not. We have good men who happen to be Progressives. Our percentage in city government is very small compared to the Democrats and Republicans, but we're a small party. We feel that if we have good men or women we'd want them to serve in government. What kind of party would we be otherwise . . . always preaching good government but unwilling to work to achieve our ends? Yes, we have some Progressives in city jobs. We're very proud that they want to serve."

An older reporter stepped forward. "One of those men is a deputy mayor. Now you'll probably have other top men in city government. Your party is becoming more and more powerful. In your twenty-three years of existence, you've provided the margin of victory for innumerable legislators, some mayors and a governor or two, even a couple of presidents. I mean, you've given some presidential aspirants the margin in this state that enabled them to win the national race. Now you've single-handedly elected a Mayor and your vote is real major league. Wouldn't you agree that you're becoming almost as powerful as the major parties?"

Lou Rabin held up his hand in a cautionary gesture. "No, that's not true. It would be misleading for any of you to say that. We have merely supported a great Mayor, and the tremendous vote we seem to be getting on our line this year may never happen again. Next year in the governor's race, and in the year after that, and after that again, we can expect to have our ordinary vote of a few hundred thousand. We don't pretend to power. We are a minor party, a small group of citizens, and we try to influence the major parties to put up good candidates that we can endorse in good conscience."

"Off the cuff, Mr. Rabin, how do you do it?" asked a young radio man.

"Do what?"

"Always manage to pick the winners."

Lou said thoughtfully, "I don't always pick winners. Not by any stretch of the imagination. Check back on the political history of this state and you'll see.

"But apparently I get credit for whatever I do," he went on. "It reminds me of that man in the Old West who charged a dollar to predict the sex of any unborn child just by looking into a pregnant woman's eyes. He even gave a guarantee; if he guessed wrong, he would later return the dollar. Naturally he was right half the time, so he made a fortune.

"Well, I'm also in that lucky position. Everyone seems to have arranged it so that I can't lose. Oh, I lose elections—I've lost most of them. But even when I do, you news people shake your heads in wonder and say I *purposely* lost it, that all I wanted to do was pull votes away from so-and-so, or to get the Republican elected because of some secret arrangement, or to prove that I hold the balance of power, or to get even with somebody. According to your tribe, whenever I lose, I win."

They smiled at the truth of his remarks and gloried in his uncharacteristic willingness to chat with them. Lou rarely gave interviews of any sort. He preferred not to be the spokesman for the party, certainly not on radio or television. One reason for this was that he still retained some of his Russian-Jewish accent—he had come to the United States when he was thirteen—and he had never considered himself charismatic with young and non-Jewish audiences.

His thoughts, in fact, had been wandering in that direction during the talk with the reporters . . . thinking about the Jewish vote as it was already apparent in the voting-district patterns, and he was ashamed. It was true that overall in the city, in Lou's opinion, decency had prevailed over the law-and-order appeal of the other two candidates. The voter had delivered himself from his baser self and in his final vote had said he wanted to give the blacks a break and try again to solve the urban problems. By voting for a man who refused to despair, they said they refused to despair . . .

But not all. His trained eye could glance at the district figures on the boards behind the television announcers and he could see the new Italian conservative strength, and he could see that the Jewish people in his city were beginning to desert liberalism. The backlash against the ghetto demands was quite apparent—the backlashinsky, he privately called it, as it applied to his people. Of course he had been forewarned; he'd heard the complaints that the Mayor cared only about the blacks and Puerto Ricans, that the Mayor appeased and bought off the blacks with jobs and money and cared not a whit for the Jews. Yes, he was ashamed.

"But we won anyway, didn't we?" he said aloud. The reporters looked at him in puzzlement. "Gentlemen, I think I have to leave now," he announced. "The Progressive Party is holding its own little victory celebration at the Norwich Hotel and they're probably waiting for me now."

He found the Mayor and his wife and told them he was leaving. "Listen, Casey, try to drop over to the Norwich later, just for a few minutes. It'll mean a lot to our people there."

"I will, Lou, I promise. After the speech and all that. But the timing will depend on when Giachetti makes his concession speech. Meanwhile let me call my chauffeur and have him drive you there."

"No, I'll walk. It's only about four blocks crosstown."

Alice shook her head with concern. "Casey, you can't let him walk in these streets at night. Please, Lou, we'll worry about you."

"Good!" said Lou. "And just to make sure I arrived safely, you'll come over later with Casey to see if I'm alive, right?"

"We'll be there. But why must you walk?"

The Progressive chairman shrugged. "I like to walk. And now I've got to worry about my next election problem, which is the gubernatorial. So I've got some thinking to do."

She wagged her head. "More thinking? Oh-oh, I'd hate to be the other guys . . ."

Those bastards. Those Democratic bastards, Lou Rabin intoned under his breath, scowling as he walked slowly and dignifiedly crosstown. Those New England Dem bastards, those upstate bastards. They were really out to screw him next year. They were treating the Progressive Party like shit, he thought. Not even once had anybody from that camp conferred with him about all that gubernatorial maneuvering, not even a telephone call!

Oh, he knew what was going on, he knew their strategy sure enough. It was clear to him months ago when the Dems appointed Jimmy Coleman as the boss of all the city's county leaders. Coleman had always been a Cameron man and his role was evidently that of an advance man for the youngest and last remaining brother of that famous family. Rabin had only to wait a few more weeks to see more of the pattern, the emergence of the behind-the-scenes chess mover, Fred O'Brian, the debonair jet hopper from rarified New England territory who had married one of the Cameron sisters and now guarded the family fortunes, a man who was also—as very few people knew—a user of heroin.

They wanted to have this state in their pocket. The New England states weren't half enough for their grand scheme. In order to get the last handsome brother into the White House, the Cameron Clan wanted to guarantee this powerful state's delegation for him in the Democratic National Convention. To do this they had to control, to own, the governorship. And the man they intended to elect as governor by remote control, by Cameron magic, Cameron organization and Cameron money, was Mr. Ambassador himself.

It was no mystery for those who would see. The plan was definitely geared to Cameron's hopes at the Convention two years hence. So this year the concentrated efforts of the Dem leaders was not on the choice for senator but on who would sit in the State House. That's where the patronage was and from whence the delegate power for the following presidential year was going to flow.

Secret polls which were not by any means secret pointed out to the Dems that the only possible candidate who could beat the incumbent Republican Governor (with all his millions) was David

Ornstein, ex-ambassador to India and Russia, a man of extraordinary prestige. He was the one man who could unify the Dems, win the election, and give Cameron the big-state power base.

The important thing for quarterback O'Brian and his Clan was that Mr. Ambassador had to owe his election to them, so that Cameron could demand his support in the eventual presidential race. As for the Progressives, they knew damn well that the little party would eventually have to get behind Ornstein. His liberal credentials were flawless and the party couldn't get out of an endorsement if it tried. Counting on this Progressive bind, the Cameron men had evidently instructed Ornstein to wait until the party came to him hat and nomination in hand, so that Ornstein need never feel any sense of gratitude or obligation for having *asked* for the party's nomination. O'Brian understood all too well that the Progressives were thinking of Casey Bohland for president, not Cameron. So he wanted Ornstein to owe his political life to Cameron's group and owe nothing to the Progressive Party. When they succeeded in winning the state from the Republicans, therefore, it would be a Cameron state.

And that was why his old friend David Ornstein hadn't once contacted him in the past year.

Lou breathed deeply of the November coolness. It was going to be a very difficult time; a knotty problem indeed for the aging party leader. Could he teach David and the Dems a lesson? Could he resist the pro-Ornstein forces and sentiment within his own party and nominate someone else, an independent perhaps, a non-Democrat? What arguments could he marshal against Ornstein?

Most disturbing perhaps was David's sudden support from the Democratic machine boys, his obvious connection with certain county leaders among the Dems like Crawford of Bucking County and Imre of Kenmore County, the machine men Lou had always fought, ancient and avowed enemies of the Progressive Party. If they were promoting Ornstein, could his candidacy be healthy? But, more important, were they useful for another round as villains and bogey men? Could he scream "boss control" and succeed in pulling the ex-Ambassador off his pedestal? Could he convince his own party members not to choose Ornstein?

As for the rest of the rumored Democratic ticket for the statewide races, it appeared to be of a piece, all Cameron people, a speech writer and ex-aides of the famous brother who had been killed. The Progressive Party would certainly be pressured to support the entire ticket but would have no trouble evading at least some of the line-up . . . the United States senator spot perhaps and the state attorney general position too.

Lou Rabin quickened his step. It was evident as of now that the Cameron people planned to kick the Progressive Party into a supine position, shove a gubernatorial candidate down its throat without a by-your-leave and try to stuff down the whole ticket. But he would teach those out-of-staters a lesson they would never forget. He would shoot holes in their homogeneous ticket and somehow succeed, though he might have to endorse the man, in bringing David to heel.

Walking briskly now in the nippy autumn night, Lou reminded himself that the incumbent Governor, Warren Wilkerson, was going to be by no means easy to beat. He suspected that the millionaire Governor was running for at least one very important reason, to keep control of the state G.O.P., so that it could never, because of a leader-ship vacuum, fall into the hands of Casey Bohland, who was, after all, an enrolled Republican. Wilkerson hated Bohland with a passion that was rare even in the passionate world of politics. He would do anything to keep Casey from building a base from which he could launch a try at the White House.

The voting public was aware of few of these deeper motivations. They saw only the obvious, and about that they were so often wrong. The columnists were saying that he, Rabin, was playing the major role as power broker and that all the hopefuls were beating at his door. In all truth, some of the Dem hopefuls had been to see him up at the union office, asking for his promise of support. None had he rejected or discouraged; he felt he had no right to do so this early in the game. The amusing result was that even when he was cool to them, even after he'd explained that he had no right to commit the party as a whole to any candidate, those men reported to their Dem colleagues and to the press that his response had been a positive one. They had to do this. Otherwise they knew they'd stand little chance of receiving the Democratic nomination. In this state the Dems needed him. His party brought in a minimum of 250,000 votes for a statewide race, and the Dems simply could not beat the wealthy Governor without that margin. They had to have Progressive endorsement of their man.

But he was not the power broker the newsmen seemed to think he was. The reporters were apparently unaware that the real operator was an out-of-stater with a needle in his arm, and that the most likely candidate for governor, David Ornstein, hadn't even offered him the courtesy of a phone call.

Yes, he would have difficulties convincing his own party to resist the Cameron ticket—the glamor was still too strong—but the Cameron people would discover they'd made a mistake in taking him for granted. He would mess up their plans. If they lost all their power in the state because of this then he'd find no reason to weep. A unified and successful state Democratic Party was not, after all, to his advantage. If he could keep the Dems out of the hands of strong leadership, in fact, Casey could emerge as the only leader . . . a well-timed switchover from the Republican Party to the Dems. Why not?

In sight of the Norwich, Lou smiled broadly. The thought was amusing indeed that both the G.O.P. and Dem leaders in the state were privately frightened that Casey Bohland might step forward and take over their organizations. How right they were! Who could say where the local brand of charisma might lead?

As he entered the foyer ballroom of the Norwich, rented for the evening by the Progressives, his friends and party officials rose from their tables to greet and congratulate. He held on to Addison Blum's hand the longest. Ad, a slight man in his seventies with silky white hair that might have come from the skull of Thomas Edison, was the party's state secretary and one of his oldest friends.

"We survive, don't we, Ad," he said quietly. "Year after year we survive."

A smile twisted the party secretary's lips. Ad had a compulsive habit of tugging at and stroking his lips, as one would a beard or mustache; in the tension and excitement of election periods he would go at this furiously, so that for days after an election his mouth was puffed up. His smile was slightly grotesque but had its usual aging charm.

"Survive?" he questioned. "Lou, you must admit that this year we did more than survive. We elected a Mayor. No, I wouldn't just call that surviving. Oh, by the way, is Casey coming here?"

"Later. He promised. Now where are our Assemblymen-elect?" Lou turned as he spoke to face two men who stepped forward from the pressing crowd: Earl Eaton, a burly black man, and Tom Valente, slim and dapper. Both beamed as he shook their hands vigorously. His eyes brightened behind the thick eyeglasses. "Well, I see our black Assemblyman and our Italian. But where's our Jewish Assemblyman?"

They shrugged. Ad said gently, "He's not here yet, Lou." Then he smiled again. "No, I'm wrong. Speak of the ghost—there he is."

Entering the ballroom at that moment was a short, powerfully constructed man in his mid-thirties, swarthy in appearance, blue-eyed, rather strikingly handsome. Ad stepped forward grinning. "Well, finally, our Winnota County Chairman and our new Assemblyman!"

His hand was extended but Shelley Greenfield strode past him without taking it. He scowled at the old party secretary, whose face became pinched as he tried to retain his smile.

"Shelley," said Lou Rabin, taking a large soldierlike step forward, "where have you been? We were concerned about you."

The young man glared at him. "I'm not staying. Do you hear that?" His booming voice caused everyone nearby to turn and fall into silence. "I don't *want* your concern!" Greenfield was shouting, red-faced. "You should have shown some concern for the people in my county who worked like dogs for my election. Why weren't *they* invited to this elite?"—he looked from one face to another—"this special gathering?"

"Lower your voice," demanded Rabin.

"I will *not* lower my voice! I came here to tell you all what I think of you. Then I'm going back to *my* headquarters in *my* county where *my* people are waiting for me."

Addison Blum touched the younger man's arm. "Shelley, please let's step outside and discuss this. We couldn't invite everybody . . ."

The arm was rudely pulled away.

"I came here just to tell you what I think of this exclusive gathering," Shelley went on. "And on my way here, what the hell does the announcer say on my car radio? I hear Lou Rabin, our great leader, said that I got elected on the coattails of Casey Bohland. After all the work my people did!" He turned to the state chairman, whose face was a white mask. "What do you mean by saying that?"

Rabin was staring unblinkingly at the ranting man. He held his chin even higher than he usually did. Nervously, Ad Blum said, "But Shelley, you must be realistic. We've never before elected our own assemblymen. Without the Bohland sweep . . ."

"No! No! He rode in on *our* coattails. Remember that. We worked for him and we got him in. We don't owe him anything. He owes *us* his political life. So let's get that straight once and for all!"

Everyone was looking at him in shock and wonderment. With a final scornful glance at all of them, Greenfield walked swiftly out of the room.

In the silence, Lou Rabin nodded slowly to himself, a disgusted curl on his lips. Then he glanced down at the party secretary. "You know, Ad, I approve of that old expression 'round the bend' to denote the loss of sanity. It's like that when you cease to communicate. It's exactly as if a person has passed a turn in the road and is no longer in sight. There's an opaqueness . . ."

An emotional man, Ad was white with trembling rage. "How dare he speak to you like that! You recommended him for chairman of Winnota County in the first place, and it was your idea to give him a chance to run for city office. He was like your protege."

Rabin's response was hard. "Well, he's not my protege now."

"Incredible!" Ad looked at the others crowded about. "Would you believe us that we only suggested him for the assembly seat to please his ego? Of course he's a lawyer and a capable man, but whoever thought he'd win, for God's sake? It never even occurred to us." He turned to Eaton and Valente. "That's not true of you two, of course. We didn't expect you to win either but we're *pleased* you won— we're *ecstatic*. But Shelley—how *could* he behave like this? I could kick myself. It's not as though we didn't have better men to run, men we'd really like to see in office." He shook his head. "But we figured it all wrong. We ran some of our best men for the boro president spots."

"Bad strategy," Lou agreed sourly.

"But thank God we got two good Assemblymen out of it," Blum added tactfully, nodding in the direction of the elected men. "Oh, why did he have to ruin this night? We've received telegrams of congratulations from all over the country, even one from Ben Davidson, the executive director of the Liberal Party in New York." He withdrew the telegram from his pocket. "Here. It says, 'May you know the same joy we knew on the day we elected four Councilmen for the first time—Clingan, Taylor, Haber and Frankenberg. May your three Assemblymen do as much for good government as our elected officials have done. Best of luck.' Oh, damn that Shelley. Lou, why did he have to ruin this wonderful night?"

The party leader said nothing.

Tom Valente was quite distressed. "Lou, perhaps Shelley didn't mean to sound as—excited and angry as he did . . ."

"He meant it."

"Maybe he misunderstood. Didn't he realize we couldn't invite all the members of the party here? After all . . ."

"Nonsense," Rabin snapped. "He knew. He was looking for an excuse for a blowup. He's trouble, that's all. He's our big mistake. Ad, we made a terrible, terrible mistake this time."

"We'll talk to him, Lou."

"Sure. But it's not going to do us any good. He was looking for a fight, looking for an excuse, an issue. But you're right, we must try." The state chairman squared his shoulders. "So let's all forget him for tonight. It's a glorious night and let's keep it that way. Ad, haven't you got any schnaps for an old man?"

TWO

"I ask you, is there anything progressive about the Progressive Party? I don't think there is. Ah, I hear a shocked silence. This is not the victory speech you expected from a man who has just been elected to the City Assembly. This is not the kind of pep talk you expected from your County Chairman. Well, tell me something, do you want a pep talk or do you want a dose of the truth?"

"The truth!" responded a chorus of voices from the nearly one hundred celebrants at the crowded Winnota County headquarters, which was housed in a loft over a group of stores. At the podium, Shelley Greenfield smiled in agreement. He'd had several Scotches and he was feeling just right.

"First I want to thank you," he said, "for the work you did in getting me elected. And on your behalf I want to tell you what I did tonight. I went up to the Norwich Hotel where the leaders of our party are having an exclusive shindig of their own—to which I had been invited, by the way—and I told them what they could do with their exclusivity. I told them that *you* should have been invited, that *you* are the real Progressive Party, that *you* are the real workers. Then I walked out on them."

He waited for the applause. When it was done they fell into an eager silence. He didn't have to raise his voice.

"For almost twenty-three years now, our party has been the private playground of Lou Rabin and a bunch of his old cronies from the labor movement—the labor movement, I might add, of more than a generation ago.

"Now I ask you, what do these old men want? Are they concerned with the life and death issues of our time? Are they on fire over the injustices to the poor and the black and the young in our country? They are not!

"Then what are they concerned with? You know just as well as I do, except nobody's ever said it out in the open before. These old men who run our party are concerned with power, their power. Power and patronage. They don't give a damn about principles. They don't give a damn about being a force for good government. They don't give a damn about the poor and the black. That *used* to be what this party was all about, but they don't give a damn about those things any more. Does my impatience with these old men offend you? Then I'm sorry. But I'm just speaking the way I feel, and I think that's what you want—plain talk."

More approval came from the crowd. They wanted it said. Publicly. There had been enough private grumbling. Who the hell was that girl, the light-skinned colored girl? Yes, yes, an associate leader in one of the clubs. Barbara something. Gorgeous. Didn't have a man by her side, he noticed. Slim. Face like an angel. Must have white blood in her. And was she ever gazing at him!

"Goddammit!" he said, banging his fist on the table before him. "We're tired of belonging to a party where a few bosses or only one boss chooses our citywide and statewide and nationwide candidates. *We* want to chose our candidates. We don't want instructions, or what they call recommendations, from an Advisory Committee made up of a bunch of old farts. What is the Advisory Committee? It's a group of the chosen few in our party who hold secret meetings where they decide on the policies you and I are supposed to support—automatically—and the candidates we're supposed to endorse.

"Sure, we're allowed to help choose our candidates—*after* they've been announced to us by the big boys. Don't fool yourselves about who chose Casey Bohland the first time he ran for mayor on our ticket and this last time. He was chosen by Lou Rabin and his yesmen on the Advisory Committee. Let me ask you a question. Did you ever hear of this party *refusing* to choose the candidate who was recommended by the Advisory Committee?"

Cries of "no" and "never" rose from the Winnota County membership. Hey, who the hell was that redheaded fellow? He worked for Addison Blum at the party state office, didn't he? A spy in our midst?

"No, of course we never refused a candidate once the big boys gave him the nod. When the State Committee or the City Committee meets to designate a nominee it merely rubberstamps what Lou Rabin and his friends have already decided. Why does this happen? It happens because Lou Rabin *owns* the committee. Whatever the great genius decrees they have to abide by."

He said this scornfully, and the crowd smiled, caught up now in the spirit of the attack. The beautiful black girl who wasn't very black at all was wagging her head as if to say, "You've done it now, Greenfield." There was something quite intimate about her charade. He caught her eye and acknowledged the communication with a courtly nod.

"This year," he said emphatically, "this coming year, we're not just going to sit back and let Lou Rabin pick the candidates who are running for the offices of governor, lieutenant-governor, attorney general and senator.

"This year the job for all progressives, big P and little P, is to get that reactionary Governor out of the State House, once and for all. He's been in there eleven long years, and we've got to make this year his last. How are we going to get him out? Can we accomplish it by playing power games and withholding our support from the Democrats—the way we did four years ago?

"Make no mistake about it, my friends, *we* put that man back in the saddle four years ago, no one else did it, the Progressive Party did it. We did it because Lou Rabin had to prove to the Democrats that he was the big power in this state, that he could swing the vote any way he wanted. So he got us to put up an independent candidate and drew away over four-hundred-thousand votes from the Democrat. That did it. That was just enough to throw the election once again to the Republican.

"We are *not* going to let that happen this year. We are not going to let Rabin play power politics with our party—not ever again. We've got to examine the credentials of *all* the potential Democratic candidates and get behind one who believes most firmly in our ideals. No more power plays—to hell with that."

They were grinning from ear to ear now. The black girl was smiling also, but to herself. He remembered about her. She had been a schoolteacher . . . came from the South . . .

"We've got to demand from our leaders the right to meet with and interview all candidates for statewide office. No more secret meetings between candidates and Rabin. We're going to meet with candidates on the county level and the club level and find out if we like them. We don't care if Lou Rabin and Addison Blum and the rest of the doddering old men say we're not supposed to meet the candidates. We don't care if they forbid it. We're going to do it. The party membership from now on is going to have a voice in the making of all important political decisions!"

He had to wait for their loud applause to abate before continuing.

"So let me end my little talk tonight with this promise. We're serving notice on the state organization, my friends, that from this day on we've stopped grumbling among ourselves about what's wrong with the party. We're announcing publicly, as of this meeting, a reform movement within the Progressive Party.

"From now on we're in battle—against the old style of power politics and political bossism that is the trademark of Lou Rabin and his cronies. We've got to do to Lou Rabin what the Reform Democrats in New York City once did to Carmine DeSapio—take his power away. Let it start in our county and it will spread throughout the state. There are many, many Progressives in other counties who feel as we do and have been waiting for us to start the reform movement. Well, tonight it's started. Now let's all drink to that."

First things first. He wanted to nail the redhaired fellow before he had a chance to leave. As for the colored girl, she'd meant all her signals and received all of his and she followed to wait at his side while he lighted a cigar and spoke to the young man.

"You're on the state staff. An organizer, right?"

The interloper nodded, smiling. "Blum calls me assistant to the state secretary. That's a hell of a title, don't you think? Like I'm in training to sit on somebody's lap." He held out his hand. "My name is Russ Pryor, Mr. Greenfield."

Shelley took the hand. "What're you doing here?"

Showing some surprise at the challenge in the question, Russ Pryor asked one of his own. "Why, do you mind my being here?"

"That depends on why you're here."

"Well," Pryor said, allowing a grin to light his face, a rather practiced act of charm, "there's this cute girl named Evelyn—you know her, of course. She invited me to tonight's shindig. You couldn't expect me to turn down an invitation from a nice girl like her." His reddish brows shot up. "Is that a satisfactory explanation for you, Mr. Assemblyman?"

"It'll do. How long have you been working at the state office?"

"Two months, that's all."

"What assembly district do you live in?"

"Twenty-eighth."

"That's here in my county. Interesting. So you'll be organizing clubs against me, won't you?"

Pryor shrugged. "I was never told anything like that. I will be trying to organize more and more party members . . ."

"Do you mind if I ask you how you got the job?"

Pryor answered dutifully. "I was looking for a job and some guy I know knows Mr. Rabin and recommended me."

"Lou Rabin, eh?" Shelley smiled thinly at the girl. "Right from the top, aren't you? Are you going to give a report on my speech to Rabin?"

Russ Pryor held up both hands defensively. "Hey, keep me out of this, will you? In the first place, I work with Blum and I see very little of Rabin. He's always in his union office downtown. I'm sure your talk will get around without my help. In fact, I'd just as well you and everyone else forget that I was here tonight. I don't think Blum would like it."

"You mean he wouldn't like you being in the enemy camp."

Pryor nodded. "When I came here it was just to be with Evelyn. I didn't realize there was going to be a declaration of war. I shouldn't be involved in that."

Shelley murmured that he could appreciate that point of view. He felt more relaxed about the young man. "So you're not going to say anything to Blum about it . . . ?"

"I'd rather not be the one who—what's that saying about being the bearer of bad news?" Pryor held out his hand for a departing contact. "So it's been nice listening to you, Mr. Greenfield. But let's forget we ever met, shall we?"

Amused, Shelley returned the pressure of the handshake. "Listen, Russ, come down to see me in City Center after I move into office." He winked. "We'll both keep it secret. We'll never mention to anyone you were there to see me."

When he dismissed the young man, Shelley turned to the girl. She was holding a drink for herself and had a Scotch on the rocks handy for him.

"I watched what you were drinking before," she said, candidly, gazing at him with quiet eyes over her glass.

"You're Barbara . . ." he offered. "A teacher or something."

"I was. I don't teach any more. Politics is a fascinating game to you, isn't it? You want to corrupt that boy."

He thought for a moment. "Yes, you're right. I like to corrupt. And, yes, you're right again, it is a fascinating game. But not just for the challenge, mind you. I want to use politics for what it'll get me."

"Which is what, Shelley?"

"Power, I suppose." He downed his drink and looked at her to see if his answer had a desired effect. His technique was to be abrasive; it had gotten him everything so far. She hadn't changed her pleased expression. He screwed up his lips. "That's right, power to manipulate people."

She still didn't respond.

"You've got to understand," he went on relentlessly, "that I'm a natural-born son of a bitch. I want to control people."

She pouted. "You're trying to frighten me. Don't you want me to like you, you big bad man?"

"I most certainly do." His eyes moved over her shapeliness. "But I prefer to establish my own terms. That's part of my way of living. I have to let everyone know right away that I can't be changed and I can't be led around. It's necessary to do this right away, so there's no hard feelings later on."

"Certainly," she said, only half impressed.

"If you take an obstinate or difficult stand right at the start," he continued, "and you're more or less accepted on those terms, then as you relent somewhat—as you might—it's considered a sign of warming up, extending friendship. That's a reasonably workable formula, don't you think?"

She wagged her head. "It's very complicated."

"Well, I'll admit that the beginning is difficult, since it's in the nature of a rebuff. And it's difficult to keep it up, especially in the presence of a beautiful woman. You feel that you want to relent almost immediately and not be so standoffish and challenging. Yet you can't. You don't. You remain hard. People come at you at great speed and—*wham*—they discover that they've slammed into a hunk of rock, and they bounce back."

"My, oh, my."

"I'm not finished. There they stay for awhile. When they decide to move in again, they circle around. They don't slam into that rock again. There's always a certain distance. That's the way it should be, Barbara."

"Ah, you used my name. I must be circling very close to Gibraltar by now. But that's my technique. I sneak up on a person. I'm like a cloud, a subjective cloud, and you know that a cloud can envelop a great big rock, even a mountain, before you can say Jackie Robinson."

"No defenses?" he asked casually. "Can anyone get into your cloud?"

She answered without hesitation. "Only special people. Very few catch my eye. I mean that literally. I live in a subjective haze and I don't even *see* most people. *My* thoughts, *my* plans, *my* needs. It never occurs to me to wonder if everyone else doesn't have a cloud around him the same way; and I do get annoyed, I certainly do, if I find that someone is trying to rub clouds with me or pierce my foggy defenses. For example, I can't stand anyone who comes on strong with charm and all that stuff. I find that very offensive."

"Obviously, I don't have much charm," he said, smiling thoughtfully.

She gazed at him. "No, you've got something else. I believe in goodness and good works—that's why I'm in the party—but my passions respond to something quite the opposite."

"And what is it they're responding to now?"

She shook her head. No, she certainly wasn't going to say his drive for power and the evil and hate that he exuded. These were the qualities she had seen before in him, somewhat from afar, though he'd tried to hide them up to now. These were the qualities that had seduced the others here tonight. As for herself, her very sexuality was somehow tied in with such a commitment, with such a conspiracy, with that very something devious that he possessed that was ready to spring. She was fascinated with the deviousness that she saw; she was eager to embrace its snaky erection which was so clearly in sight behind the self-righteous phrases of reform. Though she believed in goodness and good works, her soul was ready to spread its legs before his naked ambition.

Knowing herself so well, she looked at his swarthy handsomeness and tried to find the physical imperfections—wide pores, crooked teeth, anything—because she knew that soon any defects would disappear, that she would become blind to them, see him only in a haze of beauty. She would be captured by his beauty, as she was captured already, surrounded by it. This was the last time she would be able to find any physical ugliness in him, and even now she failed.

"What are we talking about?" she said faintly, lightly.

"I'll have to circulate right now. But not for long. Barbara, I want you to come home with me tonight."

She nodded slowly. "All right, I'll wait . . ."

Later, in the car as he drove to his apartment, he touched her shoulder, then stroked her, and she began to tremble and roll her head. He marveled at his fortune. He'd lucked in with a sick one, and he relished the sickees, who were like helpless small animals caught in the maelstrom of life's grand sexual design.

This one appeared to have no control whatever, and her helplessness had a wildly aphrodisiac effect. Oh, that excruciating feeling going through his belly and groin! He was going to give this one a ride into the land of bewilderment. No sleep for you, angel baby. What a sickee. She went for white men, that was clear. He hoped she didn't dislike black people, really black people, the way he did. Because he intended to use her to get his fellow assemblyman, Earl Eaton, in his corner. With three of their men elected to the City Assembly and only two Republicans, the Progressives became the minority party. They'd have to vote, the three of them, for choice of minority leader in the Assembly. He wanted that spot. He needed Eaton's vote.

THREE

IT'S time to call Rabin," said Fred O'Brian.

"Now?" Ornstein was taken by surprise. He glanced at his wife who was seated retiringly across the room in their hotel suite, knitting in the morning sunlight. She always knitted when she was disturbed, and O'Brian's very presence, David knew, was enough to bring forth the needles.

"I thought we were going to forego any contact with Rabin," he said almost petulantly to his manager.

"We're going to forgo what Lou Rabin would enjoy, and that's you begging and bargaining for his endorsement. It's that time of year, everybody asking everybody else to promise endorsements, but that's not what we want. All we want, all *you* want, I mean, is a social meeting. Say you want to meet him for dinner. Make it at seven tomorrow evening at the Eastern Squire Inn."

"In a restaurant? Public?" David could not avoid Ruth's frown of disapproval. "Lou would prefer a private meeting, I'm sure."

O'Brian nodded. "I'm sure too. But you make the arrangements and make it the Eastern. I'll arrange for a couple of reporters to see you there with him. Once you two have been seen together the newspeople will fill in the rest of the story. David, it's essential the impression goes out that you've got the Progressive endorsement sewed up. You'll get the designation from them anyway at their convention—they can't not choose a man like you—but the thing is that their convention is scheduled a week after the Democratic convention. To do us any good, we've got to make their show look like a foregone conclusion before our show goes on. This restaurant meeting will do it, believe me."

"But it's not the way I want to deal with Lou. No, Fred, that's using him . . ."

O'Brian didn't seem to be listening. "It's basic politics. Every time you strive for an effect you have to use something or somebody. Props are necessary. Rabin's a prop this time."

"He's an old friend."

"He's an obstacle," O'Brian insisted. "Listen, all I'm asking you to do is invite him to have dinner with you at a restaurant tomorrow night. If a reporter or two sees you there, that's not such a big thing. If the reporters want to make a big thing about your being together, then that's their business. Come on, Dave, this is basic stuff. It's got to be done. I have to get back home; I'll be flying out in half an hour. But call me later in the day to let me know if it's arranged." He stood up and nodded to Mrs. Ornstein. "Nice seeing you, Ruth. I'll hear from you, Ambassador."

Ornstein let out a long sigh and nodded several times, not looking once at his wife.

From the same hotel suite much later in the day, he called Lou Rabin at the union.

"David? Well, well, how are you, David?"

"Fine, Lou. How about dinner tomorrow night?"

"Certainly . . . I'm sure that can be worked out. Your place or mine?"

Ornstein hesitated. "Well, I thought I'd enjoy the Eastern Squire."

"No, no, David. I think we should talk privately."

"But the seafood there is incomparable."

"No, David, it'll be my place. I'll have Lottie prepare some of your favorite dishes, like the old days. Seven o'clock? Eight?"

"Seven," David said in despair.

"You know my address?"

"Yes, of course. If you're still living in the same building."

"Same place. You'd be amazed at how unchanged it is, still one of the nicest sections in the city. David, I'm happy you called. I can't tell you how glad I am." The voice seemed sincere. "See you tomorrow, old friend." Then he hung up.

Ornstein put down the receiver only to pick it up again and dial the out-of-state number at which he reached Fred O'Brian.

"Yeah, Dave, how'd it go?"

"It didn't. He insisted we have dinner up at his place."

O'Brian made a sound. "Forget that. That's bad news. No, that's gotta go. Once he gets you all softened up with his wife's Jewish food —I know how that guy operates. What's his wife's name?"

"Lottie."

"Wouldn't you know. Well, once Lottie fills up your belly with her old-fashioned cooking and a little sweet Jewish wine . . . forget it!"

"Well, what can I do?"

"What you'll do," said O'Brian, "is you'll call him tomorrow late in the day and say your schedule got all bollixed up and you have to meet someone for drinks at the Eastern at six. So could he meet you there for dinner because you'll have so little time, what with another appointment with somebody else at eight o'clock . . . ? We'll work out the exact story later . . ."

Ornstein finally agreed to this strategy, albeit unhappily, Ruth's disapproving gaze ever in his mind's eye. As planned, he waited until late in the afternoon of the next day to call Rabin, who was in conference and had to call back. By this time it was quite late.

"David, I got your message. What is it?"

Ornstein told him of the busy schedule and the necessity to remain in the area of the restaurant. Lou Rabin listened without interrupting. At the end of the explanation, he said drily, "Then I'm sorry, David. Perhaps we can have dinner some other time. Goodbye." He hung up.

O'Brian, when he was told what the old party leader had said, cursed Rabin roundly, then said with a sigh, "All right, we'll just have to fake it."

"What do you mean fake it?" Ornstein spoke worriedly into the telephone. "Fake what?"

"Leave it to me, Mr. Ambassador."

In the next morning's *Clarion*, the city's right-wing and Catholic-oriented tabloid, there was a long story on page three about how Lou Rabin and David Ornstein had met for dinner at a midtown restaurant and arranged a "deal" whereby the ex-Ambassador would be given the Progressive Party endorsement. Reliable sources, said the story, had alerted the *Clarion* to these events and the consummation of the deal.

Lou Rabin, when he read the story over breakfast, was furious. From his apartment he telephoned party headquarters and instructed Addison Blum and Milt Holloway, the party's public relations man, on the nature of the response that was to be made. He ordered a carefully worded press release sent out immediately to all news media in which he detailed a denial of having met with any Democratic candidate for governor or having made any deals with any persons—despite the inaccurate claims of a morning newspaper. Though they followed the instructions to the letter, Blum and Holloway, both professionals, knew the damage had been done. Rabin, when he arrived at his union office, instructed his secretary to turn away any calls from David Ornstein. There were two such frantic calls to which the secretary responded that Mr. Rabin was not in.

The Mayor strode out of his office with outstretched hand.

"Zeke! How are you?"

"Fine, Casey."

"Listen, come in. I've got only a few minutes, as I told you. There's a Board of Finance meeting waiting for me upstairs. But come in, sit down. Hey, give me the news. I hear you're going to try to get the nomination for lieutenant-governor."

State Senator Ezekiel Carter, a clean-cut young man with a thin mustache, smiled graciously. "Yes, I think I'll get it, Casey. There are a lot of black Democrats and people outside the party who want to see me run on a ticket with Ornstein. They'll turn that convention upside-down if I don't get endorsed by the delegates."

The Mayor was impressed. "Well, that's one way to get a designation, though I must admit I never thought of it."

Zeke was still smiling. "That's because you're not black."

"Okay. So, tell me fast," said the ever-surprising, ever-abrupt Mayor. "What can I do for you?"

"I know it's early to ask you this, but I want to know if we can count on your endorsement if we come through the convention all right— me and David."

"You mean right after the delegates endorse you?"

"Well, soon after. It'll help to cut down on our primary troubles."

Casey's eyes roamed the room as he stroked his long handsome jaw. "Don't ask me yet, Zeke. It's too early for me to make a decision. There're a million considerations."

"Like what? You don't intend supporting anyone else in the primaries, do you?"

"I doubt it. But it can prove to be a very ticklish situation. I wouldn't want to create any enemies in your party. Perhaps I'll just keep my mouth shut until you boys pick your candidates."

"All right. But afterwards, Casey, after the primaries, if it's me and David, will we get your endorsement then?" The black man's thin mustache curved with his grin. "You're certainly not going to get behind Wilkerson, are you?"

"Too early, Zeke. Too early. We'll have plenty of time to talk about all of this, don't worry."

"Right on." Ezekiel shifted in readiness to leave. "But I do want to remind you that David came out against his own party's nominee —Giachetti, I'm referring to—when he backed you for mayor last year. And in my small way I backed you up too, Casey."

It was the Mayor's turn to smile. "I'm not likely to forget those things, old friend." He stood up. "Now hit the road and let me get back to work. Oh, by the way, does David know you came to see me about this today?"

Zeke shook his head. "Hell, no. He doesn't even have the slightest idea at this point that he's going to have a black running mate."

"The Mayor's face creased with a wide grin. "Well, you can count on me to keep it a secret. So long, Zeke."

Outside, making his way down the marble steps of the City Center building, State Senator Carter suddenly started whistling. In his mind there was no doubt which way the Mayor would go. He recalled the day when he had been invited to an afternoon's festivities at the Governor's sumptuous family estate in the mountains.

It was just after the riots in the city that had proved so costly to the Governor's presidential ambitions, and all the black legislators and all the mayors of sizable cities in the state had been invited to bear witness to and share in the Governor's proclamation of a new school holiday for the state, the birthday of Martin Luther King.

It was a pleasant day to remember and a revealing one concerning the mutual feelings of Governor Wilkerson and Mayor Bohland. He remembered some of the remarks made while they were all taking the tour of the outside of the enormous rambling structure.

"Some day, fellas," the good-humored Governor said to the group, "our friend Casey here may have a home like this and a mansion in the state capital. Right, Casey?"

"It's possible." The Mayor looked about in mock appreciation. "One should never lose hope. After all, how many times have you tried to get a lease on that property in Washington? Three times, was it? But then again, money doesn't buy everything."

"Oh, it buys enough," said Wilkerson.

Inside, the visitors marveled at the Governor's famed collection of modern paintings.

"Do you know his work?" Warren asked Casey as they all stood before a large canvas of geometric blacks and greys.

Casey refused to be caught faking. "Never heard of him, whoever he is. Why doesn't he sign his name to his paintings?"

Wilkerson's brows shot up. "Because he knows that discriminating and knowledgeable people will recognize his work, that's why, Casey."

"I suppose I'm just not discriminating and knowledgeable."

"But you know what you like, right, Casey?"

"I know what I dislike."

Zeke Carter, standing alongside, wondered if they heard his involuntary gasp. He enjoyed the tour and the day thoroughly, and the next time he was near the Mayor, on the back lawn which overlooked a breathtaking view of the valley, he chose to say so. He added provocatively, "The Governor's certainly a great host, don't you think so?"

Casey looked across the valley and responded mildly, "That Gioconda smile, that charm and that hospitality. You press a button, it comes on, you press another button, it retires for the day."

"No, I think he's a sincere man," said Ezekiel, twisting the knife just a little.

"He's no man. He's an oil well. Do me a favor, Carter, stop talking about him. Let's enjoy the view. Any minute now we're going to have to go back in there and look at him again, so let's enjoy this while we can."

Zeke Carter, probable Democratic nominee for lieutenant-governor, hummed as he walked away from City Center and waved to hail a cab. No, there was nothing to worry about. The Mayor would most assuredly never endorse Governor Warren Wilkerson for a fourth term; Casey would be happy to come out for the Ornstein-Carter team. He wondered what Ornstein was up to these days. Zeke had already had a very pleasant meeting with Lou Rabin, an essential part of the winning formula, and he wondered if David had settled things in that quarter. Of course, he couldn't ask David that question; the Ambassador was liable to look at him and say, "Why, what's it to you?" Well, he would find out soon enough what it was to Zeke Carter.

Governor Wilkerson had come to his office in the city to meet with some local groups. People who would never come up to the State Capitol to see him and whose good will he wanted to earn. Now he paced up and down his carpeted private office, raised his left eyebrow, shrugged eloquently and waved his hand around in a few of his famous elaborate gestures. For a man of sixty he was remarkably energetic, mentally flexible too, and he simply couldn't understand Corbett's rigid attitude. He tilted his head at the young Senator and studied the round, rather good-looking face.

"Listen, Ron, I don't care what you do. But I just can't understand the philosophical—I mean your inability to readjust philosophically. Certainly you can see the way the wind is blowing in the state. And I've given you the scoop on my private polls. So why can't you move a little to the right in your position?"

"Because I can't," Ron Corbett said earnestly.

"But why can't you? You switched from right to left. You were a very conservative congressman, then you became a liberal senator; so why not move back the other way again?"

"No, I'm stuck. Don't you see that, Warren? How would it look if I shilly-shallied from one to the other? Even if I tried to do it gradually, it would smell."

The Governor appeared blank. "The funny thing about all of this, in my opinion, fella, is that I'm certain you don't believe that liberal line you're always dishing out."

"Hah! What about you?"

"Me? I do what I have to do. This is a liberal state and I'm by nature a compassionate man. So up to now I've been able to establish the correct balance."

"You think this is still a liberal state?"

Warren made a rubbery face. "I don't know. There's a swing to conservatism, but I don't know if it will necessarily be a permanent one. But I'm moving with it."

"Not out of conviction."

"What's conviction?"

Corbett was depressed. "It's something I'm beginning to wonder if I have either." He glanced up. "Warren, I hope I'm going to have some financial help the way I had last time . . ."

"Don't worry, fella, we'll work something out."

"And what about Washington? They don't exactly approve of me."

The Governor snorted. "Well, who the hell told you to attack the President?"

"I never attacked him," Ron said indignantly.

Wilkerson shrugged. "Well, you attack his policies and you vote against him on every issue. I don't know how you suddenly became such a goddam liberal anyway. Okay, Ron, I hope you can win with your liberals and I'll do what I can."

"But if Washington says no to me, where do you stand?"

The Governor nodded reassuringly. "We'll keep them out of our state business, don't worry. It's been nice seeing you. Give my regards to Debbie. You going home or to Washington?"

"Washington. But first I'm going to see Lou Rabin. As long as I'm in town."

"Well, as I said"—the handshake was firm and youthful—"good luck with your liberals. It's certainly going to be an interesting year."

The Senator took a taxi to Rabin's union office. He was flattered by the middle-aged secretary's obvious pleasure in meeting him and in ushering him through the door marked "President" behind which Lou greeted him warmly. Ron's ego was receptive to any show of affection these days.

"Frankly, Lou," he said, lighting his pipe and settling back in the chair with a sigh, "I'm going to need the Progressive endorsement this year."

"You deserve it. But of course I can't promise how the state delegate convention will vote."

"I know that. I'm just telling you that the administration in Washington will be out to get me. That's the buzz I hear in the back room. Buzz is the operative word. Buzz Taylor, the Freedom Party's likely candidate. Washington is going to go all out to replace me with someone who votes their way on the issues. So if you take me you'll be really stepping into a fight."

Lou Rabin nodded. "It was to be expected. You've been a bête noire to the President and I should think he'd feel obligated to get you out of the way. Well, that makes you a pal of ours."

"Thanks, Lou."

"I hope everyone else in the party feels as I do, Senator. I know I'll stand up for you . . ."

Representative Henry Simmons turned from Cousin Alfred to face his mother across the long dinner table and, as always, felt unbearably overwhelmed by her presence. She held back tonight as though wary of him; still he felt suffocated, enveloped by her. He wanted to leap across at her throat and squeeze the life out of that mound of flesh. Indeed there had been times in the past when he had broken out in sweat and trembling with the panic of knowing he could so readily kill her. God, he hoped she didn't find occasion to touch him tonight. The revulsion he experienced at her nearness was inexplicable; she was fat, but so were a lot of women he did not find repulsive. What was it about her that made him think of those grotesque paintings by Ivan Albright of fat women with dimpled and purple flesh, gangrenous lumps of humanity . . . ? He shook all of this out of his mind and smiled at her discomfort. Cousin Alfred was doing a great job on the old lady tonight.

"Aunt Lucille, I can't tell you how excited we were about the very *idea* that Hank here could actually become the Senator from this state. God, what a proud thing this will be for the family!"

Mrs. Simmons was ill at ease. "Alfred, it isn't . . . it hasn't . . ."

"And Hank, I want you to know," continued Al, lifting his coffee cup in a toast, "that I'm personally going to work in your campaign. I'm going to take time off from the store and get out there and pitch for you in any way you need me."

Henry nodded. "Thanks, Al."

"But Alfred, this is far too premature." Mrs. Simmons tried to laugh. "Don't you know how difficult it would be to get the Democratic nomination? Don't you realize . . ."

Cousin Benny waved her down from his end of the table. "Don't be modest now. You and all of us know that Hank is more qualified than the other men trying to get the nomination. They're just politi-cal hacks next to a real liberal like Hank. Why, with his record in Congress, it would be a shame, a real shame, and I mean it, if some other creep stole that nomination from under his nose. That ain't going to happen, Aunt Lucille, not if this family can help it . . ."

Cousin Milly piped up then. "This is going to be the most exciting year this family ever had. We've been boasting about Hank long before he went and became a congressman, even when he was a kid. He was always the leader, and now he's coming through the way we expected him to, and we got a right to be proud."

Henry watched his mother. She was literally stunned into silence. She couldn't believe in this family adulation of her son.

"Now listen, you people," Henry said in an almost tremulous voice, "This is damned nice of you, talking this way. Even if I can't make the race, even if I can't afford it . . ."

"What do you mean, can't afford it?" Benny asked indignantly. "Hell, we ain't a poor family. We'll pitch in."

Henry smiled sadly and shook his head. "No, Ben, you don't under-stand. To run a campaign—first a primary, then a regular campaign, the television costs and everything—well, I want to thank you for offering, buddy, but the kind of money I'm talking about . . ." He blew out his breath expressively.

"Well, Christ, you're not exactly starving." Milly was leaning half over the table to emphasize her point. "You're a lucky man. You got your mother and you got us. Listen, I'd be willing to pitch in what-ever I can afford. And your mother"—Milly turned to the bewildered woman—"is certainly not going to let you down."

Henry stared at his plate. "A man is reluctant to ask his mother," he whispered.

"That's ridiculous!" said Benny.

Alfred looked at Henry Simmons disapprovingly. "Pride's a stupid thing in a matter like this, Hank. Your mother, any mother, would give her eye teeth to see her son reach the Senate. Don't insult your mother and don't insult us by thinking that way."

Mrs. Simmons was still unable to speak.

Hank worked the conversation to another subject, the assorted children these cousins had brought into the world, their scholastic

FOUR

~~~~~~~~~~~~~~~~~~~~~~~~~~~~~~~~~~~~

"**O**NE of the reasons I appreciate you so much," he said, leaning back in the armchair as she kneeled naked before him, "is because you know your place. I mean that beautiful profile of yours pressed up against my cock. That's your place."

She pressed herself harder against him. "That's where I want to be, Shelley. These past few weeks . . . I never knew what it meant to be in love."

"Yes, you're winning me over." He grabbed her smooth black hair and turned her face to look into his. "A man would have to be completely insensitive not to marvel at the way a woman like you can love. The capacity to lose yourself, to bend to my expectations and requirements. It's as though you were made to my specifications."

Closing her eyes, Barbara kissed his erect member. "Just tell me . . . anything . . ."

"I guess it's just something a man isn't constituted to understand, but I won't fight it. After all, why should I marvel? It's the way of a man with a maid, and that's the way it's been down through the ages. But I marvel, just the way the poets down through the ages have always marveled. They must have all had deprived childhoods like me, which didn't prepare them for such privileged adulthoods. So they marveled. Do I make sense?"

"If you're saying you return some of my feeling for you . . ."

"A man cannot fail to be touched at least a little—that much I definitely return. Let me ask you a question. What about pride? That's the part a man can't understand. It's not important to you, is it? Pride, I mean."

"I don't think so."

He made a pained face. "You don't say to yourself, 'I mustn't let this man shit on me, I've got to shit on him first'?"

"No." She smiled like a cat. "I want you to shit on me. I want you to feel free to shit on me." She turned her head in his hands. "I know you can't understand. But if you've ever felt that your very existence offends nature, hurts nature . . ."

"What are you talking about?"

"It's not a religious thing," she explained quickly, earnestly. "It's nature, life, the fragile beauty and helplessness . . ."

"And you've offended it?"

She sighed heavily. "Oh, yes. And once you realize that you have a responsibility to all that is fragile and weak, to all the things and people you have hurt and might hurt in the future, then the only human thing to do is expose yourself so that you can be hurt." She laid her cheek against his knee in a tender gesture. "To expose yourself you have to trust someone. If I put my fate in your hands, if I let you take advantage of me, knowing you will—oh, I know you will—then I'm atoning. I want to tell nature or God and all the fragile, beautiful things that I can be trusted. This is the only way, Shelley . . ."

He stared ahead. He wondered if she were just dumb when it came to this stuff or if there wasn't a certain logic and sense . . . She must know, he thought, that he would use and manipulate her, and it was clear to him that she longed to be used and manipulated. He'd once asked himself whether there was any danger, psychic danger, in being a thoroughly calculating man, in using people while holding back from any deep commitment or self-involvement that served to confuse and foreshorten the view. Folklore, religion, literature and psychology all issued warnings; they all maintained that strength was weakness (and weakness strength), that wisdom was foolishness, that if one were not a fumbling, thumb-sucking idiot who saw teddy bears in the Rorschach test, one did not truly belong to the human race. Shelley had questioned his cool ambition at an early age and decided that the folklore was bullshit. The girl touched him, truly reached him in the oddest way, but he was going to use her nevertheless.

Later, she lay under his assault, arching in ecstacy, volition ebbing, giving herself to surrendering . . . losing herself, dissolving; she cried out that this was what she longed for, that she wanted to be used, violated; she wanted her autonomy taken, her liberty removed. She gave her body to him as no other woman had ever given of herself, reveling in her helplessness.

Twisting into her, he looked down at her and marveled at her submission and her passion and, over it all, at her beauty. The face was one of the loveliest he could ever remember seeing; and in contrast to the intelligent perfection of the face stared the young breasts—so *dumb*, expressionless and hurtable. He held them and squeezed and shoved himself into her until she gasped and rolled her dark eyes. Then he gripped her and soothed her, because she invariably cried, and he told her what had to be done.

She stared at him and shook her head.

"It's got to be done and you've got to help me," he said forcefully.

"But I don't know how . . ."

"You know damn well how to get a guy to like you. So either you help me or you don't." He held her off and looked at her directly. "You've got to decide something right here and now. Either we really have something for each other, either we've got a special feeling for each other, or we don't. I need you desperately to help in this matter."

"You can't want me to . . . oh, Shelley, how could I?"

"I'm depending on you. I've got to have this. *We've* got to have this. It's up, up, up for us. I can't not go up. I can't let it slip from me; otherwise I'm no good to you or to myself. You've got to make a choice about whether we go up together or sink down into nothingness like everyone else . . . until we hate each other."

She was silent for a moment, then she asked sullenly, "Where do you suggest I seduce him—at my place or his place?"

Shelley's expression was pained. "I didn't exactly say . . ."

"But that's what you meant."

"No, wait a minute!" He scowled and took the offensive away from her. "You're the one who brought in sex. I merely said get to talk to him, ask him to vote for me . . ."

"And get him to hand you the leadership on a silver platter. How did you intend that I would convince him of that. By some kind of sob story? Just to do me a favor? Oh, no, you meant put out, baby."

"I meant no such thing. You can convince him without . . . Do you think I would specifically ask you to do that. I merely said convince him."

"No," she said, "no . . ."

"You say you're a reform Democrat, Mrs. Lazarus?" Ad Blum smiled tentatively. He was not the kind of man who asked, "What can I do for you?" because that seemed too direct and rude. He merely sat behind his wide desk and blinked pleasantly at the raspy-voiced woman in the strange floppy hat, as he put his eyeglasses on and took them off again. His inquisitive expression had the desired effect.

"I wish to talk to Mr. Rabin," said Sylvia Lazarus.

Addison widened his eyes. "Mr. Rabin? He's not here. I thought you wanted to see me. That's what my secretary told me."

Mrs. Lazarus became irritable. "I'm seeing you because I was told I couldn't see Mr. Rabin. But I'm hoping you can arrange it for me."

"Perhaps I can be of some help. I mean, perhaps you can talk to me about . . ."

"Mr. Rabin. Only him."

Ad stretched out his hands. "Then we have nothing further to say, since he isn't here."

"Mr. Blum, I want the Progressive Party nomination for the 12th Congressional District. I want it so that my party will feel I'm the best choice for them because you're behind me. I want you to let them know in lots of little ways that you're behind me, that you want me and no one else, so that I can be effective in a primary against the old gentleman who has that seat now."

The executive secretary was astonished. "You intend to run in a primary against Representative Waldman? Mrs. Lazarus, I—I don't think I know who you are. Your name isn't familiar . . ."

"No, I haven't run before. I'm an attorney and this will be my first attempt at political office."

"But a congressional seat? That's a very important political position. That's in Winnota County, and of course when the County Executive Committee interviews the various candidates, you'll be accorded the same opportunity . . ."

"Mr. Blum, get me to Lou Rabin and don't give me that County Committee bullshit. You know that if he says the word, I'm in."

"What do you mean by that?" said the indignant Blum, shocked at the woman's vulgarity.

"All right, don't get uptight," she said. "I have to speak to Lou Rabin because I've got things to tell him that he'll be very interested in hearing about."

"Such as what, Mrs. Lazarus?"

"That's what I want to see him about."

"I understand. You wish to sell information of some sort."

The visitor winced. "If that's the way you want to say it, it's your privilege. But before you sneer at what I have to say, let Rabin hear it."

Ad Blum smiled slowly in his somewhat charming manner. "Such mystery! Such melodrama! Really, can't you tell me what it's about?"

"You can tell Mr. Rabin that things are being discussed by some very important people that concern you people intimately. I know something you folks don't know that you'd better know fast. Can you arrange a meeting for me?"

Blum nodded briefly. "The way you make it sound . . . Yes, I'm sure Mr. Rabin will see you."

FIVE

MAX Pizensky used to enjoy the long walks; he would stride through the city, recognized by many, perhaps the most famous labor leader in this part of the country. Now, at eighty, he walked with a bent and crablike gait and his hands and body trembled, and no one knew who he was, even in the streets of that section of the city he once ruled with his fiery rhetoric and union power. Yet, as reluctant to venture forth as he now was, he never missed an Advisory Committee meeting of the party. He arrived early at headquarters, settled into a seat in the conference room, shook hands with all the others as they came in, many of them as infirm as he. God, this was a joke! Did one ever see such a bunch of old derelicts? The average age of the committee must be seventy . . . retired union men like himself, ex-professors, a dean emeritus and a couple of scholarly authors among them. Two of them actually had to be helped to their seats; Dr. Caswell, for example, so weak he should never have left his bed.

But they wanted to be here, just as he did. They loved the party, they respected Lou Rabin profoundly; they usually voted any way Lou wanted them to vote and took great pleasure in supporting him. He had led the party brilliantly since the beginning and they saw no reason to resist his leadership. Would they go along with him this year if he did not choose David Ornstein as the gubernatorial candidate, Pizensky wondered. He had heard disturbing stories of bad feeling between the men . . . and then there was that crazy newspaper story and the denials by Lou that he had ever met David . . .

Finally they were all present, the eighteen old men, with Lou at the head of the table. He spoke softly and to the point.

"This will not be our last meeting on the subject," he told his friends, "but we must begin to formulate a ticket."

There was quick agreement on the Republican Senator, Ron Corbett, and on the black man running for Lieutenant-Governor. There was an argument, but final agreement with Rabin, on backing the incumbent Attorney General, Johnson, because of the support he had given Casey Bohland in the most recent election.

"As for our choice for Governor," Lou said to the group, "I'm inclined to favor an independent candidate this year, someone who runs on our line alone. There's at least one special reason why we may want to go it alone rather than support a major party candidate."

"We'll get a bigger vote," one of the men interjected.

Rabin nodded. "Exactly. Our history has shown that when we run an independent we get a larger vote on our line. And this year that's of prime importance because we'd like to win back from the Freedom Party the honor of being the state's third party instead of its fourth. As you all know, the gubernatorial vote determines who's in third place and who's in fourth place. When we ran an independent four years ago, we received almost 600,000 votes on our line. Unfortunately, the Freedom Party did better than we did, but this year we can reverse that, because their strong man's the senatorial candidate, not the gubernatorial. And we'll never get a high figure in our column if we merely endorse a Democrat, let's say. After all, people who like that candidate will more than likely vote for him in the Democratic column. We may have helped them decide on him by our advertising, but we don't necessarily benefit when it comes to numbers. So let's remember that consideration. We want our third line back from the Freedom Party. We stand a better chance of doing that if we go with our own candidate."

"Lou," said Max Pizensky, "let's get to the main problem. What is all this talk about independents when we have David?"

Rabin shook his head. "We don't have him. The Democrats have him."

"Well, I feel we must support him. You all know how I feel about David Ornstein . . ."

"No, tell us how you feel." Lou's face was stern.

Surprised at the sharpness in his friend's tone, Max spread out his arms. "There's only one thing to say. We must endorse him. David Ornstein is our spiritual brother. A great progressive, a great labor lawyer, a voice of liberalism throughout the world. I remember when he was the lawyer for my union. If it wasn't that he was an international figure, if he had lived in this state all these years, I'm sure he would be sitting as a member of our Advisory Committee, much as you and I. He's one of us, that's all. Of all the political figures we had to choose from over the years, David is certainly one of the most clear-cut choices."

Lou Rabin looked down at his hands. His lips were curled in distaste. They awaited his answer.

"So it would seem," he said, glancing from one lined face to another. "It would certainly seem that we should feel no hesitancy about an endorsement of our old friend David Ornstein. If you'd asked me a few months ago, I probably would have made the same plea for David as our esteemed colleague just did. But I am convinced"—Lou wagged his finger—"I am more and more convinced —that David is no longer his own man. Max, let me ask you: Has he contacted you since he came to the city?"

Pizensky, eyes downcast, shook his head.

"No—but he has contacted me," said Rabin. "And in case you don't quite understand what happened between us, let me explain from the beginning."

The men listened raptly to his recounting of the incident involving the restaurant and the false newspaper story.

"This has yet to be resolved," Lou Rabin concluded. "But we

cannot sit back and hope it will all turn out for the best; that we may be mistaken about the new David and his new friends. I am convinced that we should begin to look elsewhere for our candidate."

"Are you serious?" Max asked. "No, Lou, we have to iron things out with David. I'll call him . . ."

"I'd rather you didn't," Rabin said softly. "It's his place to come to us now. I'll make it difficult for him to come to us, but that he must do."

Pizensky waved his hand. "No, no, I'm going to call him. Lou, this cannot be a personal matter between you and David, no matter how personally you may be hurt by his actions. This is a party matter. I'm going to get to the bottom of this problem."

"Then do what you want," Lou said curtly. "Meanwhile I want to make the suggestion that we review the qualities of other candidates. I have an independent candidate in mind, a former district attorney. I'm speaking of Ken Grimes. We all know him as a trustworthy liberal and he can also supply us with an anti-crime image that doesn't hurt these days . . ."

At the end of the meeting, Lou remained glaring at the conference table, nodding briefly, stonily, as his friends filed by. When he looked up he was surprised to find all of them gone. That evening, still grim, he spoke with Lottie about the meeting, over dinner.

"You argued with Max?" she asked, distressed. Max was a special person to her; he had been with Lou, with both of them, in fact, since the beginning. Somehow this reminded her of how things had changed. She was reasonably philosophical about age because she was a fulfilled woman, busy with charity, organization work, happily married, the possessor of successful children and several healthy grandchildren. But she had a reverence for her husband and all that was her husband, which made her fearful of change for him, especially the threat of a loss of old friends. She always thought of Lou as a friendless man, even though he wasn't at all friendless, because she remembered him as a youth and remembered, too, what he had told her of his earliest years in the country.

Her husband had been born in Russia almost seventy-five years before. The son of a tailor who could barely manage a living in that hostile society, and who could promise even less to his son, Lou emigrated with a maiden aunt at the age of thirteen. In the bewildering American city where they came to settle, his first position in a leather goods factory frightened and depressed him. He was the newcomer, the greenhorn, naturally proud, naturally taciturn; the workers were unfriendly, and the hours were long and lonely. He could not be the buffoon, the butt of humor that his fellow workers, young and old, apparently thought he should be because of his foreign ways and difficulties with the language. He walked too straight; he felt a sense of mystery about himself. They resented this. And he resented them, in turn, because he could not abide to be known too easily, especially to be known as something small or humorous. He felt that these strangers did him an injustice in judging him by his clothes, his ungainly height, his thick eyeglasses and his accent, and he refused to pose as an inferior merely to placate them.

He refused to bend, to ask for friendship, to admit that he was a newcomer and that a boy needs friends. So he was lonely for a long while. When they declined to extend the hand of welcome, when they taunted, he was shocked at their rudeness. They should realize, after all, that a stranger in their midst needed kindness and welcome; they might resent a newcomer's alien presence, yet they should feel delight, too, in seeing their humdrum lives and workaday artifacts enhanced and sweetened by his freshness of appreciation.

At first he thought they were merely stupid and ignorant, even the Jewish immigrants; but then he understood that they were grim and afraid for their jobs, resenting all new workers, and that even among themselves there was too little joy and trust and solidarity. He worked long hours in the leather factory and went to school several nights a week to learn English and public speaking. He also learned about unions and was soon in secret conclave with others in his factory and in other factories, men and women of all nationalities and accents, who were proud and intelligent and fiery, one of whom was Max Pizensky; and now he had friends.

And another of these friends, a passionate Labor Zionist, was Lottie herself, a lovely woman whose auburn curls reached only as high as the knot in his tie; she became his wife before they were both eighteen years of age. She was at his side while he practiced speechmaking before a mirror; nursed him when he was beaten by the goons, the union-busters; and pridefully watched him become a spokesman for the workers, recording secretary of the union local when he was nineteen; vice-president of the international union at age twenty-three; then president of the union at thirty-seven, a tall austere, commanding man whose reputation was by no means confined to the city or to unionism. Yet she never ceased to marvel at his overriding humaneness, his gentleness as husband and father, and his fearsome morality in union affairs and in politics. For a man who loved Bach and scoffed at all romantic art, for a man who played chess with his friend Pizensky deep into the night and exalted intellect over emotion, he was remarkably indulgent with those who led with emotion—herself for example. Still, his enemies knew they were enemies, and those who betrayed him . . .

"Lou, I want you to be careful about David," she said later in the evening. "Don't be too hard on him."

"We'll see," he said shortly.

"And Max. No disagreement is worth hurting a friendship."

"We'll see, we'll see . . ."

The next day Max had dinner with his friend Ornstein and placed both of his squat hands, fingers outstretched, on the restaurant table-cloth in a gesture of openness. "Now, I've told you what Lou is thinking and I want to know what you're going to do about it."

David's tired face was intent. "Do you think he was bluffing?"

"Bluffing?" Pizensky felt helpless. "What are you talking about?"

"Max, you know him better than almost anybody. I want your honest opinion. Was he bluffing or was he really thinking of another candidate?"

The older man was suddenly angry. "The question is out of order. It is not a matter of whether Lou Rabin is bluffing or not. The question is, 'What goes with you, David?' Is this some kind of game you're playing? Here I am, in a restaurant with you. Am I supposed to wonder whether there are reporters here to see us together?"

"Don't be ridiculous!" Ornstein's face was red.

"*You* stop being ridiculous. We're not talking about bluffing and poker games. We're talking about you acting honorable with your friends."

"I've tried to call him, but he won't accept my calls. What do you want me to do?"

Max chuckled mirthlessly. "*I* don't want you to do anything. It's what *you* want to do that counts. Do you want our party's endorsement or not?"

"Of course I want it."

"Then do you want me to arrange the meeting—between you and Lou and a few of the rest of us?"

David suddenly reached across to touch his hand briefly. "Yes, I want that. Yes, thank you. You're a good friend. What do you think Lou will say?"

Max looked down at his food. "Again you want me to read his mind?"

"No, forget I asked that. I'm just nervous."

The meeting was arranged for an evening the following week at party headquarters. It would have been friendlier in one of their homes, but Lou Rabin was not in a friendly mood. He looked steadily at his old friend down the length of the conference table and disregarded the man David had brought with him, Fred O'Brian.

"David, I can't bring myself to overlook or forget what you tried to do to me."

"Lou, I ask you to forget that."

"Why did you do it?"

David Ornstein glanced at Addison Blum and Max Pizensky for help. "Can't a man make a mistake?"

"Of course," Addison said gently. "But we were hurt."

Rabin pointed a finger. "David, if you make the mistake of relying on the judgment of the group of political sharks you've surrounded yourself with it's never going to be any good. Which one of them called the *Clarion* and set up that news story?"

"Does it matter which one did it?" Ornstein asked, not looking at his manager.

"Yes, it matters. You should get rid of him. David, you've been a man of principle; you can't suddenly become a man of expediency. Be your own man."

"Lou, I have to depend on people because there's so much to do. There aren't enough hours in the day."

"Then if you must delegate authority to others, teach them principle. Don't let them teach *you*. I'm warning you, David, for your own good, your staff men will ruin you if you don't read the Ten Commandments to them—starting with integrity." Rabin pursed his lips as if experiencing an unpleasant taste. "David, we're old friends and I dislike being so blunt with you, but it is time for you to correct the upside-down relationship you've had with our party lately. You see, David—and you too, Mr. O'Brian—we're not supposed to ask you whether you want our nomination. You're supposed to ask us."

"Lou . . . Jesus Christ, this is terrible," said Ornstein. "What do you want me to do, beg you?"

The old man raised his brows. "Oh, isn't that what you're here for?"

Addison Blum made a tsking noise and shook his head worriedly. "No, no, I'm sure you didn't mean it that way, Lou . . ."

The beady eyes glared at the secretary. "Don't tell me what I mean and what I don't mean." He turned to O'Brian. "You've been trying to give the impression to the public at large that you have the Progressive backing all sewed up. Now I ask you, once and for all" —he pointed a long thin finger at the campaign manager—"whether you want to continue playing your little game or whether you want to make a formal bid for our support. If you don't want our support, if you're too proud to ask for it, there's the door."

O'Brian stared at him, white-faced, not a muscle moving. It was David who responded.

"Of course we want your support, Lou. This has been a terrible misunderstanding and I want to correct it right now."

"Fine. That's what I wanted to hear you say." Rabin handed Ornstein and O'Brian stapled sheaves of paper. "This is a six-page letter I've prepared for you David. I want you to write this letter to the Progressive Party, word for word; and when you do so I want you to release copies to the press at the same time. It's a long letter. Look it over, we'll wait. Take your time."

"You mean right now? Read it right now?" asked the astonished ex-Ambassador.

"Right now."

O'Brian was already reading grimly while Ornstein fumbled for his reading glasses, yet they finished the six pages at the same time. David removed his eyelgasses, held both sides of his face and closed his eyes. "The language . . ." he started to say.

"The language stays the same," Rabin replied shortly.

"Lou, it's such a direct appeal. It sounds as though I'm *imploring* you . . ."

"As I said before, you are."

"But the promises."

The chairman stretched out his hands helplessly. "Not so extraordinary, just good government. You promise to run an independent state administration if elected. You say you will seek the assistance and guidance of Democrats and Progressives, that your administration will dispense with politics as usual, that it will transcend purely Democratic party lines and will make use of the best men available in the state. You will, in fact, have a Democratic-Progressive coalition administration and an ethics committee of distinguished citizens from both parties to screen and pass on all job appointments and judicial appointments."

"My God!" O'Brian said under his breath.

"But Lou, that sounds like—" Ornstein held his white hair in his hands. "It sounds like I'm promising you patronage and power, that's all it says!"

It was Rabin's turn to remove his eyeglasses and rub his eyes. "I'm sorry if that upsets you," he said cooly. "But I'd much rather the public think such a thing about us than to imagine we're powerless —which is the impression you seem bent on creating up to now." Eyeglasses back in place, he squinted at the distressed candidate as through a telescope. "So when we receive the letter on your stationery, David, and see it quoted in the newspapers as well, then we'll consider endorsing you." He smiled briefly. "Is there anything else we have to discuss at this meeting?"

After the two visitors had gone, Max Pizensky remarked sadly, "He was humiliated. David was humiliated. I'm sorry I was here to see it."

Rabin shrugged. "We've all been humiliated at one time or another. Listen, when it's time for a man to eat crow, it's time for a man to eat crow."

SIX

^^^^^^^^^^^^^^^^^^^^^^^^^^^^^^^^^^^^

"WHAT I have to offer you, Mr. Rabin, is information," Sylvia Lazarus said directly. "I'm not exactly in the higher or innermost councils of the Democratic Party—I'm in the reform wing—but I've got a friend who is and who keeps shooting his mouth off to me because he thinks I'm the cat's meow. So if you give me your party's nomination, thereby giving me an edge in getting my own party's nod, and if you go to bat for me in a personal way, nobody's going to connect my sudden popularity with your sudden access to information you weren't supposed to have."

"Very interesting," Lou Rabin said. He'd investigated this woman with the ridiculous floppy hat, since she'd seen Ad Blum. She was a lawyer involved in civil rights work, a Black Panther and Republic of New Africa lover, a Commie from way back. A distasteful dish. "What kind of information are you referring to?"

"You might say it concerns the survival of the Progressive Party."

"That sounds like a very serious matter," he said. He wished she would leave soon so that he could get back to pressing union matters.

"It is, Mr. Rabin. But I need a definite guarantee from you that if I give you this information—and there will be some follow-up information as you need it—if what I give you is valuable, then I have to know I've got the Progressive nomination and that you'll go all out to see that I get the Democratic as well."

Lou shrugged, a brief spasm of his body. "Ridiculous," he said.

"What's ridiculous?"

"Everything you've said is ridiculous. Let's take one point at a time. I've heard it said that one of the things wrong with the Progressive Party is that we're the tail that wags the dog, that we really run the Democratic Party in this state. Well, it isn't true."

"It's true enough," she said. "As soon as someone's got the Progressive okay, the Dems know they might as well go along with the same candidate, because they're afraid their man couldn't make it on one line alone. Nobody ever forgets what you did to Ben Leary by running an independent for governor that year."

"Leary was a machine hack."

"Maybe so. But it proved that when you want to withhold your support you can kill any Democrat's chances. And if that's true, then the obverse is true, that when you give your favors you can put a Democrat into office."

Rabin looked at the woman under heavy lids. "Be that as it may, your second assumption—that I can guarantee you my own party's nomination—is a faulty one. Ad Blum tells me you're interested in the 12th Congressional seat. That's in Winnota County, and that means the Winnota County Executive Committee will interview all interested candidates and vote on the man or woman they think is best. The assumption that any party leader can circumvent this democratic process, which is part of the bylaws of our party, is not only a false assumption but a slander against me and the Progressive Party."

Mrs. Lazarus' look from under her hat was extremely unfriendly. "Mr. Rabin, please save your speeches for someone else. I have a very serious matter to discuss with you and we've got to be straight with each other. So let's get this one point cleared up. I know you have a democratic process in your party and all that crap, but if the reasons are pressing enough and your commitment is hard enough, then you'll tell your County Committee or the county chairman, or whoever it is, that I've got to have the party's designation and that's all there is to it. Now you and I can go no further in our discussion unless you concede right now that if my information is of real service to you then you can guarantee me the nod. That much I must have. So let's hear it."

He silently stroked his nose with his index finger, then nodded once. "Yes, let's go on. Assume that what you want done can be done. If what you have to tell me is so momentous that it could influence me, then the officers of the County Committee might also consider it a fair trade. Yes, let's go along on that assumption."

"That I can have your party's designation, you mean . . . ?"

"Yes."

"Okay. Here goes. They're going to try to legislate you out of business, Mr. Rabin. There are several State Assembly and State Senate leaders among the Democrats, and among the Republicans as well, who plan to present a bill that will effectively cripple minor parties in this state. Naturally I'm not referring to when the legislature convenes in a few weeks, but after the election, at the beginning of the following year. Meanwhile it's a hush-hush matter . . ."

The unblinking fierceness of the beady eyes made even the imperturbable Mrs. Lazarus uncomfortable as the tall man inquired gently, "What exactly is the nature of the proposed legislation?"

"It would prohibit a candidate from running on more than one line on the ballot. That means no one running on the Democratic or Republican lines can also receive Progressive or Freedom Party endorsement. Your party wouldn't be off the ballot, Mr. Rabin, but you'd have to run independents in every post. It would be the end for you."

The old man's eyes hadn't blinked once. He said briefly, unemotionally, "It's unconstitutional."

"They don't think so. They've kicked around that possibility and they've decided that it probably is not unconstitutional. I'm a lawyer myself and I've researched it somewhat and I wouldn't guarantee that you'd win the challenge in court."

After a significant silence, Rabin said one word. "Names."

Mrs. Lazarus withdrew a folded sheet of paper from her large handbag and offered it to the old man, who scanned it like an eagle without bending his head.

"There'll be more information coming as I learn about it," Sylvia Lazarus added. "And one thing more—the Governor's in on it."

The fierce look was on him again. "How can that be? He's making deals with the Freedom Party right now—that he'll go with their senatorial choice, Buzz Taylor, and knife Ron Corbett, if they'll restrain the campaign activities of their own gubernatorial candidate."

"That could be," said Mrs. Lazarus, although the arrangement hadn't been that obvious to her. "But it doesn't mean he can't double-cross the Freedom Party later. The word from the Republican contacts my friend has access to is that the Governor's been saying lately that splinter parties—that's what he calls you—are destructive and he wants you dead just as much as the Democrats do. So you've got all the big guns aimed at you this time."

"We will survive," said Rabin. "For one thing, when we interview candidates this year for the State Assembly and the State Senate we will exact a promise from each of them before we give our stamp of approval that they will never vote for a bill that would do damage to our party. I'm not sure all the promises will be kept, but I can assure you that after I have a conference with the leaders of the Freedom Party they will exact the same promises from their candidates. The two minor parties will have to be allies this year in a battle for survival, it seems. And there are other things I will do . . ."

Mrs. Lazarus wagged her head and snapped her fingers. "See, you've got it half-solved already. I've heard you're a chess player, Mr. Rabin. Now that you've been forewarned, you can plan your next ten moves in advance. I know you'll beat this thing."

Lou sat back and surveyed her coldly. "Your information has been very valuable. I'll fulfill my part of the bargain, don't worry." He wrote on a piece of note paper. "Here are my telephone numbers at the office and at home. Please call me with all new information."

Mrs. Lazarus stuffed the note into her handbag, stood up and smoothed her skirt over her ample hips. She said smugly, "It's been a pleasure talking to you, Mr. Rabin."

The Chairman of the Progressive Party nodded his head noncommittally.

Wilkerson had not seen the Mayor for many months, since before Casey's reelection, so he grasped the opportunity to speak to him here at the Catholic Charities fund-raising dinner, cocktails in hand, out of everyone's earshot. They greeted each other in friendly fashion, for appearances' sake.

"I never got a chance to congratulate you on the election," the Governor said heartily, coming on with his usual gusto.

Casey was cool. "Yes, I stayed up all night waiting for a message from you."

"You shouldn't do that. You need your beauty sleep. The story's going around, Casey, that you might decide not to run for president two years from now."

"That I might decide *not* to run? That's a switch."

Warren chuckled. "Switch and run, you mean. Seriously, Casey, I hear maybe you'll switch parties but you're going to hold off on the presidency. They say you'll be after the governorship by the time I finish my next term." He tilted his head at the Mayor. "I will have another term, you know that, don't you?"

Casey Bohland shrugged.

"Why, who could beat me?" the Governor wanted to know.

"The polls show Ornstein doing pretty well against you, as you must have heard. He could give you a race, if he runs."

"A formidable opponent," Wilkerson had to agree. "But I'll beat him. Before it's all over I'll pour enough money into it and I'll beat him." He smiled broadly. "What I'm thinking is that you, too, are counting on his being beaten. If and when I win again this year the Democrats are going to be in a desperate situation, being out of power so long in this state. They'll turn to you if they believe you can win."

"Mighty iffy, all of this," said Casey.

"No, nothing iffy about it at all. You're going to go for the presidency if it looks as though the Democrats need you there. Or else you'll try for my seat next time around. It's one or the other."

Suddenly the Mayor smiled. "I hope you're not offended that I would presume to your great office, Warren."

"No, no, my friend. I won't be here anyway, you know that. This next term will be my last, no matter what happens."

"You might even leave in the middle of it, right?"

The older man responded with a deep chuckle. "Now, now, don't start rumors, Casey. Some people are saying the President wants me in his cabinet, but that's just a lot of talk. The point is I won't be contesting you for the governorship at the time you're ready. Still, there are several good men in the state who will be."

"Yes, there's your adorable Lieutenant-Governor."

"Most certainly. A bit too much of a conservative for my taste but very well thought of. And we have some very strong men in the leadership of the State Senate and Assembly."

Casey nodded. "Well, thanks for all the advance casting. I knew all this before I came here."

Wilkerson laughed spontaneously. "Casey, I like your directness, I really do, fella. All right, I'll get to the point. Let's make a bargain. Now you know very well I'll have to give my support to any Republican who runs for governor when I retire from the job four years from now. But there's support and there's support. I can go all the way, help a man with my organization and my money, or I can merely give him token support. It depends on you."

"It does?"

"Yes, it depends on what you do this year. Casey, let me put this positively. I want you to come out in public support of me this year. I want you to—"

"Impossible."

"Why is it impossible?"

The younger man sighed heavily. "You know very well that during this last election in the city you supported my rival—"

"I had to, Casey. That was simple party protocol. But if you remember what I just said about there being all kinds of support, you'll realize that I only gave whatever lukewarm endorsement I *had* to give."

"True," said the mayor. "But when I was down and out, you'll remember, backed only by the Progressive Party, David Ornstein—a Democrat, mind you—came out to stand beside me, *against* his own party's candidate . . ."

"I know, I know."

"So I can't come against Ornstein, can I, Warren?"

The Governor leaned forward. "Okay, I'll concede the point. So I won't ask you to come out and say you're *for* me. No, Casey, all I want you to do this year is say *nothing*. Stay out of it altogether."

"I'll see."

"No, I want a promise from you. You remain silent this year and when you run for my job I'll do the same for you. I'll give your opponent only token support. Can I have your promise on that?"

"Even if my opponent is your present Lieutenant-Governor?"

"Certainly. His problems are not my affair."

"You're really quite sure I'm not going to try for the presidency, aren't you?"

Wilkerson shrugged his wide shoulders. "Nothing's certain, of course. But my guess is that the Democrats on the national scene have a few ambitious men of their own. I don't believe they're going to step aside for you. No, the script is going to be for you to switch to the Dems and support one of their men for president. Then they'll put you up for governor. After that—maybe four or eight years from that time—then they'll give you a crack at the big job."

Casey Bohland's face revealed no emotions and he offered no evaluation of the Governor's scenario. Wilkerson pressed his point.

"If you want me to remain lukewarm when you run, then you've got to remain lukewarm this year. Keep out of it. What do you say, Casey?"

The Mayor nodded decisively. "Okay, it's a deal."

"Nice talking to you," said Wilkerson, finishing his cocktail with a gulp and strolling off with a smile on his face.

She had become sensitive to Shelley's moods to an extraordinary degree. Every measure of response, whether in lovemaking or the most casual discussion, the slightest suggestion of reserve, became momentous and frightening. The possibility that he was cooling toward her was insufferable. She knew that she was making a classic mistake in her intense desire to own him, to leave not one corner of his emotional life uninvaded.

"I can't stand myself. I think I'm going crazy," she said one night, beginning to sob.

"What the hell brought this on?" he asked.

"You're sick of me, I can tell."

"Goddam right, I'm sick of you. Stop that bawling. Nobody cries in my bed."

She clung to him wrapping her slim legs around him.

"Shelley, I love you so much! Please forgive me. I know I'm acting bad."

"I forgive you." He wasn't smiling. He was cool.

"Is it Earl Eaton? Is that all you want me to do? Is that why you're mad?"

"Who's mad?" he said, his body unresponsive.

She kissed his chest and ran her tongue along his flat stomach, then moved up to whisper into his ear, "I'll go to Earl. I'll do that for you. Anything, Shelley. Say you love me . . ." She felt his penis becoming hard and hot in her fingers and moved down to lay her cheek against it worshipfully, then rolled aside.

"If I go with Earl," she said tremulously, "will you be seeing other girls. I mean while I'm . . ."

He was puzzled by her question. "Of course, I'll see other girls. What the hell do you think I'm going to do, become a monk?"

Her face was stricken pale.

"Would that make the difference?" he asked. "If I don't see any other broads?"

"Please," she said softly. "I couldn't bear thinking of you with someone else. I can do it with him, I promise. I'll do whatever you want. But you promise me . . ." He was mildly surprised to see how the tears had streaked her cheeks.

"Okay!" he said. "If that's what it takes. No girls. I won't look at another broad."

SEVEN

IT was late afternoon. Addison Blum sat at his desk, puzzled and disconcerted because it was not immediately apparent what was bothering him. Lately his memory . . . it was the oddest thing, these extended periods of blankness, frightening otherworldliness . . . Then . . . yes . . . he remembered what was nagging at him and shifted uncomfortably in his worn swivel chair. Perhaps Jesse Nelson had misunderstood. He had explained to Jesse that his help was needed in the Winnota situation, but Jesse had said—what had he actually said?—that he really didn't have the time and *didn't want to get too involved in the political problems* . . .

Addison Blum scratched his nose and worried his lip, then slapped his hand on the desk to register his decision. He telephoned Nelson at the city department where the man worked. "Jesse, there's something I want to talk to you about. Can you drop into my office after work, say about five-thirty?" Nelson said he was busy, but Blum insisted. "It's *very* important, Jesse, and it'll take just a few minutes of your time . . ."

When Nelson, a heavy-set black man, arrived, Blum sat across from him with a strained and annoyed smile and said, "Jesse, when I asked you yesterday about making yourself more available to our Winnota organization, you said you couldn't find time to help and"—Blum shook his head as though in disbelief, half-chuckling—"and you indicated you didn't want to get involved in what you called the political problems." He spread out his hands. "Now, Jesse, we're all involved in the political problems. We can't help it. As for time"—Blum looked about the room as though to find some—"well, do you think *I* have enough time for all I do? I wish there were forty-eight hours in every day . . ."

Nelson was squirming visibly. "Yes, I know how many hours you work, Mr. Blum, but I have three kids and—"

"My wife said to me only the other day," Ad Blum broke in, "that I seem to be working harder and putting in more hours, over this Winnota thing especially, as I get older. Aren't there any good Winnota County members to take some of the load off my shoulders, she wanted to know. Now, Jesse, the party went to a lot of trouble to get you your city job—Water Resources, isn't it?—and there's always the problem what with the city budget constantly being cut and people being laid off that we have to keep fighting and fighting to make sure you're not hurt by any of the cuts."

Nelson, eyes downcast, was beginning to whine. "But I work with the party, Mr. Blum. I give money at the dinners and breakfasts; I donate; I vote any way you want when it comes to membership voting . . ."

Blum shook his head. "No, no, that's not enough. Jesse, you know what a small party we are. Compared with the major parties, we have no funds to speak of, just enough to pay the rent and the staff. We don't have a big army of volunteer workers. We all have to pitch in. Let me explain. You have a car, don't you?"

The big man nodded unhappily.

"Fine, fine. Now when we call a meeting, many people can't come because they have no means of transportation or are afraid to be out at night at bus stops. Jesse, that's where we need your help. Not only in your own assembly district clubs, but in others as well. Do you like sports?"

"Sure, I like sports, Mr. Blum."

"Well, then look at it this way. What kind of football team could you have if the men running with the ball didn't have linemen to help them and protect them with interference and so on?"

Nelson let out his breath. "Yeah, I can help a little bit with my car . . ."

"And talking to people, too," the older man offered. "You'll be given some names of new enrollees that we never got around to contacting in your area and nearby districts. I want you to make an effort to telephone them and invite them to our meetings and offer to pick them up. I'll send you a list and I want you to check off those you spoke to . . ."

When Jesse Nelson left, Blum spent the rest of the afternoon on the telephone with the key men in city government who handled patronage. The executive secretary was concerned with people, the manipulation thereof. That meant getting them into city jobs, helping to promote them once they were there; that meant getting them to pay their dues in the form of financial contributions at certain times of the year, voting the right way in political matters within the party, attending and speaking at club and countywide meetings; it meant wheedling and subtly threatening, pressuring and exploiting. The old man was tireless at this. He was also the best public speaker in the party. He could step up to a rostrum, unprepared, and deliver a resounding speech of cliches and half-truths and never falter in his sincerity or appearance of sincerity. During a speech he could work himself up into red-faced anger when actually he felt no anger at all. His talent was always in demand. On the calender pad before him was a record of forthcoming obligations: a Sunday morning breakfast forum in one county where he and a district attorney would speak about drugs; a Tuesday evening forum in another county where he and a housing expert would speak on the housing shortage; a testimonial dinner in a famous restaurant where he would sing the praises of a newly appointed judge . . .

In private discussion, too, he was capable of saying what would make other men wince if they had to say it. He could speak of a political antagonist and say, "It's not a matter of political compromise or expediency. There can be no compromise. It's a matter of good versus evil, principle versus personal gain." He could say this to sophisticated men and women and feel no shame or doubt that he was being believed. He was a man of extraordinary diligence and intelligence and charm; he was a man loved by everyone until they learned to hate him. It was said his wife and children—two of whom had reached high achievement in other fields—hated him also. But this was untrue. He was so devoted to his job that they might have had cause to feel rancor, but it was not the case. His wife, who worked for the city in a patronage job, often called him during the day to worry him about how he overworked and to try to arrange their hours so that they could spend more time together. She was approaching seventy and nearly as energetic as he. She called this afternoon to ask him to meet her for dinner.

"Come on, Ad, we'll have some Chinese food. You've got a meeting with the Law Committee at seven, don't you? So get a good meal under your belt. I'll pick you up at six."

He resisted, saying he would be far too busy. In the end, though, she coaxed him into agreement. He was eager to see her, to hear her prattle about her day's events. She was a good wife, a sour old woman to others, but still sprightly in his eyes. He'd been remarkably lucky in his marriage; no other woman would have put up with him.

After her call, he felt reluctant to work. He told his secretary outside he was not to be disturbed and placed the *Do Not Disturb* sign on his doorknob. Back at his desk, he reached for the hidden bottle of gin, had one shot, then put his head on the desk to nap.

He had an odd dream, probably due to Helen's call. He dreamed he was being served dinner by his mother and he told her that he had gotten a new job, that he was going to be an employment agency. She corrected him: "You mean you're going to work *in* an employment agency." He answered, "No, I *am* an employment agency!"

He woke up in a peevish mood, called Russ Pryor into his office and spoke at droning length about organizational problems and needs.

". . . and if people ask you questions, you should be prepared to answer, Russ. Always be prepared. There are some within our own party who say that democracy is lacking." He rubbed his eyes. "Oh, you'll hear no end of the complaints. You know about the upstate dissidents and of course Winnota County—"

"Yes, I know, Mr. Blum."

"You do?" The old man nodded sleepily at the redhaired youngster.

Pryor inhaled deeply. He'd been carrying around a ridiculous sense of guilt about having met Shelley Greenfield, a lingering sense of shock that anyone could have spoken so contemptuously (he had almost applied the word "sacrilegiously") of Mr. Rabin, a lingering fear, too, that perhaps some of those who had seen him with Greenfield had long ago repeated it to Blum, who in turn was waiting for Russ to say something. The whole thing was ridiculous. What he must explain was that the meeting was accidental, that he had not at the time realized where Greenfield stood on party matters or that there was any such thing as party disloyalty . . .

"Mr. Blum, there's something I want to mention. It's been on my mind . . ."

Addison Blum was staring at him with a look of horror. Pryor moved back in his chair, then looked over his shoulder to find some explanation for the older man's transfixed expression. Blum's lips were working.

"Did Lou—did Mr. Rabin send you?"

"What?" said the frightened young man.

Blum's face was screwed up. "Oh, this is terrible!"

Pryor rose from his seat, shaking his head in puzzlement.

"How could you do this?" Blum screeched. "Sometimes I'm forgetful, but to send you—"

"Mr. Blum, please—what is it? What are you talking about?"

Suddenly the old man stiffened and stood to face him. He glanced down at his desk as if searching suspiciously for an object, then narrowed his eyes as he looked up again.

"Nothing, nothing," he said shortly, containing himself. "Yes, we'll talk again . . . I've got a lot of work to do."

Russ nodded. "Yes, of course," he said, edging away from the desk. As he left the office he felt a tingling sensation along his spine as though expecting that something was going to be thrown at him to speed his departure.

When he closed the door of Addison Blum's office behind him, Russ stood against it for a moment, enjoying suddenly the sensation of discovery, of secret knowledge. Excited, he could not remain in the office another moment; he decided to rush down the elevator, to sit somewhere over a cup of steaming coffee and savor a knowledge, he was sure, that others did not possess, about what was happening to the old man.

In the street, his mind filled with the thought of Shelley Greenfield. No, he wasn't going to call Shelley; he wasn't going to tell anyone. He knew vaguely which side was the right side to be on in the circumstances, but none of them needed to know why he was ready to join them. It was as though Shelley were standing next to him, beckoning him. Now he felt ashamed that he had thought of rushing down for a cup of coffee. Scotch, that's what Shelley would order. How in God's name could he have thought of coffee?

EIGHT

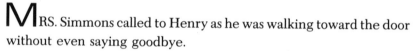

MRS. Simmons called to Henry as he was walking toward the door without even saying goodbye.

"Please sit a while and have lunch with me. You have no time these days to spend talking to your old mother."

"You're right," he said, entering the dining room. "It's time for a long session with mother. But don't make it too long."

She didn't quite know how to interpret his cavalier response; she decided not to react.

"I remember when you were younger." She smiled as he helped himself to a sweet roll, "You used to help me in investment matters . . ."

He shrugged. "I always had a good head for those things. But you have advisers for all that."

"It was more fun talking things over with you. Oh, how I wish you weren't so intent on being a great man. Then you'd be able to spend more more time just being a person. I think you're too ambitious, Henry."

"Too ambitious?" he repeated.

"Yes. Why not be just an ordinary lawyer. You're not really cut out for such a big job, Henry. In all your time in Congress you've only brought out one piece of legislation, and that wasn't very—"

"Oh?" He was beginning to lose control. It was time to go. "Don't worry mother, it's going to work out just as we planned. It'll work out fine."

"I'm sure, dear, but . . ."

"I couldn't do this without you, you know that, mother."

"Henry, you're not going to start asking me for money, are you?"

Surprised, he turned on her. "Who the hell said anything about money? You called me in here, I didn't call you."

"Don't get angry, please. I haven't the heart to argue any more. I'm feeling a little under the weather today as it is."

He became solicitous. "Then don't eat too much. And after lunch, why don't you go upstairs and take a nap? You know, I think you worry too much about money. Put that out of your mind. There's no need for us to talk about that ever again."

"Henry," she said, "I think you should know what I really think."

"Yes?" he said warily.

"I have to admit it. I'm still not sure about giving you all the money I promised. What guarantees do we have—"

"Guarantees?" Suddenly he was shouting. "You want guarantees about politics? All right, I'll give you guarantees. I'll deliver. I'll show you that I can't lose. All right, once and for all. You wait, I'll show you guarantees . . ."

Earl Eaton had never been to Greenfield's law office before and he was not impressed. It was housed in an old office building, near the courthouses, that contained dozens of small-time operators like Shelley, and the blond receptionist was as shoddy as the building itself.

Shelley let him into his private office, closed the door, invited him to sit down, and seated himself behind the desk.

"Okay, Earl, we're alone. Let's talk."

The black man made no effort at friendliness. "I've been instructed to vote for you for minority leader," he said. "I'm sure you know who gave me those instructions. But it isn't going to be that easy. I don't come across that easily."

"Oh?" Shelley leaned back comfortably. "Is there something else you want?'

"Plenty of things. Let's start with whether or not you'd be the right leader for the three of us."

Shelley's eyes widened. "I'm the *only* leader. Neither of you two guys are lawyers, you don't really know the first thing about legislation, drafting bills . . . Come on, Eaton, don't kid me. You'd be scared shitless to be the spokesman for the party in the Assembly. You don't want to be leader. You don't even know if you can carry off the greatness that's already been thrust upon you. So don't bullshit me."

Eaton was sour. "You're too damn smart for your own good."

"Fucking right, I am. And I'm sure you realize Valente's not the one for the job."

"I don't know. I wouldn't sell that man short."

"He's a putz and you know it. Come off it, Eaton."

The black man was visibly unhappy with the way the conversation was going.

"For a man who wants something," he said, "you sure don't know how to be tactful, do you, Greenfield?"

"You want tact? No, you wouldn't be here talking to me if you hadn't already made up your mind. If you weren't going to vote for me, all you had to do is not vote for me. But here you are trying to justify a bargain you made in bed. What's the matter with you, Eaton? Can't you be honest with yourself?"

Earl expanded his rather massive chest. "You wouldn't understand. I have a sense of responsibility—"

"You're full of shit, Eaton. You've just got a stiff prick for that beautiful girl."

For a moment it looked as if he would leap to his feet. He breathed deeply, then shook his head. "That's not it at all. I'm a black man. When I get power, when a black man gets elected, it's a responsibility. It's too big a responsibility just to throw away—" His voice dropped. "How can *you* understand what it means to be a black politician?"

Shelley laughed. "You think I don't understand? Oh, I understand all too well. I know exactly how you feel. A black politician feels a great sense of obligation to serve his people."

"Well, maybe you do understand, but—"

Shelley flicked his hand in a pointing gesture. "It's *you* who doesn't understand, Earl, my friend. You haven't looked behind the meaning of your dedication and seen the racism that's hiding there. You feel the way all black politicians feel, that they must do everything they can to forward the cause of the blacks. They also feel that the white politicians should do everything possible to serve the cause of the blacks. It reminds me of that old Russian saying—'What's mine is mine, what's yours is negotiable.' Now what would you think, Earl, if I felt a burning sense of obligation to serve the whites? Or only the Jews? How would you react if all the Italian politicians in the country got together to work out strategies so that more and more Italians could be elected to more and more offices? You'd scream racism, wouldn't you? But you blacks are doing that all the time—pushing for blacks on tickets, forming caucuses, always pushing for *your* legislation, *your* people. I tell you, friend, that looks like racism to me."

Eaton was remote and cool. "Like I said, for a guy who wants my vote . . ."

"Have I got it?"

Earl put his large hands on the desk. "Under one condition. She stays with me. This is no one-shot deal for me, man, I want her. She's not going back to you."

Shelley was thoughtful. "That's interesting. How does she feel about that kind of arrangement?"

"She'll get used to it. But that's our bargain, Greenfield, you and me. You don't take her back, even if she comes back."

"Okay," Shelley spread out his hands. "It's a deal."

Eaton's lips curled. "You know, there must be some good things about you for her to feel the way she does."

"Of course," Shelley said brightly, standing up in an act of dismissal, "but I can't very well exhibit them in a room without a bed, can I? Be seeing you, Assemblyman . . ."

After he showed Eaton out, he tweaked the blond secretary on the nose and said, "Honey, this is my day for deals. No screwing for you this afternoon; I'm saving myself. Get me the *Daily Ledger* on the phone. I want to talk to Bill Sokolov. He's a reporter."

Bill Sokolov was available for lunch; but sitting across from his sweating, buck-toothed countenance in the busy downtown restaurant was certainly not conducive to Shelley's appetite. He watched as Bill accepted the envelope and counted the money, his shrewd eyes narrowing.

"This amount every month?" asked the surprised reporter. "That's a nice piece of change."

"Yes, it is."

"I'll be glad to take it, but I have to warn you. I couldn't possible deliver whatever it is you think I should deliver."

Shelley held up his hand reassuringly. "I'm not going to ask you to deliver all the time. Look, Bill, this is an investment for me. It's worth every cent. Because when you can deliver I'll make it count. After all, what the hell have I got after four years on this job? I couldn't get reelected, not as a Progressive. That'll never happen again. So I've got to make my name during these years as a minority leader, if only as a personality."

Bill smiled. "Or as the new Lou Rabin of your party."

"You can't tell. Those boys are old. Somebody's got to step into the picture. Incidentally I want to be known as the titular head of the party. I want you to use that expression."

"Sounds sexy. I get it. My job is to help build up your image. Whatever small thing I can do for the money, Shelley . . ."

"You may think it's small. But when you consider that there are only a few newspapers left in the city and that yours is considered the one that carries the liberal viewpoint, it's a wise investment."

"My pleasure . . ." Sokolov grinned, showing a full set of teeth, while he pocketed the envelope.

Shortly after two in the afternoon, Russ Pryor came to Shelley's office. He had telephoned several days before to make the appointment. It seemed to Greenfield that everything—but really everything—was falling into place.

"How are the old farts up at headquarters?" Shelley asked, lighting a cigar.

"Rabin and Blum? They're fine. Did you ever think, Shelley, how remarkable it was that those two guys managed to make—to create this party, and how they've kept it going all these years?"

Shelley nodded distractedly. "It was touch and go plenty of times."

"But you don't see it as a remarkable thing?"

"No, not really."

"I see it that way. To win over enough enrollees from the two big parties . . . It's been one of the most successful third-party operations in the country."

"There was a need," Shelley said briefly, "and they filled it. I don't look at these things romantically."

"You're not giving them due credit. Think of the work, the organizing it must have taken!"

"All right, it took a lot of doing. What's your point?"

"Nothing. But it seems a shame to take it all away from them, that's all."

"Ah!" Shelley blew smoke toward the young man's face. "Now we come to it. You think I'm being a meanie to take it all away from them, is that it? Pryor, I'm going to lean over in one minute and bash your face in." He smiled. "But I won't. Because you wouldn't be here if you weren't ready to come in with me. What is it you need, kid, justification? You feeling sorry for the old boys?"

The orange-red eyebrows were drawn into a frown.

"Well, don't be," said Shelley. "After all, I always thought we were living in a democracy, where the rank and file have the right to disagree with the leaders, even to push them out. But it seems that people like you are so enamored of their leaders, so awed by their wisdom, so sure that only they have the right to lead . . ."

Pryor's expression was still one of puzzlement. "Is it simply that the rank and file are always going to push up and out? I mean, force the old leaders out for new ones?"

"You're goddam right!" Shelley leaned forward as if he were indeed going to carry out his physical threat. "That's life, boy!"

Pryor felt, once again, in a very physical way, that same fascination he had experienced the night of the Winnota County celebration when Shelley had been elected to the Assembly. He's a dangerous man, he thought, and he's so much stronger and surer than I am, not only about the party but about everything.

Now he felt invigorated, alive. Yes, he wanted to be part of this force; he was tired of himself, he wanted to come alive, have a purpose, a cause. Shelley seemed able to do that to him, bring him alive, whereas Rabin and Blum inspired him not at all. He realized that Shelley might be guilty of opportunism, political opportunism; but in his personal candidness there was a fierce honesty in the man which attracted. Rabin, on his part, was so secretive and dourly cynical in his relations with people, and his righteousness was far from attractive. The ambition of Greenfield held fascination if only because of its nakedness . . .

"Listen, Russ," Shelley said in a more friendly tone, "Nobody owns a political party. It belongs to the members. So you get that sentimental shit out of your head. They may have started it, but it's time to move over for youth. Don't you forget that. Hell, Russ, you'll never get anywhere in politics, and you'll never make any right decisions, if you've got soft ideas like that clouding your brain."

"It was just a thought."

"A lousy thought. It's a law of nature, boy, the young move up and the old move out. The sooner the better."

"I guess there's no arguing that."

"Sure, let them go to Florida and retire."

"Or let them drop dead."

"That's right—or let them drop dead. Remember that." Shelley stood up and began to pace the room. Then he stopped to point with his cigar. "Okay, so let's talk about you. You've got a little job with the state office. You're earning a little more money than you're used to. But I don't need to tell you it's a small job and there're bigger things to be had."

"Can you get me a better job?"

"Something can be arranged when we're ready. I'm in a good position."

"What kind of job?"

Shelley grimaced with annoyance. "I don't know right now. I suppose a legislative aide or even a deputy commissioner spot or something of that sort. We don't have to pin it down now."

"Yeah, but what do I do right now?"

"Work with me on reforming the party, that's all."

Russ Pryor smiled briefly. "But I'm on the state payroll, I'm with the very people you're working against. And I'm not really sure—"

"Sure you're sure. Look, Lou Rabin and Addison Blum are on their last legs one way or another. You know it too, or else you wouldn't be here talking to me. There's a goddam power vacuum in this party of ours a mile wide. I'm stepping into it. Anyone who wants to help me—well, I pay my debts."

Pryor nodded thoughtfully. "But what can I do to help you?"

"The first thing you do is continue what you've been doing all along, working with Blum. I want you to be my inside man. Report everything that's important to me and sabotage them any way you can. Every new group or person you bring into the party, tip me off so that I can get to them . . ."

At four-thirty, after an hour's drive to outer suburbia, Shelley arrived at the estate where he was to make his last deal of the day. There was a butler, which he should have expected, and an intimidating interior, which he should also have been prepared to shrug off.

But now and then he preferred to give vent to astonishment at riches, because there was something unreal and ridiculous about too much wealth, and he frankly stared at the rich decor, the subtly lighted carpet that seemed to purr, the immense Florentine paintings, curved windows, paneled walls, elaborate fireplace and the spiraling staircase peeking just beyond the bend of an archway, from which Simmons finally came out to greet him.

"You're not used to this kind of house, are you, Shelley?" Simmons said, shaking his guest's hand briefly.

Shelley glanced at a dazzling chandelier. "I didn't think *anybody* was used to it. Imagine growing up like this! How'd you stand it?"

"Fortitude. I want you to come in to meet my mother. There are also a couple of kids here. College boys. They're going to be volunteer workers—in Corbett's headquarters."

"Oh?"

"I'll keep them on a little weekly retainer." Simmons smiled. "You need someone on the inside to inform you of what the opposition is planning, don't you?"

"You're absolutely right, Hank. I've made arrangements like that myself up in various quarters and I can vouch for the plan's effectiveness. Listen, Hank, how come you want me to meet your mother? I've known guys who wanted me to meet their sisters, but mothers never."

Simmons stretched his neck uncomfortably, as if to free himself of his collar. "This is serious business, Shelley. My mother—well, she's in on all my operations. Hey, I'd better get in there and escort those kids out before you go in. They wouldn't want to be seen. So wait out here a sec, okay?"

"Of course. I understand." Shelley repressed a smile. What a jerk this guy was!

The college boys were ushered out by Hank, his arms around their shoulders, their eyes downcast as they went by Shelley. They seemed to be of the opinion that if they didn't look at him he wouldn't be able to see them.

Mother turned out to be a grand surprise, a sweet and pleasant looking fat woman; he had expected a son-dominating virago or at least Ethel Barrymore or Gladys Cooper. She extended a pudgy hand from her chair.

"Are you on a retainer too, Mr. Greenfield?" she inquired to her son's dismay.

Shelley nodded. "In a way, yes. I'll be getting a substantial hunk of change, but unfortunately not on a weekly basis."

She let out a long breath. "Henry's been bringing home all sorts of people who are going to help him win the primary and the election. Can you guarantee me that he's going to win?"

"*Mother!*" Simmons broke in, red-faced with anger. Shelley

merely tilted his head. "I guarantee only my end of it. I'm not selling the product, Mrs. Simmons, only my services."

"I like you," she said suddenly.

"That's because I like *you*, and my charm flows most freely under exactly these circumstances; mutual appreciation, I mean. Quite seriously, I believe your son will win the election. This is basically a Democratic state, Hank is a natural politician, he's got the best advertising agency working for him, loads of dough, and Ron Corbett is in real trouble even within his own party. Do you remember what happened in the Charlie Goodell-Dick Ottinger race in New York State? Well, Ron Corbett isn't the man Goodell was and your son is as good a man as Ottinger. At least I hope he is. The important thing, though, is that we don't have a tough opponent like Jim Buckley to beat out. I believe your son can make it. As for me, all I'm going to try to do is get him my party's nomination. I'm only a little cog in your smoothly oiled machine."

"An important cog!" Simmons said enthusiastically.

"I'm glad to have met you." The fat hand came out again.

"My immense pleasure," said Shelley.

NINE

CONGRESSWOMAN Luella North, a spindly black woman, listened to the pussyfooting chairman on the podium of the Democratic convention carry on about the Lieutenant-Governor nominations and felt an old and familiar mixture of rage and exhilaration. She knew what she was going to do in just about a minute and the thrill of her daring was like something sexual, leaving her weak even before she did it. All she had to do, she reminded herself, was whoop it up and whip it up the way she used to do in church, crazy hallelujah, and she would whip up this whitey audience just the way she wanted to see them.

The pussyfooting white bastard up there was actually bullshitting about the virtues of the many persons who had been mentioned in recent months as possible nominees for Lieutenant-Governor. Bullshitting a mile a minute, when everyone knew the word was in for Zeke. The black word was in. Fifty black leaders and legislators in the state had called a press conference just last week—while she was busy in Washington—and given out the warning that it had better be State Senator Ezekiel Carter for that Lieutenant-Governor spot or the Democratic Party could expect a general exodus of blacks from their ranks and their voting totals come Election Day. Jewboy Ornstein had picked up the ball the very next day and announced that his future candidacy for Governor was inextricably wedded to the candidacy of Zeke Carter for the second spot; they were a team. He was smart, Ornstein was, acting even before the convention, and acting as if he were Zeke's patron and champion, when in reality Zeke's position on the ballot was the only foregone conclusion of the day.

And now she would do the same. Pretend that the Democratic Party had not already been blackmailed into a decision before the party bosses could even begin their wheeling and dealing. Without a word, Congresswoman Luella North leaped from her honored seat in the front row, walked up to the podium, and yanked the microphone away from the astonished chairman.

"*Get off and let me speak!*" she raged at him.

"But Mrs. North . . ."

"*I want to speak!*" she screamed. "*Oh, my brothers and sisters! My fellow Democrats!*"

After that she was lost in ecstasy, tears rolling down her thin cheeks as she bellowed into the microphone.

"*This is a new era. Your old politics are dead, dead. You cannot overlook the black people any longer. If we blacks don't get represen-tation here today, you will not see a single black going into the voting booths to pull down a Democratic lever this year. This year the blacks will vote against you.*"

Through her tears she saw the shock in their eyes, the horror on Zeke's face in the front row, his mouthing of "NO, NO . . ." but nothing could stop her. She opened her mouth as wide as she could, so they could all register the niggerizing of her face, knowing how the screaming through her large, aggressive teeth could stir the whites to rage.

"*So this year, at this convention,*" she went on, "*there will be none of this shilly-shallying about who's going to be nominee of the party for Lieutenant-Governor of this state. This year it's going to be a*" *black man. This year it had better be a black man or you Democrats have had it. Zeke Carter is the man we want!"* Now she was screeching at the top of her lung power and the blacks in the audience were on their feet, cheering and applauding. *"If we don't get representation here today with the nomination of Zeke Carter,"* she said waving her arms, *"there will be social upheaval in the cities of this state . . . social upheaval that will make the riots of a few years ago look like play-acting . . ."*

When she was done there was applause, but far less than the reporters had anticipated; she'd certainly shaken up the hall, though. They looked for her while the chairman sheepishly remounted the podium and pounded for order from the distracted delegates, but they could find her nowhere.

The Congresswoman had managed to elude the reporters and make her way to the rear of the hall where she engaged Victor Longstreet, the upstate industrialist who was challenging David Ornstein, in private conversation.

"You're going to fight them, aren't you?" she asked, still breathing heavily. "You're going to go all out in the primary, aren't you?"

Longstreet was puzzled. "What are you talking about, Luella? You just about did me in up there. By sewing it all up for Zeke Carter you sewed it all up for Ornstein too. Don't you realize that? Carter already promised Ornstein he'd only run with him. They're a team."

Eyes shut, she wagged her head vigorously. "Don't be ridiculous. I didn't sew it up for Zeke Carter. That was all sewed up a week ago. I just tried to undo it today. Didn't you see me. I turned off half the white people in that audience out there. You'll be getting the benefit of that backlash from now until Primary Day."

"I don't understand."

"Listen; they were blackmailed into taking Zeke but they wouldn't admit it before. Now I shoved it in their faces and they have to admit it. And they won't like it."

He was dumbfounded, "But why, Luella? Why'd you do it?"

"Because I'm the most important black politician in this state and thats the way it's going to remain. I don't want that good-looking, lovable son of a bitch getting elected and moving me out of first place in the hearts of my people. I won't have it. I want you to win that primary, Vic, and I want you to do it with a white lieutenant-governor. If you need my help during the primary, I'll be there. I'll find an excuse to turn against Ornstein and come out for you."

Longstreet, still dumbfounded, managed a weak smile. "Great, great. Then I'll be calling on you."

She waved. "See you in church."

Shelley was intent and thoughtful as he spoke to those at the table. After county meetings some members liked to dawdle over coffee in the cafeteria next door; there was a group of eight tonight, including Russ Pryor who had joined them at the cafeteria. "If we could only get control of enough counties so that we could swing the delegates our way and get ourselves elected to the state chairmanship . . ."

"You mean *you* get elected to State Chairman," Russ Pryor clarified, smiling at his friend Evelyn.

The broad man breathed deeply and blinked as if coming out of a trance, "Sure, why not? We could really make this party hum."

"But you don't really care too much about the party—I mean the principles of the party. You don't really want to fight for progressive legislation." Russ cringed inwardly as he said this, for he expected an outburst of denial. Instead Shelley raised his brows and contemplated him for several seconds before saying calmly, "You've become critical, I see."

"No . . ." Pryor now wanted to retrace his steps. He'd been showing off for the girl and now he was sorry. "I just wanted us to be a little more honest with each other, that's all."

"You feel I've been dishonest with you?"

Pryor squirmed in despair. "Oh, I didn't mean it. It's just that— well, I don't always feel you're very strong on what you sometimes preach."

"I see." Greenfield leaned forward, his blue eyes intense. "Russ, boy, I like you, I really do. I like you enough to sit here and listen to you call me a hypocrite and not push my fist through your gorgl. Friends don't talk like this, Russ. Friends don't call each other hypocrites. Have I called you a hypocrite or other names that describe other disgusting qualities, have I, Russ?"

Pryor swallowed. "I'm sorry, Shelley . . ."

The others at the table watched in discomfort. Greenfield suddenly reached across and put his hand on Pryor's shoulder. "Russ, do you know what I really want to achieve?"

"You want us to have more of a voice in party affairs," said Pryor. Shelley watched as some of the others nodded in agreement.

"No," he said. "I'm much more ambitious than that. I'll admit it. I want us to have more than a voice. I want us to turn this party around, upside down if need be. A complete overhauling is what I want. We've got to stop asking for a mere voice in party matters. To hell with that. Listen here, you yokels, I want you to be much more ambitious than that, much more."

They waited silently for him to go on. He did in a softer tone.

"Listen; I want us to start thinking of taking over this old, creaking party—taking it over. What the hell is the matter with us? Are we so unsophisticated and unassertive that we can't *demand* that the old men step down and turn over this political organization to those who want to use it as a great force for public good?" His voice rose, so that persons at a nearby table glanced up. "For Chrissakes, this goddam party doesn't belong to those old buggers. It belongs to us. If they don't want to give it up then we've got to take it from them . . ."

TEN

~~~~~~

LOU Rabin arrived at the hotel ballroom when the nominating convention was almost ready to begin. To his annoyance, he found that he had to pass through left- and right-hand sideshows presided over by Henry Simmons and Ted Michaelowitz. The Democratic candidates for United States Senator and State Attorney General respectively, along with aides and signs, were on display in the lobby immediately outside the ballroom, receiving abundant attention from the media. Their signs decried a lack of democracy in the Progressive Party.

"There's Rabin now," said a Simmons aide. The chairman was blocked from entering and the television lights blinded him. He cursed under his breath as a microphone was shoved in front of him. "Mr. Rabin," the interviewer asked, "why won't you allow these candidates to address the delegates at your convention?"

Lou answered glumly, frankly bored with the question. "The answer is simple. We don't have Democrats or Republicans speaking at our nominating conventions any more than we would expect to have Progressive Party candidates speaking at their nominating conventions. They have no right to address our delegates. This"—he waved at their signs—"is just a circus, a publicity stunt."

Suddenly the microphone was snatched away by Shelley Greenfield, who barked into it, "That's not true. The delegates of the Progressive Party *want* to hear these men. But Lou Rabin, the boss of this party, won't allow us to hear the truth. He wants to shove his own candidates down our throats."

Lou made a face and began to elbow his way through, despite the calls of the newsman. Score one for Shelley, he thought. Now that all the delegates had had to pass through Simmons and Michaelowitz and their signs, the conflict inside would be considerably heightened.

Seated on the dais, before it was time for him to step up to the microphone and impart the recommendations of the Advisory Committee, he scanned the three hundred or so delegates and tried to determine the number of persons involved in the hurried groupings, caucuses, forming in various corners. It was alarming to admit the visual testimony that the figure of insurgency could be as high as fifteen or twenty percent. Was that possible? Could there be that much strength among his enemies?

He remembered how it was when he, Max Pizensky, Ad Blum and so many others now dead had fought for control of the Labor Alliance Party almost thirty years before. The Communists had the power then and they were shocked to learn that non-Communists could fight just as passionately and tenaciously as they. In the end, however, he had failed to oust them; the anti-Communist faction had to leave to form its own party. And in a few years, when all the responsible liberals had flocked to the new party, the Progressive Party, he was given the satisfaction of chairing the growing organization as it surged ahead of the Red-tainted Labor Alliance Party on the ballot and eventually forced it out of existence.

The fight against the Reds went on in the labor unions too. He and Max, fighting side by side, had led what was eventually and properly called a "purge" to get the Communists out of union leadership. God, what floor battles they had had at those meetings and conventions!

In those days labor was at the forefront of progressive politics, bringing talent and a special fire into the political arena. Labor knew how to debate, how to fight; and his own leadership in the union had led him naturally into political leadership.

There were always battles, but right from the beginning his lone decision was able to swing the party and the party was able to swing the state in gubernatorial and presidential elections; and soon anyone running for even minor office in the state came to depend on the margin of victory he, Lou Rabin, could provide. He succeeded in helping reformers to fight the machine; soon his voice became synonymous with conscience, and his approval as indispensable as the seal of *Good Housekeeping.*

From a small beginning he had brought the party forward and imbued it with a moral vitality that made it one of the outstanding third-party movements in the country's history, greater and more effective and enduring than the Farmer-Labor Party of Minnesota, the Progressive Party of Wisconsin, the Liberal Party of New York or even the Socialist Party that preceded them all. He knew he was hated in some quarters and this disturbed him not at all. The sad thing was that although he was loved by many he didn't care much about that either. That was the unfortunate fact of aging, he had discovered: the increasing indifference he felt towards the passions he inspired. Most of those who hated him, he liked to believe, considered him the one who had deprived them of the spoils of politics, grasping men whose acquisitiveness he had pointedly and purposely frustrated. And that characterization of an enemy—albeit an intra-party one—fit Shelley Greenfield as well as any of those hungry politicians he had put down in the past.

He was certain he could deal with Greenfield and his troops in short order. He looked to his right at Ad Blum, who was at the microphone reading off the order of business—nomination of state-wide candidates and of the party's own Executive Committee from the State Chairman down. There was no danger here today; the majority of delegates were his people, loyal or indebted. Ad had the proxies of enough non-attendees in his pocket to counter any insurgency. The important thing was to soothe the regulars, to maintain their confidence in the leadership and in the ultimate triumph of the singleness of purpose, the pleasant agreement of purpose, that they had come to take for granted. He must not allow the dissident voices to disturb the others or to stir doubt.

When Lou Rabin rose to address them at the microphone, under the intense glare of the televison lights, there was enthusiastic applause and no rude sounds of disapprobation. He knew when the rudeness would erupt.

"My friends," he said, "today you will decide on your statewide candidates for this year's election. A little later you will also decide on the officials of your party, your choice of a State Chairman and a State Executive Committee for the next two years. All I want to do now is present to you the recommendations and the viewpoint of the Advisory Committee of our party regarding our statewide candidates for this year.

"After I finish, some of you will want to express other viewpoints; and our Executive Secretary, Addison Blum, who is chairing this convention, will call on all who wish to speak. My hope is that all these viewpoints will be discussed and that each delegate will respect the rights and the opinions of his fellow delegate, even if he represents a minority opinion, and that in the end we will all rally behind the majority decision, whatever that may be. Our strength is in unity. The very quality that distinguishes membership in the Progressive Party is unity of purpose . . ."

As he expected when he began to name the Advisory Committee choices, the response was thunderously enthusiastic for David Ornstein as the gubernatorial candidate and for the black man, Ezekiel Carter, as Lieutenant-Governor.

"You have noted, I'm sure," he went on, "that the two men we have recommended so far are Democrats. Historically we have supported Democrats in most elections, national and state and municipal.

"But all of us can remember instances when the party supported Fusion—an alliance of the Republican and Progressive Parties. Five years ago, when Casey Bohland, a Republican, ran against a Democratic machine candidate for Mayor, we supported him, as we have supported other good Republicans in the past.

"Now there is nothing strange or inconsistent in such a policy. We don't belong to the Democratic Party. We're for good government.

We're for clean government. We're for effective government, from whichever party it comes.

"So this year the Advisory Committee has recommended to you some Republicans as well as Democrats for our statewide ticket. For United States Senator and for Attorney General the Committee has submitted its recommendation of the incumbent Senator, Ron Corbett, and the incumbent Attorney General, Walter Johnson."

A concerted roar of disapproval came at the same time as applause, which eventually drowned out the negative manifestations. As he went on, to extoll the records of these two men, the dissidents booed and interrupted his speech many times and loyal party members turned to glare at them and murmur in puzzlement and anger. For the faithful there was a dismaying realization that in the last year the core of rebellion had grown in size and bitterness; it was as though strangers were among them.

When Lou Rabin had finished and the objectors came forward to speak into the standing floor microphone, their nominations of candidates were accompanied by vitriolic attacks on the party leadership. Simmons and Michaelowitz were praised by those who nominated them and those who seconded, and Rabin was damned along with the two Republicans he championed. There was angry reaction from the loyal majority, cries of "Go home, you jerk," and "Traitor" and Liar" and some actural scuffling on the convention floor. The dissidents also put forth a slate for the Executive Committee, topped by Shelley Greenfield as State Chairman and an upstate professor for Executive Secretary. This in itself was a shocking heresy to most of the membership, because never before had the leadership lineup of the party been challenged; it was inconceivable to some that any person could actually aspire to stand in Lou Rabin's shoes or that there could be an Executive Secretary other than Addison Blum. The wild applause that greeted Shelley Greenfield as he came to the center of the floor was a chilling revelation for some of the older members.

"The Progressive Party," he shouted into the microphone, "has been run for almost twenty-five years by a bunch of old men who owe their allegiance to only one man—the boss of all bosses, Lou Rabin!"

He waited for the outburst of catcalls to die down before continuing.

"I'm calling for a new democracy in our party. I'm calling for a chance for all of us to speak with the candidates at the top of the ticket from both major parties, to invite them to our clubs, to question them on issues, to let them speak before us here in the convention.

"Why, may I ask, are we being deprived of the opportunity to hear Henry Simmons or Teddy Michaelowitz? Why must they stand in the lobby like beggars? What is Lou Rabin afraid of? Is it that we might begin to learn how to think for ourselves?

"I'm calling for open primaries, where all Progressives, not only this convention of delegates, may vote on our candidates. Most of the delegates here, as you and I know, bear an allegiance to the state leaders and will do anything Lou Rabin and the Advisory Committee tell them to do.

"Well, I'm for the abolition of the Advisory Committee and I'm for the removal of the boss of all bosses, Lou Rabin."

The Greenfield supporters responded enthusiastically on cue. They applauded too when he ended the speech with his seconding of the nomination of Simmons for United States Senator.

Following Greenfield, Addison Blum stepped up to speak, his face reddening, his voice deep and ringing.

"A small faction of our party has been attacking the party and its leadership in the press and over radio and T.V. as being undemocratic, autocratic; they say we're conducting a purge, that we're stifling dissent. I say this is false!

"There has been no purge in the Progressive Party. Give me the name of one person who has been forced out, give me the name of one person the leaders have *tried* to force out.

"No, these are lies, deliberate lies disseminated by an organized faction that is determined to take over power no matter what the cost or by what method. They have repeatedly attacked the state party and its democratically elected leadership. And never, never do they have one good word to say about the party, its work and its program. They function separately as an anti-Progressive group with their own meetings, their own machinery, public statements, press conferences, even candidates for party and public office.

"Now I want to say one thing about this whole idea of having Democrats speak at our convention or enter our primaries. If they did so it would mean the destruction of our party. For us it would be suicide. We can't let the major parties come in and use our primary the way they would use a battlefield. They'd manipulate, try to buy off the voters, influence them. We can't have them meddling in our internal affairs."

He went on with the theme, and when he was finished the majority of delegates was on its feet applauding, for Addison Blum knew how to bring an audience to its feet.

Then came the roll-call vote on the nominations. The party leadership choices prevailed, but to everyone's astonishment the dissidents collected almost twenty-five percent of the vote. If it had reached twenty-five, the party would have been obliged by state law to hold primaries in which Simmons could have challenged Corbett and Michaelowitz could have had the time and the platform to plead his case against Johnson. The Greenfield faction was jubilant at the outcome. They had not expected to find so much support among the delegates. Now they had new names to add to their forces, and next time, next time . . .

The Rabin leadership slate was elected by the same three-to-one margin, yet the chairman remained grimly staring ahead in his seat on the dais. The significance of rebel growth to this proportion within little more than a year—since Shelley had become county chairman and begun his treachery—did not escape the man who had once tried to unseat and then had destroyed the leaders of another party long ago . . .

ELEVEN

SHE lay beside Earl and tried to lose herself to the feel of his lips on her body, her breasts, then the finger and the tongue searching between her legs. When she found the slightest flicker of warmth she fastened on it to urge it into flame, but it refused to ignite. She pretended; when he thought she was ready he rolled on her and plunged deeply into her while she waited for the hot breath of passion to move from his body to hers. She squeezed herself around his cock, willing herself to tremble, longing to leap to that other plane, the level of abandon . . . His endearments were wet and warm against her ear and she fought the need to turn away, to think of Shelley. Oh God, Shelley, Shelley . . .

She hated whites. All her youth, in those Southern shanty towns, the bitterness toward the white oppressor had driven her to a frenzied scholastic brilliance that astonished her slow parents and frightened the black men. She fought off those blacks who tried to kiss and rape her, hating them, hating the whites for making her own people so vile that she could not accept them. She fought off the black men like a frightened animal, and she was in her twenties before her body asserted its rights and took possession of her. By then she was quite sick with her hatred for whitey, unable to face her nature, already the murderess of a white girl. She was twenty-two exactly when she saw the first man who was to become her lover.

He was waiting for her in front of the school building as she stepped from the bus. A schoolboy monitor from the eighth grade was speaking to him and then pointed to her as she approached, while the man watched her with expressionless blue eyes. He was a rough-looking man who probably worked at one of the factories. His shirt was rumpled as if he had slept in it or had not slept at all. He waited sullenly beside a dull black automobile that had been driven and dented for many years and had one orange fender. It was parked at the main door where she must pass. He spoke slowly, in a sad insolent monotone.

"You're Miss Williams? I'm Aggie Sullivan's brother."

"Agnes? Won't she be in school today?"

"No, she won't."

She waited, but the man simply looked and looked at her as if he could not really see her features. The street was very still. Finally she said, "Is something wrong with Agnes?"

He nodded. "She's dead."

She stared numbly and saw the pain hidden in the unshaven face. She could not get used to the thought that one of her sixth-grade pupils had suddenly become large and majestic and wise and stone-like. Then she wondered if Agnes's brother had come to explain and apologize for the girl's absence. But another look into those eyes that had not slept told her that the man was angry and his wrath was directed at her.

"But how—" she started to say. And that was when he spit in her face.

The monitor on the steps saw it all and gasped so audibly that she snapped her head about to share his surprise. She saw the boy and then she saw the sky. And she knew at that moment, for the first time in her young-old life, that the earth truly turned in this universe of sky and that she was standing alone. She felt the earth move beneath her and she was rigid with fright. Somewhere in this vastness she tried to seek out the person of Agnes' brother, and by the time she succeeded he was entering his car. He drove off before she could decide whether she wanted to scream at him or weep. She had not done either of these things for so long that a decision was required.

The students whispered all that day of the morning's incident and the death of Aggie Sullivan. They had found Aggie's body last night at the railroad tracks. It was said that a train had surprised her while she crossed the section where the switches converged. She was afraid to go home and was running away; such was her plan; this was what she had told a friend. The friend knew why and so did all of them when they read the report card in the pocket of the dead girl's dress.

"It's not *your* fault, Barbara," one of the other teachers, a white teacher, assured her. "She deserved every mark you gave her. You ought to call the police about that man. You could have him arrested!" But she didn't want to discuss it and she hated the woman for trying to break her silence.

She knew whose fault it was; that she had been far too severe in grading the child. For the first time in her life, in her brilliant nunlike career of frozen hatred, she had lashed out, the sharp pen tight in her fingers, and had expressed her scorn, heaped it upon a sullen white child with vacant blue eyes. And now that it was done, she could see how futile and inhuman it was. The girl was twelve, a stupid, noisy, disruptive, arrogant pupil; since she had killed her, the girl no longer seemed any of these things. Now the sullen face hung like black stratus over the earth, a leaden sculptured presence.

Barbara Williams had reached a point in her life when something was bound to happen to her. Such an event was foretold, not because fate decreed it, not because things were going too smoothly, rather because she had been so selective in her exposure to the world that she was doomed to encounter life with devastating suddenness. One day, as it were, the flap of the tent would blow open.

Expiation, forgiveness, she would have these or she, too, would die, or so she believed. She could run away, of course; the time was right for that. The spring term was over, could end today if she wished. The next few days were administrative, designed to allow the children to run away from *them*, the boys to do Catherine wheels out of the yard, the girls to sing the traditional taunts. She could be off today, on her way east to see a friend or two, or to Europe for the summer, and she need not even return in the fall. Still, her few friends and her teacher status and the old, tired, widower father she visited back home in the South meant nothing to her, were no longer of this new world, this strange universe set in a midwestern city, where Aggie Sullivan reigned in her heaven.

So that evening Barbara made her way to the funeral chapel. What she had meant to do was to stand before the parents of the child and wait to be struck or at least show to them that she was willing to be struck, or something equally expressive of the abject posture of her thoughts. However, she did not get to see the parents. She contrived to arrive late at the chapel, when most of the mourners would have left, and as she stepped from the taxi, the only person she saw in the street light was Agnes' brother. He was standing against an expanse of brick wall, drawing on a cigarette cupped in his palm, as though he had practiced a lifetime of hiding this habit from his parents; or perhaps he held secret conversations or said prayers in his palm, as one would to a carved white angel in a niche in the church. When he saw her he drew thoughtfully, inducing an angry red glow in his hand, behind which his eyes, too, glowed, the look of the white man she had always despised; then abruptly he flipped the cigarette into the street and blocked her way with his thick body. "*Are you crazy?*" he muttered.

She was so frightened of him that she was speechless. She shook her head.

"Then what the hell are you doing here?"

How could she explain? He glanced over his shoulder.

"You can't go in *there*, for Chrissake. Get in my car."

Humiliated, she looked about and recognized his automobile. Her throat vibrated in an effort to cry, but it was no use. She walked slowly to the car. The front door was open, the seat was worn and scratchy against her legs where the burlap threads came through.

She watched him enter the chapel and understood she was to wait for him. When he came out finally, he was hurrying. He slid behind the wheel and started the motor without a glance at her or even a word.

It was dark outside of the city. Once away from the buildings, in view of the night, she could see too well the curve and exposure of where they were; and she trusted the man beside her that the car would not fall into that up-down blackness that was the universe. He drove, and in the headlights' glare the onrushing trees and poles genuflected with ancient rhythm; and up in the sky, beyond the atmosphere, so she had been told, all was black and pure white and there were no colors. He drove to a hill and there stopped and bent his head to the wheel. Then he moaned and she heard that he was sobbing.

Oh, my God, if only . . . if only. She knew she would do it, even if he struck her. A tentative hand to his shoulder. His face, turning to her, was terrible in grief. She drew him and held him, and the wet of his cheeks and his lips were on her thin dress, and her pores seemed to open and her heart was big and grateful, and her body was on fire. He held her so hard, caressing, that her body trembled and arched and strange sounds came from her.

". . . to my place," he said.

The place he called his was a furnished room—no, two rooms—in a small building. In the parlor was a faded green couch. In the bedroom a light bulb hung unattractively from the ceiling. Then the darkness came and she went crazy the moment he touched her.

At dawn, the light was strange. An alarm rang and the blue-eyed man beside her stumbled from the house, to go perhaps to his job or to the chapel, she knew not which. Soon she dressed. There was no reason to report to the school; there would be goodbyes and exchanges of addresses, and she would exchange this address with no one. What needed to be done was clear out her own quarters, have everything shipped home, except for some clothing, and pretend to her landlady that she, too, was leaving immediately for home. She would say nothing of remaining for the summer. It would be a summer, no longer than that.

She walked on this errand, from his rooms to her own. It was but a single day since yesterday, but the landscape of the city was bi-zarrely disarranged, like those perception experiments she had wit-nessed at the university, where the shape of a room made children appear taller and more Godlike than adults and much sport is made of the warped perspectives. She thought of the night and what had been done and began to burn in her groin. How astonishing to con-template that at any time, while she simply walked across a city, so many things were happening behind so many doors and nothing was ever the same afterward.

That night he returned late. He was drunk. When he snapped on the light and saw her lying on the couch he gaped at her and howled and slapped his thighs and circled about her in mock disbelief. Then he began to wheeze with laughter and say lewd things about school-teachers and other supposedly prim types, and he smirked and smirked and taunted and eventually violated her. He seemed to have decided that his initial form of greeting outside the school building, spitting on her, held the formula for his success, and his variations of physical abuse were so shocking as to numb her very soul, even as they thrilled her body. Her summer had began.

During the night he agreed that she might stay, might live with him for a few weeks, if she so desired; and that night, all night, she prayed in the midst of her sexual frenzy and her fright that from this place of depravity she might emerge into humanity.

With wonder she learned the way a life can change. Overnight a viewpoint can encompass a world that had been rejected as a matter of course, or had not even been thought to exist. After some weeks, she found that she could do what she had set out to do, and that was to pull the blanket of humanity over her eyes and her body and hide from that glimpse of the sky.

The world that was his was one of drunkenness. There were his friends, some of them neighbors, voices and bodies out of that face-less world of white men. Sometimes he contrived that his friends should meet her, always casually, in his apartment; a form of boast-ing, for she was nothing if not beautiful. Those times were night-mares. They drank and played cards or merely drank, these shifty-eyed men, and as they drank they saw her wince at their language and they became so filthy in their talk that she was the game, not the cards. He stopped them when they tried to touch her, but he made her stay and listen and saw that she suffered each word.

Yet there was admiration. Her own life had never been precarious, in a physical sense, and so this surprised her, the lucky courage of men, the drunken ones she now numbered as legion. She saw them stagger so often, her keeper and his friends, and she marveled that they could so expose their bodies to harm. She marveled, and she admired the belligerent confrontation with life that carried these dumb brutes, and their women too, through their brawling evenings and nights. When he came home drunk and alone and she tried to assist him, he became abusive. When she became loving, he became sadistic. When she tried to understand him, he was wary and insulted, for he did not consider that his masculine self required so much effort in the knowing. She spent her own savings to shop and to prepare dinners, whether he came home or not, whether he spoke to her or not, whether he was drunk or sober; and some nights he did not come home at all. These times she locked the door to keep out his friends. He actually beat her only a few times, if only to enforce, lest it atrophy from disuse, his astonishing license to insult with impunity. He occasionally remembered, and she somehow reminded him, that she was there to be punished.

As for her days, she rarely left the apartment or the building, except for the brief shopping excursions. The neighbors, the women, frightened her, and she had no patience or heart for even the most ordinary social purposes. Friendship, that constant surging of ego against ego, was a forgotten, tiresome game. One needed vanity to play the game and that was the quality in her that the summer had drained. She cared for nothing, thought of nothing. Nor were there books to fill the hot shimmering hours, for she had shipped her books south. In the apartment there were some of his comic and detective magazines, but these she never opened; and her mind even refused to generate thought out of idleness. Even when she stared at the monotonous dotted pattern on the old parlor wallpaper her vision did not leap to make designs. Nothingness, heedlessness, these were the blessings.

Then it was over. His parents had found out about her living there, his priest too, and she must leave. He said, "I'm going out for a while. Don't be here when I get back."

Earl lay heavily on top of her, spent and happy. "You come all right, baby?" he asked doubtfully.

"Sure, honey," she said. "That was great."

TWELVE

THE group consisted of six members of the Winnota County Executive Committee, and Lou Rabin endeavored to give them the impression that he expected friendship and cooperation from them, as though the absence of Shelley Greenfield for the moment wiped out all hostility.

"To get to the heart of the matter and discuss the reason I've asked you to stop here to Ad Blum's office for a brief meeting this evening, let me start by saying that I respect the right of each county to nominate its own candidates. The delegate convention has already had its meeting and nominated the party's statewide choices for Governor and United States Senator and so on. Our local candidates —I'm referring to State Senators, State Assemblymen and United States Congressional Seats—those are for County Committees to choose.

"The 12th Congressional District falls in your county. The seat is presently held by Sam Waldman, about whom the best that can be said is that he is a somewhat liberal Democrat and rather innocuous for the most part."

One of the older Winnota County members shook his large greying head. "That hasn't been our attitude in past elections. Up to now the Progressive Party has endorsed Waldman, and the state leadership has never objected."

"Because we've had no one better to choose from," Rabin supplied quickly. "This year, in the opinion of some of the party leaders, you've got a far superior choice."

"Darned right," a young man piped up enthusiastically. "Lazarus. Sylvia Lazarus. I couldn't agree more, Mr. Rabin."

"Well, thank you." Lou was pleased. He glanced at Addison Blum who sat inconspicuously on the side couch. The meeting had been called in this informal setting, rather than in the conference room, in order to make the committeemen feel important and relaxed. The young man who had spoken was apparently one of the few Addison had approached privately during recent weeks; no doubt he had a city job of some sort. If he would use these few cooperative ones to sway the others . . .

"Mr. Rabin." It was the beautiful black girl, Barbara Williams. "I've heard of Mrs. Lazarus and I can commend her efforts in civil rights and women's rights. In fact, she's quite militant and I can tell you she's caught the imagination of some of the black organizations in the area. But Waldman has a good record and he's got senior status—he's on several important committees in Congress. That makes him a very effective liberal legislator, not just a crusader."

"And it's also true," another member offered, "that in the Democratic primary Waldman is certain to win. Why should we go with the loser and make an enemy of an old friend?"

Lou Rabin's lips curled. "He's not an old friend, not really. He's had a very little rapport with the party, very little respect for it . . ."

"But a good voting record in Congress and he's the probable winner in the primary. What's the advantage of taking this Lazarus woman?"

"Plenty of advantages." Lou looked about at the younger members. "Just think of the interest that we as a party can evoke in the youth and minorities of your district, throughout the city in fact, if we take on the task of championing a real fighter, which is what this woman is. Don't underestimate this woman. She's got a certain kind of down-to-earth appeal. Like Louise Day Hicks in Boston and Bella Abzug in New York." He went on to enumerate Mrs. Lazarus' background and mentioned some of the support she seemed to have in the Democratic Party.

"I beg to differ with you," said the grey-haired member. "Most of the Democrats I've talked to hate her guts. They say she's got a big mouth, they say she's a Commie, they say she's one of those Third World babes who has no use for the Jews, even though she's a Jew herself. I don't see what the hell's so attractive to you about this woman, Mr. Rabin."

"All right." Rabin raised his hands. "So she's not attractive. I mean, she's not attractive to veterans like us"—he looked straight at his adversary—"who know the kind of tradition she represents, veterans like us who recoil from all that Marxist rhetoric. But I'm telling you that a lot of the youth and a lot of black people don't share our aversion."

There was a momentary silence during which he stared at the one who had challenged him. Actually he agreed with the challenger in every particular and he hoped the man had not perceived this truth.

"Mr. Rabin," the man said softly, "did you make a deal with Lazarus?"

Lou Rabin glared at him and sat up stiffly in his chair. "I don't make deals," he said sharply. "I've given you my opinion . . ."

The discussion went on long enough for Lou to realize he was not going to succeed in changing their minds. Only then did he ask them to think about it and of course to vote any way they saw fit. After they had filed out of the room, Addison said, shaking his head, "I don't understand why you didn't just tell them the truth."

Lou shook his head. "Because we can't afford to have that story get around. If I told them about the threatened legislation against us they'd leak it to the press, either intentionally or not, and our vote this year would be practically zero."

"I hadn't thought of it that way . . ."

"Oh, no? You should. Would you vote for a lame duck party that might not even exist after next year? And there's something more.

I refuse to accept even the thought of such legislation. It's a humiliation to me. I want it kept quiet at all costs, because if it becomes known it becomes real. And it's not real."

Addison Blum did not dare remark that it was real.

The Chairman reached for his coat, said good night, and walked thoughtfully to the elevators. When he came out of the building, he saw the black girl.

"I've been waiting for you," she said. "I think it's time somebody tried to get you and Shelley Greenfield to end this feud."

"Oh? Are you speaking for him officially?"

"No, not officially," said Barbara Williams. "He doesn't know . . ."

"That's what I thought." The old man raised his brows. "You fancy yourself a peacemaker, young lady, but I don't think there's any chance of your supplying the magic formula to bridge the gap, not simply out of your sentimental good-will."

Barbara lifted her hand tentatively. "But suppose he does want to talk peace. What would your reaction be? Would you simply turn away any overture?"

"Turn it away? I should say not. Peace is to both our advantages. This rupture is damaging to all of us. I've been angry and disillusioned. But it's not the first time I've had to sit down and negotiate a peace settlement, even within our party. After all, there have been great breaks and many little splinters along the way, dating back to the old Labor Party Alliance days and the union defection a few years ago . . . most of which I'm sure you're well acquainted with. Oh, I know how to sit down and listen to the other side of a story. But we must have one party, Barbara. And when a man is voted down on a given issue, voted down on a democratic basis, then he has to bow down to the will of the majority."

She shook her head sadly. "That sounds to me like you're not going to bend on anything."

"No, that's not accurate. I'm at my office if he wants to talk. But on his part it has to be a returning to the fold."

"Mr. Rabin, I want to ask you another question. Is there anything personal in your disagreement?"

"Certainly. I've been greatly offended. It was I who recommended Shelley as County Chairman in the first place a year ago. It was I who recommended his running for the Assembly. I do feel betrayed. But that doesn't mean I'm inflexible in the matter of healing this wound —a wound to the party rather than to me, because all that adverse publicity has hurt our image."

"Then you're willing to meet to talk with him."

"Always." Lou Rabin pursed his lips. "But you're making a mistake. He doesn't want to talk with me. He may say he does but he doesn't mean it. He figures it's to his advantage to prolong the turmoil, that he'll become a more powerful figure in the eyes of the Democrats and other groups he wished to court if he continues to shine as my major adversary in the party." He let out his breath. "Barbara, your good intentions will be to no avail, because you're viewing all this as a personal rather than a political matter."

"Well, I see it quite personally," she said softly.

"So I notice." The party chairman nodded. It was strange to see pity written on that usually sour and acidulous countenance. "All right, do this—tell him I've extended an invitation for an immediate conference, just between him and me. This week. My secretary will phone him tomorrow and set the time."

She nodded. "I haven't seen him lately, but I'll get the message to him."

"Fine. Good night, young lady."

Two days later, Shelley was seated across from Rabin in his office at the union. Rabin had decided to agree to the suggestion of a meeting because he wanted peace and he also wanted to fulfill his promise to Mrs. Lazarus. For the moment, the older man prolonged an unimportant telephone conversation with a union representative so he could keep Shelley waiting, possibly slow down and subdue the man's obvious readiness to do battle.

He watched Shelley light a cigar and shift his heavy shoulders. A formidable, energetic man, Rabin remarked to himself. And perhaps it was a good thing that Greenfield had come forth this year to do battle. Who knew what he might have been able to achieve if he tried for power after . . . well, after Lou Rabin departed from the living? No, that was faulty reasoning. Shelley was smart enough to realize he had to create his image of leadership while the old leader was still alive. After the Chairman's death he could be lost in the scramble and would indeed have little if any claim to leadership. Now . . . he had to make his name now as the one and only man vying with Lou Rabin for the hearts of the party members. Shelley could only come alive while Lou Rabin was alive.

And Lou Rabin murmuring into the telephone, most assuredly intended to live. He knew that the climax of any efforts to unseat him would come two years hence, when the delegate convention voted again for state officers. Every two years, in fact. How many of those meetings were left for him and Addison? Quite a few, certainly. Yes, Shelley was gearing up for the next two-year confrontation, and he was sure the young man felt very strong. Why shouldn't he? After all, in his first year of rebellion he had captured almost twenty-five percent of the delegates; he had every reason to feel confident.

When he hung up the telephone receiver, Rabin went right to the point.

"Shelley, I want to talk about Sylvia Lazarus."

The younger man blinked his blue eyes with amusement, then began to shake his head. "Lou, you amaze me. How could you have stepped into it so blindly?"

"Explain that, please."

"This Lazarus thing. How could you have been so naive as to hand me an issue like that on a silver platter? The choice of a Representative from one of my districts is a county decision and here you go ahead and try to dictate—"

"I'm not dictating to anyone."

"And threaten people in my county with their city jobs."

"False," said Rabin.

Shelley waved his cigar. "You amaze me. I'm going to drag you through the mud on this issue—it's exactly the issue I need to get the ball rolling. I'm going to fill the newspapers with it whenever I can; you might as well know it." He made a pained face. "Let me ask you a question. What the hell kind of deal did you make with that loudmouth broad? Or was it with the Reform Dems? Whatever it was, it must have been a lulu for you to do such an unwise thing."

"There is no deal."

"Okay, so there's no deal."

Rabin smiled grimly. "Believe it or not, Shelley, I thought maybe you and I could talk peace today or maybe some kind of truce or rapprochement. But everything you say, the minute it comes out of your mouth, turns into a declaration of war. I'll grant you one thing: you're a very direct man."

"I believe in being direct. You should call things by their right names. It disarms the enemy."

Rabin agreed sourly. "Yes, it is disconcerting."

"Knocks the weapons right out of the opposition's hands," Shelley went on. "There's nothing worse than the power of unsaid words, Lou. So you've got to say the words. Simplify, articulate, confront all mystery and insinuation."

The chairman raised his brows. "At whatever the cost in human relationships? When there is confrontation, Shelley, sometimes the face of one of the parties must be erased, and there is not much to be said of a person who would purposely create situations where faces are erased."

Shelley chuckled and blew smoke into the air. "I always knew you were a gentleman of the old school," he said with renewed amusement, "but I didn't know you were an oriental gentleman. That's what's wrong with you. That's why you dislike me so much. Because you're a real gentleman. A slob like me shocks you so much just by being honest and natural that you overreact. You're like a guy who doesn't talk much, but when he does open up he's liable to say too much. So when a gentleman like you hates, he hates too much. You want to break me, bring me to my knees. *You're* the one that's not willing to compromise, Lou. All I want is a chunk of the power you've got. I want to wheel and deal a little, the way you do."

Rabin's face showed disgust. "You wouldn't know what to do with power if you had it."

"Oh, you're wrong. You mean, would I continue the battle for good government—to use your expression?"

Lou Rabin half-nodded, half-shrugged.

"Probably I couldn't help doing some of that," Shelley said blandly. "But that's the difference between us. You kid yourself into thinking you want to reform government, but actually you only do the things you do because they make you feel Godlike and powerful. Me, I believe in power for the party as a primary factor. You're the truly vain and power-hungry one, not me."

"I don't see that," said Rabin softly. "I do understand that you've been castigating me publicly for my insatiable need to exercise power and my patronage activities."

Shelley waved that away. "No, I just say that because it's what the yokels want to hear. What I really object to is that you don't seek *enough* power and patronage for the party. You're concerned only with your own vanity and if that gets satisfied you'll sell the party short."

"You'll have to explain what you mean."

The younger man pointed to the walls of the chairman's office. "Too many pictures up there, you know what I mean? Too many photographs of you with the famous politicians—mayors, governors, presidents . . . 'With warmest regards to my good friend Lou Rabin' and all that crap. I once heard it said by a ballplayer—Bob Feller, I think it was—that trophies are for amateurs, the professionals take cash . . ."

Rabin scratched his nose and looked up at the ceiling, to answer with a half-smile.

"I've always said I was only a political amateur."

"It's not right." Greenfield was no longer amused. "You should be pushing your people into public office all over the state and in Washington. You haven't done that. Only in the last few years, and only in city government, you've started acting the way a politician's supposed to act." Shelley moved forward in his chair. "Like that story you tell about how the President invited you for dinner at the White House—five or six years ago, I believe it was. I think you said you'd be a few minutes late because you had to drop off at the hotel to pick up your wife and the President said never mind, he'd send his private limousine to pick her up at her hotel. Now that's one of the favorite stories you like to tell. It's like putting these pictures up on the wall. And it's a nice story, a sweet story. But do you know something, Lou, you gave that President the Progressive Party's endorsement that year and he never gave you anything. You didn't get one job for any of our people for that endorsement. The President bought you very cheap. An invitation to dinner and a special limousine for your wife —that's too cheap. You're not a power broker, you're just a vain old man, and I think you're kind of silly."

Lou Rabin nodded several times. "I suppose it's futile," he said, "for me to ask you, before we forget, whether anything can be done about the Sylvia Lazarus situation."

"No, not altogether futile." Shelley sat back. "But let's talk first about some city jobs for the people in my county."

Rabin stared down at his restless fingers. "There have been no openings."

"That's not true. You've given out jobs to a few black boys in my county that I've heard about."

Rabin shrugged. "Not very many, and the blacks need our help."

"So do my boys."

"Let's be honest, Shelley. There's no comparison between the help a black needs and what one of your friends may need."

Shelley was adamant. "There's a perfect comparison. My friends need jobs just as much as black boys. And you gave these jobs to the blacks because you want to own them and have a tight little group in my county who will mobilize against your enemies at a moment's notice. Like against me, for instance. Don't give me any bleeding heart routine about poor blacks. You know how I feel about them . . ."

Lou's face was expressionless, his voice calm. "I don't appreciate hearing you scoff at what you call the bleeding heart routine. Bleeding hearts have been responsible for most of our decent legislation—"

"And all the permissive legislation too," Greenfield cut in rudely. "Look, I know your game. You want everyone else in the party to be all gush and a crying towel and then we can leave the big decisions to you, isn't that the story? Well, I don't buy it. I want to be in on the decision-making." He pointed his finger jabbingly. "The name of this game is patronage, and I want some of it for my boys."

Coldly, and seemingly from afar, Rabin shook his head slowly. "No, the name of the game isn't patronage. It's principle."

"My ass!" said Shelley, staring at him intently.

Rabin had had enough. He sighed. "Good day, Shelley. It's been interesting seeing you again. I guess we just can't talk to each other."

Shelley shot up from his seat and walked out of the office without answering. A moment later, Rabin's secretary entered. She had heard the raised voices and she looked at him cautiously to see whether he was still upset. He seemed merely pensive.

"I'm ready to take that letter, Mr. Rabin . . ."

"Esther," he said thoughtfully, "you've been with me about eight years now. During those eight years you've seen this union get smaller and smaller and lose its power. I wonder if that's the way you think of me, too, as a man whose effectiveness has been diminishing. I never thought of it before, but it occurs to me that you never knew this union when it was still a yeasty place, when it had vigor." He shook his head. "Pity—you have the wrong picture. You've missed the best years, the growing years."

Esther, a woman in her early fifties, was mildly surprised at his reflections. "Do you mean I've missed the best years of the union or of you?"

He chuckled. "That's a good question. Both. Both."

"Then I'm sorry I missed them," she said with a smile, shifting her steno book.

Rabin dictated the letter she'd come in for, feeling somewhat sheepish and distressed, because he knew he was actually flirting and he felt just a bit of a fool. Marvelous woman, Esther. Tactful, too.

THIRTEEN

~~~~~~

"I'LL bet you can make them change their nomination," Bill Sokolov said excitedly. "Go up there with a bunch of your Young People's Army and insist that they support your Puerto Rican candidate instead of that hack DeSalvio. Go up there and take the place over, a sit-in."

Bernardo Rodriguez was wary. "I wouldn't want any trouble with the cops."

Sokolov waved away the possibility as ridiculous. "Never. They'd be too embarrassed, they'll be afraid of the publicity. They're all Jews up there and you can get away with anything with Jews."

"You're one yourself, aren't you?"

"That's how I know. Soft. Weak. I hate them. It's perfect for you, Bernardo. Jews are the soft underbelly of the establishment. Why do you think the blacks are going after the teachers and landlords? Do you think they'd try that shit with the Italians in the Sanitation

Department or the Irish in the construction gangs? No, you go after the Jews . . ."

Rodriguez didn't especially like the Jews and he found Sokolov one of the most distasteful, though he was careful not to show it. The man was all teeth like Harpo Marx in the old movies and equally as ugly, a true creep who seemed to love violence. But he was smart and he was right about this. The Jews were the most vulnerable, and a man who wanted to change the established order should never forget it. A sit-in, a takeover just the way they did in the churches. It could be a perfect tactic for putting a political party on the spot. He looked at Sokolov curiously.

"Hey, man, I've been wondering about something. You seem to know so much about them. Don't tell me you once belonged to the Progressive Party!"

It was a shrewd question and Sokolov sensed that he couldn't lie and perhaps didn't have to. "Once," he said, "once upon a time. I didn't fit in."

Rodriguez laughed. "Do you ever?"

That pleased the reporter. He felt a surge of comradery. "Bernie, would you believe it—they invited me to leave, called me a Communist. They think a populist is a Communist!"

"Crazy, man. They're really in the nineteen-fifties, ain't they?"

But privately Rodriguez had tagged Sokolov as a Commie-Trotsky nut a long time ago. He had a very clear-eyed notion that the various radical causes he and the reporter engaged in from time to time were pinkish, but he didn't give a hoot one way or the other. He was surprised that people like Sokolov really cared so much about being tagged for what they were.

"Somebody telephoned you about fifteen minutes ago—someone named Randy. I told him you'd be home soon. He wants you him back. You know, he sounded to me like Randy Payton Jones."

"He was," Earl said brightly. "That's who the man was."

Barbara caressed her cheek. "It was so strange, Earl, picking up the phone and hearing that sexy cultured accent . . . I grew up hearing that voice of his, the most famous black politician of all time, I guess; the lover, the wastrel, the profligate, as big a crook as every white Congressman he sat next to . . ."

"The one and only," said Earl.

Barbara was impressed. "I didn't know you knew him."

"We've met once or twice. But now he needs my help. And through certain intermediaries we're arranging something."

"I hope you're going to tell me what it is."

Earl mixed a drink and gave thought to whether he wanted to go on. "Well, look, Barbara, this is confidential. I don't know if I should —" He looked at her unhappily. "You've got to promise me, that's all. It goes no further than you, okay?"

"You don't have to tell me anything," she said in a soft voice.

He gulped his drink. "Oh, hell, I'm anxious to tell you, honey. He wants me to run for Congress in his district."

"I don't understand," Barbara said in puzzlement. "Isn't he running again?"

Eaton responded with spontaneous laughter. "He's running, all right. But he's got a primary to get through. They're out to kill him this year."

"Where do you come in, Earl?"

"Simple. I tie up the Progressive nomination so it can't go to Luther Kennicut. The Democrats, or at least the Reform Democrats, are trying to replace Jones with Kennicut, and it's going to be a rough primary between the two of them. The Progressives are all set to go for Kennicut—they've never been able to tolerate Jones—and that just might give old Luther boy an edge in the primary. So it's my job to make sure he's deprived of that edge. I can run without giving up my Assemblyman seat, so it's no hardship. Am I surprising you, Barbara?"

"A little," she said wonderingly.

"Well, that's the name of the game. You do something for me, I do something for you."

"What's Jones going to do for you?"

"He's done it already. Who the hell do you think supplied the cash and the manpower for me when I ran for the Assemblyman's seat in the first place? Now it's my turn to pay back the favor."

Barbara threw up her hands. "Boy, this is a hot one! Here I thought you were the straightest"—she smacked her lips—"and all the while you've been wheeling and dealing with the best of them. I don't know what to think about it."

Earl made a face. "Then don't think at all. Listen, this isn't a game for sweet little boys and girls. You wouldn't be playing fair yourself now if you start sermonizing—"

She shook her head. "No, not that. In fact, I'm impressed."

He looked at her intently.

"Really," she said. "It impresses me favorably. I don't know why . . ."

He watched her with amusement. "I think you're ready to make love. Am I right?"

She nodded wordlessly.

"You say you had a call?" prompted Addison Blum. "What exactly did he ask? Did he want to join one of our clubs?"

"Yes, he—"

"Winnota County?"

"Yes, that's true," Russ said. "He told me he lived around Sixty-second Street and wanted to know if we had a club there."

"And what did you tell him?"

Pryor shrugged elaborately. "Oh, I merely told him that I didn't have all that information and that he should write in and we'd be in touch with him, call him in for an interview."

"Good. Good. Russ, was it your feeling that he was pumping for information? Did you feel he merely wanted information about any new clubs we've been forming?"

"That's possible, certainly . . ."

"You see, Russ, these past few months people have been registering in the Progressive Party who are not truly interested in joining our party. They want to aid in a takeover."

Pryor frowned. "A lot of people? I mean, I suppose there may be a few, a neglible number—"

"Nothing is negligible!" Addison breathed deeply as though to still an inner excitement. "Russ, we've got to be very careful, very careful. Examine every call, every inquiry. The other side, Greenfield's group, seems to be getting too much information about our organizational movements."

"All right, Mr. Blum, I'll be careful." It was said as a promise and also to calm the distressed man. "I agree," the young man added, "that we should certainly keep alert about this, but I'm sure it'll never prove to be a significant number of people . . ."

Addison snorted and fell into silence. Russ, raising his brows slightly, knew he was being dismissed from the room. "I'll be going home now, Mr. Blum."

"Yes, yes, it's late."

When he left, Addison became uneasy. Lately the office was scary and so still at night. He jumped, startled, as the telephone rang. His private line. When he picked it up no one answered. He sat nervously after hanging up. It had happened before. Some people knew his number and were harassing him.

How many evenings had he spent in this office, or in the other quarters the party had rented over the years, neglecting his family, working into the night? He'd never given much thought to it, the aloneness.

But tonight it seemed so still. Or rather he could hear such creakings and seeming presences as had gone unnoticed at other times, other nights. They had frightened him with those telephone calls, reminded him that he remained alone, that he left the outer doors open—he had never locked them because party people often visited him at night and his own office was so far to the rear that he would not hear someone knocking. He had never feared before. But in recent months he had been learning to live with fear. The memory blanks were worse and more frequent, and the unaccountable storms of anger, the black and red rages floating before his eyes, were the most frightening moments of all. How many evenings of late had he stood at the window feeling the urge to leap? He was becoming afraid to leave his office, to leave the building, because the streets, he was convinced at some moments, were dark torrents of sea that he dared not enter. Yet it wasn't only a physical fear, it was the loneliness and strangeness of becoming old. It was as though the telephone caller were Death. Life was just not fair. The most organized and efficient man, it seemed, could not prepare himself for these vagaries of age.

It was almost eleven in the morning when Bernardo Rodriguez and his Young People's Army invaded the state headquarters of the Progressive Party to stage a sit-in. Bernardo, tall and princely, strode through the double doors announcing gaily, "Hello, hello, hello, hello . . ." followed by a troop of considerably less princely Puerto Ricans, veritable Fidel Castros in khaki and jeans, some in their teens, some in their twenties, a few comely females and Bill Sokolov, the reporter.

"What the hell!" said the plump secretary who was seated outside Addison Blum's office. "Hey, what're you people doing?"

"We're taking over, sweetie," said Rodriguez, and without further discussion they barged into Addison Blum's private office where they swarmed over the terrified man's desk and chairs and couches with cries of, "Let's get comfortable, we're here for a long rest," and "Oh, how soft . . . I sleep here tonight."

Blum was pale. "What is the meaning of this?"

At this time, staff members of the Party, alerted by the secretary, entered the room, Milt Holloway among them; he frowned when he spied the smirking Bill Sokolov amidst the revelers, for he knew too well the reporter's capacity for trouble-making. The Puerto Ricans had fallen silent. There was now sufficient audience and it was the proper time evidently for Bernardo Rodriguez, the leader, to state his purpose. He stepped to the center of the room and made a speech punctuated by opaque Marxist phrases and transparent threats.

"We are going to remain in this office for days and weeks if necessary," he summarized, "until the Progressive Party reverses its endorsement of Joseph DeSalvio in the Forty-third Assembly District and gives the endorsement to the Puerto Rican candidate, Ceasar Nunez."

"*What?*" said Holloway. "You must be kidding!" He looked across at Blum who was tight-lipped and silent behind his desk as Rodriguez handed out a mimeographed press release. It read:

FOR IMMEDIATE RELEASE

The Puerto Rican people of the 43rd A.D. have been grossly insulted by the sick and decadent action of the Progressive Party in its endorsement of Mr. Joseph DeSalvio, a Democratic District Leader and Boss, as its candidate for the State Assembly. The Young People's Army has announced a new era in politics in this city. The Young People's Army will not allow the Progressive Party, a tool of the oppressive capitalist system, to impose this candidacy on Puerto Rican voters. This is a flagrant contradiction of the essence of an acceptable philosophy of progressive government. The Young People's Army refuses to accept this decadent state of affairs. On Monday of this week from 11 o'clock on we will be at Progressive Party headquarters and will remain there until we are given satisfaction.

The era is over when central party headquarters will dictate to its local constituencies what takes place. The paternalism of previous years must be brought to a halt immediately. The Puerto Rican people in our city and the nation will decide their own destinies and will not be dictated from above.

Holloway scanned the release, then leaned over Addison Blum's desk.

"They're tresspassing. Do you want me to call the police?"

Blum nodded and spoke softly. "Call them but explain that we only want someone on hand to keep order. We don't want any arrests. That would only bring publicity. And you'd better telephone Lou Rabin and the chairman of the Executive Committee of Greene

County. They're going to have to be the ones to decide whether they want to reevaluate their endorsement."

Holloway was incredulous. "You mean you're actually going to consider changing a nomination just because—"

"It's up to the County Committee," Blum said with a slight shrug.

A police captain arrived, accompanied by two patrolmen, and wrote down all the pertinent information. He spoke with Holloway and Blum in Holloway's office.

"I don't know why you don't let us drag them down to the station," he said. "If people like you won't allow us to arrest these people, they'll never stop their crazy sit-ins and confrontations."

"No, no, no," said Blum. "They don't seem to be disorderly, and we'll have to wait until this evening for some of the county leaders to get here and meet with them."

"All right." The captain was pleasant and businesslike. "I'll leave two patrolmen here to watch things."

In the evening, Lou Rabin and seven members of the County Executive Committee sat in Addison Blum's office, where additional chairs had been brought in from the conference room, and talked it out with Ceasar Nunez. For by this time the Puerto Rican candidate the Young People's Army hoped to promote (Rodriguez, it turned out, was his campaign manager) was also present.

A thickset, handsome, olive-skinned young man, he sat much of the time frowning in heavy thought. He was a lawyer, as were seven members of the opposition he faced; he took himself very seriously, believing that he was a deep man and a man of destiny. But he was no match for Lou Rabin and seven lawyers. As Bernardo Rodriguez, Bill Sokolov and the others listened and observed, and tried at times to interrupt, the lawyers befuddled Nunez with so many legalisms, complications, ramifications and veiled threats of political blackballing for the rest of his natural life that after a few hours he was perspiring and fervently seeking a face-saving exit from the whole mess.

This the solemn and somewhat bored chairman of the Progressive Party was pleased to supply. While Sokolov scowled and the weary Young People's Army strained to listen, he explained to Nunez that in order to reverse a nomination, a County Committee meeting—which involved sixty or seventy persons—would have to be convened—reconvened, actually—and that only the County Executive Committee, of which there were eighteen members, could make the decision to call together the larger group. Seven of these Executive Committee members were on hand tonight, said Rabin, gesturing to the gentlemen around him; the rest would have to be canvassed by telephone the next day.

"The problem *you* have to face," said Rabin, pointing at Ceasar Nunez, "is whether you want to continue this sit-in or not. I can tell you this. Many of the County Executives here tonight and many of those not here are going to be influenced in their decision by your attitude. If they feel that you're trying to pressure them, to put them over a barrel with these kinds of tactics, there's going to be tremendous resistance to any consideration of your petition. Now you decide; talk it over among yourselves. I'm just giving you the facts. There's a good chance for your success, now that we've heard your part of the story, but it's up to you . . ."

The Puerto Ricans, some demoralized, some merely trusting and eager to believe the old man who sounded so sincere, argued heatedly among themselves while the seven lawyers smoked their cigarettes and pipes and engaged in soft desultory conversation. They knew better than to leave the room while they had their opponent on the ropes.

Rodriguez held for continued militancy but was argued down. He stomped out in disgust. Bill Sokolov followed him to the hallway near the elevators. "Get the hell back in there. What the hell are you doing out here?"

Rodriguez shook his head wearily from side to side. "It's no good. Ceasar got talked out of it and the rest of the boys are losing interest. I can't get it together again."

"You *can't* give it up! Don't be such a shmuck, for Chrissake. Get the hell back in there."

"No good. Now shut up, will you."

Sokolov snarled. As always, his physical unattractiveness offended the handsome Puerto Rican's sensibilities. But Rodriguez restrained an angry remark and turned to walk away.

At two in the morning the Young People's Army marched out after having extracted promises from Lou Rabin of fair play and an energetic attempt on his part and his colleagues' parts to get the Executive Committee's authorization to reconvene the County Committee.

"We'll be on the phones all day tomorrow," Rabin assured them.

When the last Puerto Rican had disappeared through the outer door, he turned to his smiling friends and said with such anger that they were shocked. *"How dare they!"*

The lawyers were no longer smiling. He glared at them.

"Let's go home and get some sleep and try to forget they even thought they could do this to us."

"You mean we're not going to call another county meeting?" one of them asked.

He looked at the man with disgust. "A political party is not bullied by gangsters. There will be no meeting. They're lucky we didn't arrest them."

FOURTEEN

━━━━━━━━━━━━━━━━━━━━━━━━━━━━

IT was handshaking time in a lower-middle-class section of the city, mostly Jewish, and the ex-Ambassador painted a smile on his somber face and did what he could to unbend. The old people loved him, had always admired and respected him—he was the lawyer, the world figure, they'd always wanted their own children and grandchildren to be. "I've always admired you, Mr. Ambassador . . ." and "I'll vote for you, don't worry . . ." were typical responses.

He was gratified but he found it difficult to get into the spirit of the thing today because of Luella North's attack on him the day before. What the hell was the matter with Luella? Out of nowhere the black Congresswoman had decided to call a press conference and criticize him on the grounds of racism, saying he had put up posters showing himself and Zeke Carter in the black neighborhoods, but in white neighborhoods he'd used posters featuring only his own picture. Whatever had possessed the woman? He'd assumed, now the primaries were over and he and Zeke were the standard bearers, that she was on their team . . . Who the hell could figure politics out? Someone like Shirley Chisholm, the only other black woman in Congress, would never do a thing like this. But Luella seemed to have her own deals going. There was even a rumor that she had ambitions to run in the presidential race and was already trying to exact promises of a cabinet post for the privilege of her ultimate support. Glumly Ornstein shook hands and smiled on cue.

Hank Simmons turned up after a while. The two candidates had set aside a few days this month to campaign together, or at least to touch base in public, if only for minutes. There had been comment in the press about Hank's rancor because Ornstein, coupled with Republican Ron Corbett on Progressive Party campaign literature, had been slow to identify himself with his fellow Democrats. Today was to demonstrate that Democrats stick together.

Hank arrived with a swarm of aides and a sound truck that deafened the ear and drowned out the gubernatorial candidate's attempts at conversation with people on the street. Hank Simmons walked at the older man's side, smiling for the cameras, while his aides intercepted all who tried to approach Ornstein and shoved campaign buttons and literature into their hands. Ornstein had no buttons and no sound truck; he had a tight budget.

In the midst of his stroll, a rasping voice bellowed from behind, "David, why don't you get that fuckhead Simmons out of here? All he's trying to do is cash in on your popularity, and he doesn't even have the grace to walk ten paces in back of you where he belongs. That goddam sound truck of his is so loud, who the hell can hear you?"

Ornstein spun around and faced Johnny Kieran, the writer. Short and squat, with the face of a truck driver or a fighter and a street-gang accent to match, the Irishman was already in his cups, though it was still early in the day.

"Dave," said Johnny, putting his arm around the candidate, "I'm going to teach you how to finesse a prick like Simmons. How long is he supposed to join in this walking tour?"

"Only about a half-hour, Johnny. Then he's going across town for an endorsement or something."

"Good." Kieran, who had run in the mayoral primary a year

before, considered himself a pro in such matters. "What you'll do for this half hour, Dave, is come in with me and have a pastrami sandwich. I want to talk to you anyway. And by the time we're finished, fuckhead will be gone."

Ornstein was impressed. "Hey, that's a good idea!"

"All my ideas are good. Come on, there's a delicatessen. I'm going to give you a private lesson in communicating with the people." The writer turned around to bellow at the newsmen and Ornstein's aides. "You guys wait out here while Dave and me go in for a bite."

Seated at the corner table, after the order was delivered, Kieran said, "The first thing you have to learn, Dave, is how to stop being so goddam stuffy. People respect you but they also want to know you're a regular guy. That means when you blow your top, you blow your top. Especially when you talk to reporters."

Ornstein bit into his sandwhich and nodded. "There are times when I become angry . . ."

"Genteel, genteel . . ." Kieran's face, cheeks puffed with pastrami, grimaced in disgust. "What you need is a lesson in talking plain English. I'll teach you some basic words—fuck and shit. Now say after me. Fuck. Come on. Fuck."

"F . . ." David hung his head. "I can't."

The writer looked at him philosophically. "Ornstein, you're going to be a failure all your life."

Outside once more, they were glad to see that Simmons and his sound truck were gone; they separated with slaps on the back, the candidate to meet more of his public, the famous writer to visit the nearest bar. As planned earlier with his staff, Ornstein walked two blocks south until he came to a vacant lot; there he made a speech to the local residents who stopped to listen, while the newsmen scribbled. Ornstein glared over the lot, which had been purchased by the state four years before with the promise of turning it into a 400-bed treatment center for drug addicts. He waxed indignant.

"Four years ago, when the state bought this property with taxpayer's money for almost a hundred-thousand dollars," he exhorted the small audience, "it was a rat-infested vacant lot. Now, as we stand before it today, it is still a rat-infested vacant lot.

"Governor Wilkerson made us a lot of promises about what he's going to do to alleviate the drug problem. I say the governor has broken all his promises, I say his narcotics program is a failure . . ."

After the speech, it was handshaking and strolling time again. By this time he felt a little better. He walked into stores as he passed and spoke heartily to proprietors over counters and to the pleased customers. In the street, as people came forward to shake his hand, he looked them in the eye and worked at projecting his sincerity. One young woman said, "I can't tell you what a great honor this is." He was touched. He called to an unshaven old man who seemed afraid to approach, "How are you friend?" The man smiled and said, "Why don't we go sit in the park, just you and me? There's a lot I want to know about you."

An aide broke in. "David, you don't have time for that kind of stuff."

"I'm sorry," he said to the man, moving on.

A little girl, perhaps seven years old, came up to him.

"Are you my grandpa?"

He grinned down at her. "No, I'm not your grandpa."

"You look like my grandpa."

"That's because I'm Jewish," said the candidate, glancing about to see if anyone had heard his joke. Johnny Kieran was standing at his elbow. "Did you hear that?" Ornstein asked.

Kieran nodded. "You should have told her to go fuck herself."

"It's hard for me to explain. You don't understand Shelley. He's so *alone*. He has no party."

"What?" Earl laughed loudly. "What did you say? He has no *party*? What the hell's that got to do with anything? You mean the Progressive Party? Who the hell cares about a party?"

She closed her eyes. "No, I didn't mean it that way. But it's true that they'll never take him back into the fold, the state leaders, I mean—"

"You thinking of him as a man without a country or something?"

"Earl, he's cut himself off from more than just a political affiliation. He's really a man without attachments. They're all pretend attachments, just the same way he fools the public into thinking he has some feeling for the black people. He hates the black people."

"You're telling me!"

"He's split down the middle. You can't pretend to love what you hate. But I think I'm the only one he's got some feeling for. I'm all of it together for him, what he loves and what he hates."

"Don't be such a dumb broad. He doesn't love you, a black girl. Are you crazy?"

"He kind of loves me. That's something I can tell. He loves me."

"Barbara, he sent you out to get me to vote for him. I want you to remember that. He also agreed that you should stay with me, permanently. He doesn't want you back. Doesn't that make any difference to you?"

She got up and said without facing him, "I'm going to make myself a drink. Do you want one?"

He shook his head. "No, I want to talk about this. It's important, Barbie. He really doesn't care about you."

She returned to stand in front of him and pressed the cold glass against her smooth cheek.

"Earl, he could send me away from now until doomsday and I'll keep hoping he'll call me back. I can't help it, I simply can't help it. Maybe one day it'll just dry up and I'll feel nothing. But right now I go on fire just to hear you talk about him."

"Thanks." Earl looked at her and thought he saw her lip tremble. "Listen, I'm the one who should be crying," he said. "Well, maybe you don't have any pride but I do. So any time you want to go back to your white massah just say the word . . ."

"No, Earl, I'm not ready to go back. I want to live with you. If you want me."

"Of course, I want you, for Chrissake."

"Maybe I'll be able to forget him."

"I doubt it."

She sniffled. "I wouldn't be so upset if it wasn't for you. You're so much better, so much finer than I ever expected you to be, than I had any right to expect—"

"What do you mean you got no right to expect? You got every right in the world. What the hell's the matter with you, Barbie, don't you know who you are? You're one of the most beautiful-outside and beautiful-inside people I ever met. Barbie, when I say I'm in love with you I mean it. I want to make a life with you."

This time she really burst into tears.

"Aw, Christ," he blurted, "cut that out."

She couldn't stop herself. "I know you hate when I cry. But you're the one who's making me do it. You've got to stop being such a beautiful—oh, if I could rip him out of my mind I would, Earl." She shook herself wildly. "I'm making a mess of everybody's life. I ought to leave you both. That's what I'll have to do."

After a pause, he answered. "I wouldn't want that. I think I'd rather leave things the way they are, even if they're up in the air, than not see you at all." He went to her. "Look, sweetheart, I'll help you work this out. I'm good for you girl. You let me help . . ."

FIFTEEN

THE Wyndham Heights section was one of those pockets in the city where an older generation of Italian-Americans lived in well-kept two-family houses. Many of the homeowners were existing on paltry union pensions and social security. The houses were their special investments in life, their security, their symbols of independence and pride.

Suddenly these quiet residents of the city became vocal. This occurred when they were informed that the city was going to demolish their homes in order to build a new elementary school.

"There are several perfectly good sites—city land, in fact—that can and should be used for the new school," argued the spokesman for the homeowners, pointing to dozens of empty lots in surrounding areas. "Our immediate neighborhood doesn't have to be used at all."

Then Dino Spinella, a City Assemblyman and a Democrat built along the physical lines of New York's one-time Mayor Fiorello La-Guardia, jumped into the imbroglio and became the champion of this

Italian community as he had championed other Italian communities in the past. He succeeded in changing a neighborhood issue into a citywide issue and did a bang-up job of publicizing the plight of the homeowners who were destined to be paid inadequately for their homes only to face high rents elsewhere on their limited incomes . . . He also drafted a bill in the Assembly to block the demolition proposals and ran about City Center like a dynamo on roller skates convincing his Assembly colleagues to stand up for the homeowners.

Naturally he solicited the support of Tom Valente, even though he was of another party. Tom, idealistic, young and Italian, agreed wholeheartedly and promised his vote in defense of the homeowners. Valente then agonized over whether he dare approach his minority leader to arrange for solid Progressive Party support for the Spinella bill. Lately Shelley Greenfield and his office premises in City Center had become off-limits to Valente. Shelley had spacious rooms and a staff of six persons which were supposed to be available for the needs of the three party Assemblymen. But Valente, inasmuch as he was a Rabin supporter, had been cooly shut out. He knew he could not approach Shelley and Earl on this issue, even though they would surely be inclined to vote on the side of compassion over bureaucracy. It was a pity indeed that the minority party in the Assembly was unable to offer a united front for good legislation.

Tom Valente was stunned when, the morning after he had been approached by Spinella, he received a telephone call from Shelley asking him to stop in and see him about the Wyndham Heights situation. He hurried to the minority leader's office. Shelley greeted him in his private office, lit a cigar, offered one to Tom, which was accepted, then said, "Tom, this bill that Dino Spinella's putting up later this week—"

"Yeah, I talked to Spinella, and I'm glad as hell you're interested in this, Shelley."

Greenfield waved his cigar. "Sure, I'm interested. I want to kill it. I want to stop this goddam crap and let's go ahead with the demolition."

For a moment Valente couldn't even speak. Finally he said hoarsely, "You're against it? You want to tear down—"

"Goddam right! That's what I called you in here about. I want a solid Progressive vote on this matter to vote down Spinella." Suddenly he looked up. "Oh, I see. It's the Italian bit. Spinella got to you, eh? Oh, come on, Tom, you didn't buy that sob story, did you?"

His visible contempt for the homeowners brought out the fire in Valente.

"Shelley," he cried, "what the hell is the matter with you? These are working people, people on small pensions, some of them living on social security alone. How can the elected Assemblymen from the Progressive Party vote against them, especially without even taking the trouble to listen to their arguments?"

Greenfield gave him a look of disgust. "Don't make me cry."

"Is it just because they're Italian? Do you figure those people don't vote for you anyway, Shelley? Maybe that's what's wrong with us Progressives, maybe we ought to stand up for *all* working people, whether they voted for us in the past or not. How are we ever going to win them over?"

"Why don't you wise up, Valente?" The minority leader leaned back in his swivel chair and rolled the cigar in his mouth. "Cool all this sob stuff and let's face the facts. The facts are that all the arrangements have been made. We can't let a handful of wop homeowners hold up all the machinery that's already under way."

Valente responded indignantly. "Fuck the machinery! These are *people* we're talking about. They want us to look at other sites for building the school, that's all. What the hell's so unreasonable about that?"

"Everything!" Shelley shouted back. "Everything's wrong with that if you happen to have a financial interest in the demolition company that's going to knock down those beat-up shacks."

"What?"

"That's right. It took months and months to get it all set, and now you want us to start waltzing around and wondering if the school's going to be in this neighborhood or in some other fuckin' neighborhood. By the time all this publicity runs its course, lord knows who'll jump into the bidding for those jobs or whether there'll be any houses to knock down at all. I don't want any more waiting, I don't want any indecision—"

Valente was staring at him with his mouth open. "Did you say you have a piece of the demolition company?"

"Not me, you sap, my folks. They hold a piece of it under another company name. What the hell're you looking at? There's nothing wrong with my parents having a piece of the action. *Somebody's* got to own things."

"That's not the point," Valente insisted. "You shouldn't be voting on this issue. You ought to disqualify yourself. You certainly have no goddam right at all to try to organize a bloc to vote down those poor homeowners."

Shelley sneered at him. "I got as much right as anybody else. You don't want to vote my way, then don't. But don't stand here lecturing me." He rose from his seat. "Excuse me, Tom, I've got work to do. You don't want to cooperate then you know where the door is . . ."

Valente walked numbly to his own desk in the office shared with the other Assemblymen. He stared at his telephone, began to pick it up, then pulled his hand back. No, he'd go to party headquarters later this afternoon and talk about this privately with Addison Blum; there was no Assembly session today, so he'd be free to leave. What to do about Greenfield was going to have to be a party decision. Blum would of course call in Rabin and some of the key men in city government, as well as some Advisory Committee members. Yes, he would leave all decisions to them.

Tom let out his breath in relief. No need to rush into anything. The Assembly wouldn't be voting on Spinella's bill until early next week at the earliest. There was plenty of time for the party to take a position on how to handle this delicate problem. God, he was hungry! He looked at his watch. A few Bloody Marys before lunch wouldn't hurt either, he thought, shaking his head.

He wasn't back from lunch more than a half hour when the newsmen were upon him.

"I'm Bill Sokolov of the *Ledger*," said the buck-toothed one.

"Sure," said Tom tentatively, "I remember you, Bill."

"I'm Alston of the *Tribune*," said the very tall one. "And this"— he gestured to a slight man—"is Tim Dunne of A.P."

"Yes, boys, what can I do for you?"

"Mr. Assemblyman," said Sokolov, "can we talk privately to you—in the press room?"

He followed them to a corner of the City Center press room, where Sokolov did the talking.

"There's been an accusation at Progressive Party headquarters that Shelley Greenfield is involved in a serious conflict of interests. He's been asked to resign his position with the Assembly because of secret connections and secret meetings with the principals of the Parkside Demolition Corporation. Do you know anything about this, Mr. Assemblyman?"

Valente slapped his hand against his cheek. "Well, I—is this the company that's supposed to do the demolition work on those homes in Wyndham Heights?"

"Yes, that's the company. Can you back up your party's accusation, Mr. Assemblyman?"

"They said that up at headquarters? I mean, I do know that he has a financial interest in the company—"

They were all leaning toward him. "You say Mr. Greenfield has an interest in Parkside?" the A.P. man insisted. "How do you know that, Sir?"

"He told me. Not him, not him, his parents have an interest. They own part of the company."

"And what is his position on the Spinella bill?" asked Sokolov.

"Who, Shelley?"

"Yes, Mr. Greenfield."

"He's against it, of course. He asked me to vote against it. But I told him no dice," Valente was quick to add. "I told him I was *for* the Spinella bill, no matter what he said."

The *Tribune* man whistled juicily. "When did this conversation take place, Mr. Valente?"

"Just this morning. I mean, of course I was going to do something about it. But I wanted to confer with my party officials first. But as long as they've already found out about it, as long as it's out in the open . . . Jesus, this is terrible, isn't it?"

"Thank you, Mr. Valente." The *Tribune* man signaled the others with a tilt of his head. "What say we go see Greenfield now, eh, boys? Thank you very much for your help, Mr. Valente . . ."

Alone, Valente returned to his office and sat heavily behind his desk. He rested his head in his hands. Then he telephoned Addison Blum's office. The switchboard girl informed that he was busy on another line. "Have him call me back as soon as he can. It's very important," Valente instructed.

It was at least twenty minutes later before the Executive Secretary returned the call.

"Sorry, Tom, I've been extremely busy. What can I do for you?"

"Some of the press have been to see me about Greenfield. I just wanted to let you know I talked to them."

"About what, Tom?"

"They asked me about his connection with the demolition company. I figure that as long as you broke the story—"

"I didn't break any story. What are you talking about? What demolition company?"

Valente filled him in on the Spinella bill and the homeowner's plight. He also recounted his morning meeting with Greenfield. Blum remained puzzled.

"I don't know what to tell you, Tom. We didn't speak to the newspeople. I'm the one who speaks for the party—hold on a minute, I want to call Milt Holloway in here." There was a long silence, then Blum returned to the telephone. "No, Tom, he doesn't know the first thing about it. Now if the Public Relations Director didn't make any statement and I didn't—listen, did they mention who said this?"

Tom was now scratching his forehead. "No, they just said he was accused by the party, so naturally I thought you made the statement."

"All right. Now listen carefully, Tom. Get to those newsmen fast. Are they still in the building?"

"I think so. They were on their way to see Shelley."

"Good. Get to them right away. Find out who told them about this in the first place. And then get back to me. I'll keep my line open. I won't take any other calls."

Beginning to feel an unaccountable sense of panic and lack of control over events, Valente ran through the corridors to Shelley Greenfield's office. "Is Shelley in?" he asked Dottie, the pretty blond girl who sat outside the private office.

"No, I'm sorry, Mr. Valente, he's gone for the day."

"What about the newspapermen? Were they here?"

"Oh, yes, they were here about a half hour ago. But Mr. Greenfield hasn't been back to the office since lunch."

"Then they didn't have a chance to talk to him?"

"No, they didn't. I don't know where he went or how to get in touch with him. I'm sure he'll call in later . . ."

Loosening his collar as he left the office, Valente hurried to the press room. The *Tribune* man, Alston, was the only one of the trio he found there.

"Hi," he said. "Did you get to speak to Greenfield?"

The gangling reporter shook his head. "No, he wasn't in. But we put the story through as it is."

Valente made a pained face.

"Why, what's the matter?" asked the alert newsman. "Something wrong?"

"Well, maybe we should have held it up."

"What for?" Alston reacted with traditional coolness to the idea of withholding news for any reason. "You did tell us the truth, didn't you?"

"Of course. But Jesus, don't you verify a story?"

The tall man was quite annoyed. "Hold it, man. I know my business. I tried to speak directly to Greenfield but he's just not available. We can't even locate him. Now I can't hold back a story like that. And neither can the other boys. We have two separate sources of information and that certainly makes a good story."

"Who? Who have you got besides me? Who'd you speak with up at the party."

"His name was Pryor, I think." Alston pulled out a notebook and thumbed the pages. "Here it is. Russ Pryor, assistant to the Executive Secretary."

Valente stared at him. "That kid told you this story? How'd you happen to talk to him?"

"He called a news conference outside the *Ledger* offices."

The Assemblyman, bewildered, thanked Alston and went back to his own desk to telephone Addison Blum. He repeated what he had learned.

"Very, very strange," Blum said in a soft voice, so soft that it betrayed his apprehension, as though someone had knocked the breath out of him. "I can't imagine what Russ is up to. I can tell you that he didn't report to work today and the office manager called his apartment and received no answer. Tom, I think you'd better come up to my office. I'm going to call Lou now and a few others. We'll have to put our heads together on this."

By the time Lou Rabin arrived to join the others at party headquarters they had begun to understand the extent of the debacle. The radio and television stations had already made mention of the accusations as stated by Pryor and Valente. The evening *Ledger* was out on the stands as well and page three was devoted almost in its entirety to the accusations and to Shelley Greenfield's reply. The reply seemed to go on and on; indeed it ran to a back page.

Valente shook his head wonderingly at a copy of the *Ledger* spread before him. "I don't understand when Greenfield made this rebuttal," he said. "I mean, he wasn't in his office."

"What difference when he made it?" Lou Rabin said testily. "He may have checked in with his secretary, found out the newspeople were looking for him and then got the *Ledger* on the telephone. Or"—the party chairman narrowed his eyes—"he might have purposely been out of his office so that the reporters would not have to delay in sending in the accusation story—he wanted to make sure it got into today's news—then he got together with this reporter at the *Ledger* for the reply. You realize, Tom, why he wanted this reply in tonight's newspaper, don't you?"

"No . . ."

"Well, it should be obvious to you." The Chairman was as ascerbic as ever. "He has now made it extremely difficult for me or the party to issue a statement explaining that we never made such accusations, that this Russ Pryor character doesn't speak for the party. Lord knows how I would have got around and explained what *you* said, since you are an elected official and an important member of the party, but at least I could have attempted to neutralize the effect of what Pryor said. That kind of statement on my part *might* have worked if I said it *before* Greenfield had a chance at his rebuttal. Now if I say such a thing, it will merely look as though I'm running scared, that I meant to smear him and I'm trying to back away because he caught us in a lie."

Lou Rabin fixed the Assemblyman with a beady stare. "I hope you've learned something, Tom, that under no circumstances do you ever publicly accuse someone in your own party of wrongdoing. I hope you realize that in his rebuttal he has utterly destroyed your claim to integrity and probity, that you've hurt yourself immeasurably. I hope you realize that you've helped tarnish my image, too, an image of honesty and fair play that I've spent a lifetime in building. Have you read his reply?"

Tom was ashamed to admit he read at approximately half the speed of Lou Rabin or Addison Blum. "I didn't quite finish it . . ."

"Well, finish it," said Rabin, "and I'll leave it to you to judge what harm has been done to the party."

Greenfield's reply accused the party, particularly Lou Rabin, "the boss," of trying to smear and ruin the Assembly Minority Leader because he refused to buckle in to the Rabin dictatorship.

It accused Rabin of attempting to dictate County Committee choices for public office and threatening those County Committee members who had city jobs with the loss of their jobs—if they didn't vote the Rabin way. It accused Rabin of conducting a purge, of attempting even to intimidate and oust elected officials like Greenfield, who dared to resist his commands, by such dirty smears and lies initiated by Rabin henchmen—the party employee named Pryor and Assemblyman Tom Valente.

These were lies and they would be shown to be lies, said the rebuttal. Greenfield insisted on a full investigation. "I dare anyone to show or try to prove any connection between me and the Parkside Demolition Corporation," Greenfield was quoted as saying. "Russ Pryor lied when he made the allegation that I had been seen with principals of that company. I don't even know who the principals of that company are!

"And as for Assemblyman Valente's claim that my parents own a piece of the Parkside Corporation, that is not only a vicious lie but a stupid one. If Tom Valente and his boss Lou Rabin had bothered to do a little basic research they would have discovered that I have no parents and in fact I don't have a single relative on this earth. If

Lou Rabin and Valente and their Smear Committee have decided to give me rich parents they should have done it when I was three years old and went to live in that damned orphan asylum." A parenthetical note in the newspaper article explained that Assemblyman Greenfield had spent his youth in the old Unity Orphan Asylum that used to stand in what was now Lowell Park. The home was shut down when Greenfield was sixteen, at which time he went to work and put himself through night school, earning his degree at the City University, then went through law school the same way.

"And as it happens," the quote from Greenfield went on, "I am *not* against the Spinella bill. Assemblyman Spinella came to me about the problem of the homeowners and I told Dino I wanted time to study the situation and I'd let him know where I stood in a few days. My decision at this point is to vote in favor of the Spinella bill. I believe the city can and should find another site on which to build the new elementary school. I'm outraged by Tom Valente's lie that I've been trying to organize support *against* Spinella and against those beleaguered homeowners. Like his other lies, it can easily be disproved. I challenge Valente to bring forth any other Assemblymen that I'm supposed to have attempted to organize against those homeowners.

"One final point. I want to express my gratitude to the *Ledger* for allowing me to defend myself against the smears leveled at me by the Rabin faction of the Progressive Party. In order to answer the same accusations made over radio and television and in other newspapers, I am calling a news conference in the press room at City Center at ten tomorrow morning."

At the news conference the following morning, Shelley Greenfield offered two surprises. The first was his announcement that he would introduce a bill in the Assembly making it a crime for any lawmaker in that body or any highly placed city official to have financial interest in any firm doing work for the city, whether it be construction, demolition, consultant, law or other services. The newsmen realized that many Assemblymen and mayoral aides had such financial interests, including some who were members of the Progressive Party, those loyal to Lou Rabin.

The second surprise came when Greenfield introduced Russ Pryor, assistant to the executive secretary of the Progressive Party, who confessed before the television cameras and the radio microphones and the newspapermen that he had lied in his accusations against Assemblyman Greenfield and that he had been put on to this lie by Lou Rabin and the other party leaders.

"I am ashamed of what I have done," said Pryor, "and I am ashamed that Lou Rabin made me do it. I can no longer remain in the employ of the Progressive Party, not under this kind of leadership. I am resigning as of now. If Assemblyman Greenfield and the other party reformers who want to democratize the party and make it a decent party again will have me, then I'd like to offer my services in their fight against the Rabin dictatorship."

SIXTEEN

ONE morning, Milt Holloway, the party's public relations man, walked over to the Garfield Hotel to see Mike Long, Ornstein's press man, in order to get copies of all the publicity releases and position papers the Democrats had been sending out for the gubernatorial challenger. While Long, a thin, balding, cadaverous ex-newspaperman, was thumbing through the filing cabinets, Bernardo Rodriguez came into the room to talk to a secretary.

"Rodriguez!" Holloway said. "What're you doing here?"

The handsome Puerto Rican blinked at Holloway without recognition. "I'm working for Ornstein."

Milt vaguely remembered reading that Rodriguez had become an Ornstein aide, a liaison with the Spanish-speaking voters. He wagged his head at the ubiquitous young man. "Hey, I'll bet you don't remember me at all, do you?" he asked.

The tall Latin waved his hand airily. "Did I once take over your church or something?"

Holloway threw back his head with laughter. "Come to think of it, you and your Young People's Army have taken over a few churches, haven't you?" He suddenly decided—a small victory indeed, but a gesture he wanted to make—not to explain who he was to Rodriguez. "So long, Bernardo, nice seeing you," he said, and turned away. He walked to where Mike Long was busy at the files and asked, "What the hell is Rodriguez doing here?"

"Don't ask," Long said with disgust.

"You know what he did to us, don't you?" the public relations man offered. "He and some of his thugs pulled a sit-in at our office to try to force us to switch our nomination on some uptown candidate."

Long nodded that he knew. The ex-newspaperman had a face that was shaped like and portrayed a sourness very much like the farmer in Grant Wood's *American Gothic* painting. "What the hell do you think he did to us?"

"He pulled a sit-in here?"

"Damn right. We couldn't get him out. So we bought him off by hiring him. He threatened to make a big fuss about how Ornstein is neglecting and screwing the Puerto Rican voters. All that crazy bullshit. But who needs that kind of publicity?"

"He blackmailed you for a job then. Well, that's one way to get ahead in the world."

"He's useless. I think the Puerto Ricans hate him and Ornstein made a great mistake. When you think of all the real Puerto Rican leaders in this country, like Diaz in Chicago and people like Badillo and Guzman and Segarra and Garcia, look at the kind of creep we end up with."

"Well, keep him busy with the filing cabinets and the secretaries. Try to keep him away from the public."

Long shrugged. "None of my business. I'm just the press man around here. I'll let the geniuses upstairs worry about it. Here, take this pile of stuff. There's a copy of every release and position paper I sent out, up to date . . ."

Lou Rabin sat in the Mayor's office and nodded. "Naturally I want you to come out for Ornstein," he said, "but I realize you may be hurting yourself."

"Don't worry about me, Lou."

"Oh, but I do worry. I'm not the one who's got a whole political lifetime in front of him, who hopes to be in the White House within a few years . . ."

Casey Bohland scratched his chin and looked at the Progressive Party Chairman with some puzzlement.

"I thought you said it would be the smart move for me to endorse Ornstein. I recall you said that only a few short weeks ago, that I'd better start cultivating the Democrats. Are you changing your mind?"

The old man smiled sheepishly. "No, not really. But I'm getting cold feet for you. I want you to weigh all the factors. If you endorse David, then Wilkerson will never rest until he ruins you. I've been hearing bits and pieces of stories from upstate people about the kinds of things he might have in mind if you—"

"Oh, screw him. I can take care of myself. And, yes I've heard the stories too. He's going to try to make my administration look like the worst and most scandal-riddled since the Teapot Dome. I think he's a load of hot air."

"No, he's not, Casey. That's the one thing he's not, he's not hot air. And he's the one person you seem unable to think clearly about. So that's why people like me have to think clearly when we help you make decisions."

The Mayor laughed joyfully. "See, how can I get hurt? I've got people like you ready to look out for my welfare, so how can I get hurt? Lou, isn't it important to you that I endorse David?"

Rabin agreed. "It would be a great blow to my standing if you didn't."

"Then let's not even consider anything else." Casey stood up. "Your party's Annual Dinner is next Tuesday, right? And I'm one of your guest speakers, correct? Why don't I announce that I'm endorsing David at that auspicious occasion?"

"Yes, that would be nice, Casey."

The Mayor shook his head wonderingly. "You know something Lou—you have the most extraordinary way of asking for things."

Rabin smiled. He smiled all the way back to his office in the taxicab. He felt like a proud father.

Later in the day he received a telephone call from Ron Corbett that made him feel like a distressed father. The Senator was low in spirit; the Vice-President and other members of his party had been attacking his liberal and un-Republican record, and these attacks were beginning to take their toll.

"Senator, I'm beginning to think we did you no favor by endorsing you," Rabin said softly into the telephone. "But I never imagined when we gave you our nomination that we'd prove an embarrassment to you."

"No, Lou, don't be ridiculous."

"The way things are turning out . . . It's a conservative year. You've got to hold on to your Republican constituency. If they don't resent us they may resent your association on our line with Ornstein. Let's face it, they feel loyalty to Wilkerson, our good governor. He's got them in the palm of his hand."

Corbett sighed. "Yes, there's some truth to what you say. But I still have faith in the good fight and so should all of us. It's that rotten Wilkerson who's giving me heartburn. He won't give me a cent over what he promised me months ago—chickenfeed for him. And now that isn't anywhere near enough, what with the television you have to have, and all the money Simmons is pouring in."

"The governor's playing ball with Buzz Taylor," Lou said gently.

"I know. And I've got to keep smiling and telling reporters he really supports my candidacy. And those jerky statements he makes when someone asks him who he's for. He says, 'I supported Ron Corbett and I continue to support him . . .' He sounds like a man whose wife asks if he loves her and he says, 'I married you, didn't I?' "

Bernardo Rodriguez stood on top of the car and used his hands as a megaphone. *"Governor"* he shouted, *"you do nothing for the Puerto Ricans. We won't vote for you. Suck my cock, Governor . . . I have a big, fat Puerto Rican cock, Governor . . ."* He said this again and again.

Wilkerson stopped speaking to the street gathering only for a moment or two. He looked hard at the insulting heckler as though he wanted to remember the face. Though his aides and some of the newsmen were aghast and furiously angry, the governor remained seemingly composed; he resumed speaking over the sound of Rodriguez's high-pitched obscenities. Bernardo's friends finally convinced him to desist from further interruptions.

But the damage had been done as far as Wilkerson was concerned. He knew how to hide his feelings, but he was raging. Not only at the Puerto Rican, whom the newsmen had identified for him as an Ornstein aide, but at a complex of events: that other Puerto Rican who had once triggered a riot and thereby cost him the presidential nomination; the perfidy of Casey Bohland at that time, and again, this week, when he had announced at the Progressive Party dinner that he was supporting David Ornstein, despite his promise of neutrality . . .

That other Puerto Rican . . . what the hell was his name? Oh, yes, Miguel Perez, the governor recalled, getting into his limousine after the street rally . . . Miguel Perez, a Housing Commission policeman. The incident took place two and a half years before, just at the time of the presidential convention in Coral Gables. Perez had spent his evening off, a Friday evening, in his apartment, watching television with his mother and a brother who had come for a visit. Glowering in the back seat of the car, Wilkerson was amazed at his instant recollection of every detail. He remembered that Perez was thirty-four, separated from his wife, and had been on the Housing force for eight years.

At two o'clock Saturday morning the visiting brother left. Perez, who had run out of cigarettes, accompanied his brother to his residence, only two streets away, then, on the way home, stopped off at a bar, reportedly to buy a pack of cigarettes.

In the bar Perez was greeted by a man, a Honduran, whom he had once met briefly through an acquaintance. This man was with a friend, both already quite drunk; they invited Perez to have a bottle of beer at their expense, which he accepted. Before Perez had a chance to finish his beer, the two men stood up to leave; they explained that they intended to go next door to a counter diner for something to eat. Perez remained to finish his drink. When he left the bar, after drinking only the single bottle of beer, it was approximately three in the morning.

Upon emerging from the bar Perez had to pass through a crowd of blacks who were standing in front. He heard and saw one of the crowd shouting: *"That's what happens to you Puerto Ricans when you come around here, you motherfuckers!"*

Perez then saw a man doubled over, staggering toward the gutter, hurrying to escape the crowd and to get across the street. He followed the man and caught up with him at the opposite side of the street, on the curb of a gas station. Here the man finally fell, face up. It was Perez's friend from the bar, mortally wounded, blood all over the front of his shirt. Perez pulled up the shirt and saw an ugly wound on the left side of the stomach. He asked the man, "What happened?"

The Honduran, who was to die two hours later in a hospital, said in a weak voice, "I was jumped by the crowd across the street."

"Who stabbed you?"

The wounded man, propped up against a sign pole, pointed to a man who had by now stepped forward from the crowd and was approaching them from across the street, waving his fist and shouting threateningly at Perez (who was in civilian clothes and not recognizable as a policeman): *"Come on, you Puerto Rican Motherfucker, come on and get yours!"* The wounded man pointed to this threatener and told Perez: "That's the man who stabbed me."

Perez stood up and walked toward the shouting man, holding forth his police shield. He called to the man, "I'm a police officer." The man stopped. Then suddenly he turned and dashed back through the crowd. Perez ran after him, calling, "Stop, I'm a police officer!" The crowd impeded him but he finally broke loose and chased the running man west and continued calling after him to stop. When the man refused and was on the verge of escaping into the hallway of an apartment building, Perez fired a shot that caught the man in the leg.

Though hit, the fugitive continued running, this time toward the basement entrance of an adjoining building. Perez fired a second shot, again, miraculously, hitting the man in the leg. He followed the man into the basement and there found him on the cement floor in a collapsed state, two bullets in the same leg.

He put handcuffs on the prisoner and went out to call for help. The nearest police call box was on the corner; he told the station to send help and an ambulance. Just at the moment he hung up the phone, he saw a patrol car passing and hailed it. He explained that he had a wounded prisoner in the basement. The two patrolmen, who happened to be white, accompanied him to the basement. There they were met by the same angry crowd of blacks who had been in front of the bar. They shouted at Perez: "That's the one, that's the one who shot your son!" Perez was then pounced on by a woman who tore his shirt and scratched his face. The crowd then jeered that Perez didn't have to shoot, that he hadn't identified himself as an officer, that he was wildly drunk. Inside the basement the officers found the prisoner unconscious; but his pockets had been ransacked, emptied by his friends of any evidence of weapon or even identification. While they were in the basement the crowd of blacks attacked all three policemen. They beat the white policemen into unconsciousness and they cut the screaming Perez in the face, arms and chest.

Hearing the approaching sirens, the blacks scrambled out of the basement, leaving their wounded friend behind as well as the policemen. They ran through the streets as a group, shouting, seeking other "Puerto Ricans" to attack. Three unlucky men were severely beaten and cut and one woman was raped. Blacks came out of buildings to join the attackers. By morning a war was on. Puerto Ricans, Cubans, Jamaicans, Venezuelans, Ecuadorians, Hondurans and Dominicans alike—all considered "Puerto Ricans" by the mob—were the targets of beatings, knifings and shootings by blacks.

Retaliation was swift and vicious. The rumor had spread that the housing policeman Miguel Perez had been castrated as well as cut elsewhere on his body and this seemed to ignite the Spanish-speaking community to rage. Rifles, pistols, knives materialized out of nowhere and blacks were cut down. During the day, street fighting broke out between the two factions in several parts of the city, battles with knives, sticks, rocks and guns. In the evening, bombs were exploded in several movie houses showing Spanish-speaking films.

Then the looting started. Every kind of store in the black and Puerto Rican sections was broken into and looted of its stock. Juveniles of both warring groups forgot their fight and looted and laughed together; it was a holiday for the young. Policemen were helpless to stop them—they had orders from the Mayor not to interfere with any of the looters—so bands of marauders moved from one street to another, breaking windows, invading.

The Mayor and other city officials met with black and Puerto Rican leaders in what turned out to be long angry sessions for airing of grievances. Promises were made to stop the fighting and the looting but no results were immediately forthcoming. What started as a ravaging of the Spanish areas by the blacks soon spread to their own streets, then to the white sections. White law-and-order advocates marched to City Center singing "God Bless America" and gave warning to all the minorities that a spillover of violence to the white community would bring white wrath upon them.

But the spillover could not be stopped. Store windows were smashed in all-white sections and white store owners were attacked, some killed. Overnight it became a war between whites and blacks. Law-and-order rallies protesting police leniency were held in several parts of the city. Rumor spread throughout the state that black militant leaders were swarming into the city from all points in the country to lead what they called a guerrilla war. Window smashing became fire bombing. Now streets were filled with thousands of blacks freely looting. The crowds threw rocks and bottles at passing cars, dragged out white motorists and beat them, then overturned their cars and set them on fire. Molotov cocktails were hurled through the night air. When firemen responded to the eerie night conflagrations, rocks and sniper fire greeted them. The police who came to protect firemen were also subject to brick throwing and sniper fire; they answered by shooting over the heads of the threatening crowds. The rioters grew uglier and bolder in the face of official timidity. Direct confrontations with police riot squads and increasing sniper activiy from the anonymous ghetto buildings were hourly occurrences.

Governor Wilkerson moved to contain the violence by setting up roadblocks and cordons of state police to keep the guerrillas from leaving the city and extending their activities to other cities in the state. Blacks in cars were stopped and searched; they were arrested if found with any weaponry. Mayor Bohland never seemed to be available to speak with him on the telephone, so Governor Wilkerson rushed to the city for a personal meeting. "Casey, we've got to put a stop to this immediately. Tell me what you need—anything. The state and all its resources are at your disposal."

The Mayor smiled and leaned back in his chair at his City Center office. "You're taking this harder than I am, Warren. Has the Florida convention got anything to do with your offer?"

"This is no joking matter, Casey. No, I won't kid you. I stand a chance for the Presidential nomination this time around. But this mess looks bad for me. Promise the rioters anything, but end this fast. I'll make it up to you, I swear to you."

"Yeah, you sure want that big prize." Casey Bohland was still smiling. "All right, Warren, I'll do everything I can."

"Have you enough police?"

"Sure, we've got plenty of police. The trouble is keeping them cool."

"That's right, that's right." Wilkerson was perspiring. "That's the key word—keep it cool. Listen, Casey, I'll going to be in constant touch with you on this. Now I want you to answer my calls immediately. I don't care what you're doing, drop it and return my calls, understand that?"

The Mayor made a face. "Well, sometimes it gets pretty hectic . . ."

"I don't care. I want you on that phone when I want you. That's an order."

Bohland lifted his head slowly and gave him a long level look. Wilkerson massaged his face.

"Oh, I'm sorry, Casey. I didn't mean to sound that way. I wanted you to know how urgent this is, that's all."

Casey Bohland nodded icily. The Governor was beginning to feel despair. "Is it okay, Casey? I mean, will you forget I said that? Just remember that a friend needs you now, and if we can work together on this, pal, you'll have a friend for life."

"Certainly, Warren."

"Good . . . good . . ."

The Mayor had taken some actions but they had proved futile to halt the rioting. All the bars in the city were closed down, yet there was liquor available from looted stores. Curfews were simply disobeyed, and when arrests for violations were attempted there were desperate confrontations and battles with the police. Hundreds of blacks and Puerto Ricans were arrested on charges of carrying dangerous weapons and for assaulting policemen. The pattern of guerilla warfare was evident when police discovered they were being diverted to investigating and quelling disturbances or fires in one section of the city while firebombers spread havoc in other, usually white, neighborhoods. Under the no-kill edict of the Mayor, the police riot control squads were helpless. Any white civilian on the wrong street at the wrong time was robbed and beaten; rape was commonplace. Following the black firebombing of a building in a white neighborhood, a group of over three hundred construction workers invaded a black section "to break some heads." Several whites and blacks were killed in the ensuing battles.

On the morning of the fifth day of rioting Mayor Casey Bohland went on television and radio and publicly asked the Governor to send in the National Guard.

Wilkerson was stunned. "What the hell is the matter with that crazy bastard?" he cried to his aide. "Here I've been trying to call him all day yesterday and all morning and he never returns any of my calls. Then he does this. Why the devil didn't he check with me first?"

"The newsmen are out in the hall, Governor. Television's out there, too. What do you want to do?"

"Send them in. I'll show them who's in charge in this state."

"Are you going to call in the Guard?" the newsmen wanted to know.

"I am not! Most emphatically, no!" said the Governor. "That's a panic move. You all know the kind of massacres that have taken place in other states and on college campuses when the Guard was brought in. Every time they do that fifty to a hundred people get killed. No, it would look to the rest of the country like a panic move and that's what it is."

"Then what are you going to do, Governor?"

"What I'm going to have to do is get in there myself and take charge. I'm going to arrange an immediate meeting with all the leaders in the black and Spanish-speaking communities of the city. My assistants are busy right now arranging such a meeting. I'll handle all the negotiations myself at that meeting."

It was a dramatic meeting, held in the bombed-out office of a black community center. The leaders of the black and Hispanic groups came prepared with lists of demands and the Governor acceded to almost everything they requested. He promised to change the composition of the State Legislature to create openings for more minority representatives, more districts in the minority areas. He promised enforced quotas of minority hiring in the Police and Fire departments throughout the state. He listened to the demands from those representing Muslims, Nationalists, United Afro-Americans and other black-power organizations; he agreed to pour money into ghetto communities in the form of payoffs to those influential enough to keep peace, and to the housing and poverty projects and block associations they would control.

The rioting stopped almost immediately and the governor was proud. But the oily smell of bribery became an embarrassment as the blacks boasted of their conquest and as the response from other parts of the country came in. Only then did Warren Wilkerson realize his mistake, that he had projected an image of timidity in the face of rioting by refusing to call in the Guardsmen, that he was considered to have acted as a weakling under pressure of blackmail rather than as a clever negotiator or conciliatory genius. The comments from political leaders, especially those at the Florida convention, were of disgust at his "weak-kneed capitulation to the militant thugs."

Later, when he saw that all delegate support at the convention was slipping away, he could only think that Casey Bohland had been the one who had sabotaged him. He could not imagine why the Mayor had chosen to thrust the National Guard decision onto him publicly and with no warning as he had done, but it was clear that the act of doing so had precipitated Wilkerson's defeat in Florida.

"Are you all right, now, Governor?" his aide leaned from the front seat of the limousine to ask.

Wilkerson, nodding to himself, his thin eyes almost closed, refused to answer.

SEVENTEEN

D AVID Ornstein had been on tour upstate and did not hear about Rodriguez's behavior until he was back in his hotel suite that evening with his wife and Fred O'Brian.

"I want that man thrown out of our headquarters!" he raged into the telephone. "How *dare* he insult the Governor! I'll call the Governor myself to apologize. My God, what trash we have to deal with in this business! That man is never to cross my sight again, do you hear me?"

O'Brian was wagging his head as the candidate hung up the telephone. "Maybe you shouldn't have fired him so fast, David."

"I should have fired him long ago. God, the scum I have to deal with! Fred, I think if I had known what the political world was like—"

Ruth Ornstein broke in. "Hah, do you think Fred would have told you?"

O'Brian, seated at the edge of an armchair, looked at her with cool hostility. David turned in surprise. She was standing, drink in hand, slight, trim, still so remarkably pretty; but her eyes were blazing with anger. She never could tolerate O'Brian and he seemed to squirm under her glare.

"Are you restless?" she asked. When he deigned not to reply, she began to breathe heavily, working herself up. "If you're restless, why don't you go in the bathroom and have yourself a fix?" she said.

"Ruth!" David Ornstein was pale. "How dare you say such a thing? Fred, I apologize. I can't tell you—"

"Go," she said to the seated man. "I can see he's ready. He's at the edge of the chair, see." She smiled mirthlessly. "Talk about people you have to deal with in this business! Go, Fred, take a fix. How often do you have to put the needle in yourself? Every hour? Every two hours?"

"Stop this talk immediately," David ordered. "Fred, you'll have to forgive my wife. We've been under great strain these last few weeks . . ."

"I hate them!" She wouldn't stop. Her breast heaved and she moved about, but she kept looking at Fred O'Brian. "I hate all the disgusting people who are ruining our world. They laugh at refinement of any kind and I'm supposed to love them. Well, I despise them. I'm supposed to cry when I read in the newspapers that they kill each other or they die of overdoses. Why am I supposed to cry?"

"Ruthie, this is unforgivable," her husband said, shaking his head.

"Why? Why am I supposed to cry for those poor, poor junkies who pistol-whip old men in the parks and in the subways? Am I supposed to cry just because they're young? Everyone tells me I'm supposed to be sad because they shoot extra-strong stuff or extra stuff into their veins. Well, they should *all* take overdoses. If I had my way I'd buy the strongest stuff in the world and spread it all around the state. Let them all take overdoses."

"Are you finished, Ruth?"

"No. I want to say it. Why shouldn't I say it? I'm sick of being told what's nice to say when all these disgusting people are taking over our world. Go, go—"

To Ornstein's astonishment, O'Brian had risen and was indeed going toward the bathroom. Ruth followed him. She shouted through the closed door. "Take an overdose! Can you hear me? Take an overdose!"

David drew her away from the door. "I want you to go downstairs to the coffee shop or just stay in the lobby." he told her quietly. "Don't come back for at least an hour. I'm going to have a private talk with our friend."

"All right, David." Her eyes were wet. "I hope you realize that he is taking a shot in there."

"I realize."

When O'Brian finally emerged from the bathroom, David apologized for her.

O'Brian sat down heavily on the couch and listened without blinking an eye.

"I've been on the go constantly, Fred, as you know." The ex-Ambassador sat across the room and sloshed his drink before his eyes as if to discover impurities. "So she's been on edge lately. I mean, I'm rarely home and she worries about me . . ."

Fred O'Brian looked up at a corner of the ceiling. David suddenly leaned forward.

"Fred, I think you ought to pull out. I mean, go home."

The thin man stared at him with expressionless waiting eyes.

"Yes, that's what I think." Ornstein stood up and began pacing. "A reporter made a remark to me the other day. He told me that someone's been working hard to spread stories about your addiction. He said the newspapers and the wire services have agreed to sit on it. They'll try to do that anyway. After all, you're not a candidate . . ."

"I see." Fred's voice was clipped. "As long as I remain behind the scenes, they'll treat me kindly."

Ornstein sat down again and tried to make sympathetic contact with the other man.

"It'll be for the best if you go. The public and our opposition needn't realize that you're no longer with me, but I do want you to go. There's really nothing else for you to do here. Go back to your own state."

O'Brian smirked. "Sure, but if I handed over some money, you wouldn't mind my being here, would you?"

"Well, the truth is, I had expected financial help at one time."

"The family considered that. But then we realized you weren't going to win anyway, so we reconsidered."

"I can understand that," said David.

"Evidently my organizational work and my general expertise weren't enough."

"No," the older man admitted. "At one time . . . well, I did think that anyone who had handled the Cameron campaigns knew everything there was to know . . ."

"And now you think differently."

"Now I think I can run my own show. After all, you're not exactly John Mitchell or Steve Smith."

"And you," the other man snapped back quickly, "are no Arthur Goldberg."

"How right you are. Fred, at the beginning I followed your instructions, and I did many things that were not reflective of my true nature." His voice lowered tactfully. "My wife should never have said the ugly things she said to you. I think, in your way, you've tried to be a good friend. I sincerely apologize for her, and I'm sure she'll do so herself in the future. But I understand what's upset her so much. I stopped being myself for a while; I let other people do my thinking for me."

"Politics is complicated, David. You can't do everything alone."

"Yes, you're right." He pursed his lips in a thoughtful grimace. "But from now on, for better or for worse . . ."

The thin man was suddenly on his feet. "Okay, friend, I got the message."

"No hard feelings, Fred."

"No hard feelings at all, Mr. Ambassador."

When Ruth returned and David explained what had been resolved with Fred, she evinced no triumph or satisfaction. "It had to be," she said simply.

David embraced her. "I'm sorry I ever started with this," he said. "We ought to go back to the house, leave this damned city. Politics sickens me now. I don't know what I thought it was all about at one time. I don't know what about it I believed in so fervently. But I can't seem to recapture that spirit."

He felt her lack of response, her unwillingness to help him develop his mood, and he knew it meant she was beyond his thoughts, ahead of him.

"David," she said softly, "you mustn't admit defeat yet."

He released her. "Sometimes it's wiser to back off. Oh, I don't mean I won't finish the campaign and do right by all the people who are supporting me." He had moved to the bar and was mixing himself another drink. "But now I feel that I don't really want to win. Perhaps I never wanted to win."

She saw only that he was hurt, that the prospect of losing was too painful; at one time he did indeed burn to win, and the losing had hurt him far more than she'd guessed it would.

"And you wouldn't regret it the rest of your life?" she asked. "I mean if you let Wilkerson win it? Are you ready to retire from public life? Never to involve yourself at all? Are you ready for that? We could travel more. Visit the children more often. You could work on the book."

Ornstein gulped his drink and chuckled with sudden good humor.

"You are a marvelous woman. You've actually managed to make yourself believe, and to make me believe for just an instant, that I have a choice in all this. The truth is I have no choice. I'm going to be whipped and you know it. So our retirement or semiretirement is not going to be as voluntary as you'd like to paint it. But, no, I wouldn't retire to travel or write a book. I'd go right back into practicing law, you know that."

"Will it hurt very much if you lose, David dear?"

"It'll hurt. It *has* hurt. Because the polls show it—I've lost sweetheart. I'm merely adjusting. You know, when a man says he no longer wants something it may mean he knows right well he isn't going to get it. That's probably what's happening to me. Self-protection or something like that."

She came close to kneel and to lay her head on his chest. "Forget that self-protection stuff. I'm here to protect you. Just the way I've always been here."

He kissed her lightly, distractedly, on the cheek. "Poor Lou. He wanted me to win. At first he resented my being thrust upon him, but after we got started he wanted me to win more than anyone in this town. He's a good friend. He never lied to me, that man. He humiliated me, but he did it for a reason and he didn't do anything behind my back. And he was right, too. Only today I finally did what he wanted me to do right from the beginning, get rid of that unnatural man I've had around my neck. Casey's been a good friend also, don't you think? I guess you realize that by the time he publicly endorsed me he knew very well he wasn't endorsing a winner. But Lou is the real friend. My losing's going to hurt him more than it does me. In this state it's every Democrat for himself. But the Progressives were out there on the streets for me. They worked very hard, those people . . ."

EIGHTEEN

~~~~~~

THEY sat about in chairs in the plush hotel room, the three Democratic leaders, facing the old man named Lou Rabin. One of the Democrats was the State Chairman of his party, another was the National Chairman, the third was a Senator from New England who expected to run for president. The State Chairman said:

"It's simply this, Lou. We're tired of having you run our show. You're just a tiny splinter party and yet you end up having too much say in our state party affairs. Every time we want to nominate a man we have to tremble and wonder whether you're going to approve him, endorse him. Lou, that's not right."

The National Democratic Chairman spoke also.

"We don't have this trouble in other states, Mr. Rabin. This is the only place we're having this kind of situation. You're destroying our traditional two-party system. This isn't France, you know. And thank God for that. The multiparty system has brought France to her knees more than once. Mr. Rabin we've got to pass some kind of legislation to take the sting out of your tail."

The Democratic State Chairman chimed in. "We want to end your inordinate influence in our party business."

Lou Rabin had listened unblinkingly. He turned to the handsome presidential aspirant. "And what have you got to say, Mr. Cameron?"

"I'm in agreement with my colleagues. This is an important state. I don't have to tell you that. The Democratic Party has been weakened considerably by many forces, your party among them. It is time for us to strengthen ourselves. Conceivably, if we allow things to continue as they are, you could contribute to the ruin of our state and even our national organizations. In the past you've influenced or actually determined our choices of governors and mayors and all levels of legislators. We intend to cancel out your power within our party."

Lou digested this thoughtfully. "Gentlemen," he said, "the outlawing of second party endorsements is illegal and unconstitutional. I would fight such legislation."

"We'd expect you to," said the State Chairman.

"But if you should succeed," Rabin continued, "it could end up hurting your party more than mine. It could boomerang. If we can never endorse your candidates, then of course we have to run independent men and women in every spot on the ballot. This could siphon just enough votes away from your candidates to cause your defeat in many districts."

"We'll have to take that chance," said the State Chairman in a bland manner that indicated that he did not consider it a serious threat. "And while we're at it, Lou, I should mention a second movement that's afoot in our party. Whether we pass legislation outlawing a second line for candidates or not, we may decide to change the rules within our own party organization. We can simply impose rules within our party prohibiting cross-endorsements. All our candidates will be obliged to sign pledges and to make public announcements of their promise to refuse second-party endorsements and stick by the rules the party establishes—or they'll lose our support in their primary races."

"Yes, I've heard of that movement, too," said Lou sourly. "But you may discover, gentlemen, that your candidates have minds of their own. They may feel they need our endorsement and are willing to be heretics. You may split your ranks more than they're presently split."

The reaction of the three party leaders showed that they feared this not at all.

"Mr. Rabin," said the National Chairman, "you called this meeting, not us. It's been an inconvenience for us to come to your city, but you did ask to have the three of us here. Is this all you wanted to say? If so, it hasn't been worth the trip."

Lou chuckled. "Then I'll make it worth the trip. I want you to understand, gentlemen, that the kind of legislation you're planning to put through against my party's endorsement powers, and the kind of internal prohibition of cross-endorsements that you want to write into your party regulations, will be a great blow to the Progressive Party. I admit that if you do these things you will successfully take the sting out of our tail. But that's only true as long as we continue to be the party we have been up to now, a non-aggressive, non-militant, middle-of-the-road, sensible liberal kind of party. Our power up to now has been in our endorsements of candidates. In a way we've always been like a political Citizen's Union or Good Housekeeping Seal, giving our stamp of approval to the candidates of one or the other major parties."

"And now?" said the man who would be president.

"Well, if you think this old warhorse is going to sit back and let you destroy him, you're mad. You would leave me no choice but to become more aggressive. I mean, if we have to run a complete slate of independent candidates, then our entire philosophy must change. We would have to offer an alternative philosophy to the kind of liberalism both our parties now offer."

"Such as what?"

Lou Rabin shrugged. "No doubt we would have to move considerably to the left. And if I were you, gentlemen, I would begin to feel some consternation about that."

"Go on," said the National Chairman, hitching up his chair.

Lou raised his brows over the eyeglasses. "Ah, I see that you're becoming aware of the possibilities, aren't you? I don't know if you men realize that this country, this entire country, is just waiting to be galvanized by something a little bit left of center . . ."

"Are you getting national ambitions?"

The old man shook his head. "Not at all. But I have been approached by various groups throughout the country who would like to form an alliance with us. After all, we're the party that ran and elected the most beautiful mayor ever seen in this land, and we happen to be the most enduring and respected third-party movement in this country." He held up his hand. "No, let's forget the national scene for a moment. I'm concerned with state politics, not national politics. Right in this state there's a very substantial left-of-center, far left-of-center, even radical—"

The State Chairman interrupted with a wave of his pudgy hand. "They'd never join you. You're more discredited in their eyes than we are. They have to vote with us. Your party represents the old type of liberal they despise."

"True, true. But I can change that party image overnight. I can accept many of the alliances we've been offered. I can call for conglomeration with radical and strong black groups. I can bring their leaders in as vice-chairmen and Advisory Committee members in my own party. Don't forget, my friends, that I'm already having a lot of pressure to do just this kind of thing from some of the dissidents within my party. And it could prove a strategic move if I were to take the lead in this new young philosophy.

"It's not difficult for me to do all this," Rabin continued evenly. "And I'm not afraid to make the move. After all, at my age, what have I got to lose? But it would be impossible for your party to do any of these things. The Democratic Party cannot afford to make public alliances with radicals and revolutionaries, because you've got to hold on to your center. But *I* won't have to worry about that, will I? I'm sure you gentlemen realize that if I do any of these things I will increase my party enrollment at least threefold and my power considerably. And, my friends, it might be impossible for me *not* to go in this direction *if* you persist in punishing me for being a tail that sometimes tries to wag the Democratic dog. Furthermore, it might prove impossible for me to stop such a movement from becoming a nationwide phenomenon."

"You're bluffing," said the National Chairman of the Democratic Party, visibly disturbed. "You're too old to be that ambitious."

"No, I'm too old to be afraid of the consequences." He looked directly at Kevin Cameron. "On the national level I could destroy any Democratic candidacy. And calling me a spoiler would deter me not in the least. I've been called that many times."

They fell silent, glaring at him.

"Don't force my hand, gentlemen," he said softly. "We all agree we've got to get the Republicans out of that White House. So let's work together toward that end. Don't force me to help the Republicans win the next few elections. Let us think this matter through, gentlemen . . ."

"I predict," Lou Rabin said with a sigh, "that there will be no legislation against minor parties in the next two sessions of the State Legislature."

Ad Blum seemed doubtful. He glanced at Max Pizensky and the other old men seated about the conference room table and said, "I can't imagine how you achieved that."

"Simple. I threatened them."

Max's brows shot up. "With what?"

"With my age. When you're playing poker with younger men, age is the best bluffing hand you can have. I simply let them believe I'm so old that I'm liable to do any crazy thing—because I'm so old that I've got nothing to lose. They're young, with a lifetime of potential before them, and they can't afford to make the wrong decisions; but what have *I* got to be so careful about? So I told them I'm just liable to do nutty things like open up our party to the whole radical left and maybe even make a national party of it."

Rabin leaned back majestically. "I've been bluffing with my age since I was fifty-five. And it works better every year; the older I get the more they believe I'm just crazy enough and don't-give-a-damn enough to do anything. Of course, what they don't know is that I feel even younger than they do, and I expect to live longer than any of them. But that's because I'm a fool."

Addison was shaking his head. "Well, I wish I could feel as much confidence as you do that they've backed down."

One of the ex-professors chimed in: "Perhaps you went too far."

Lou Rabin denied this. "Gentlemen, we may lose our hair and our ability to fornicate but let us not lose our nerve. I tell you I scared the living shit out of those men. And do you know something, what I was saying to them about a national effort began to sound so good and so convincing even to me that I'm now taking the idea seriously . . ."

The others looked at him skeptically. He smiled and spread out his hands. "You'll admit . . . it could be interesting . . ."

NINETEEN

H ENRY Simmons paced the hotel room, "I can't stand this waiting. You wait and you wait and you wait for Election Day and you've
got no control over what's going to happen. Goddam these contact
lenses, I can never get used to them. Jimmy, do you want me to tell
you why they're bothering me so much? It's because I want to cry
all the time. That fucking Corbett, that son of a bitch. Why doesn't
he just fold up his tent and get the hell out of the contest?"

"Take it easy, Hank. You're doing okay."

"I'm doing shit. A two-way race and it would be my state. Boy, and
I'd make it my state, you'd better believe it. I'd whip this party into
line like it hasn't been whipped since—I tell you, it's all mine except
for that prick Corbett."

"Don't worry, they're switching over, all the liberal voters will
switch over before the end. We've got labor working with us now.
We're going to have a blitz of big newspaper ads signed by all the
unions. 'Don't waste your vote on Corbett, don't split the liberal vote

and elect Buzz Taylor'—that kind of thing. And, yeah, I almost forgot. That guy in the Progressive Party—Greenfield, that's it. He's going to switch over to you."

"Switch over to me? I bought him years ago!"

"Of course you did," said Jimmy patiently, "but now he's going to do it like it's a big revelation and like his whole party's beginning to switch over to you because of the danger of a split vote giving a narrow victory to Buzz Taylor. So we're going to arrange a news conference with him making the announcement . . ."

"Jimmy, how do we know all this is enough?"

"We're doing everything we can."

Simmons was scornful and mocking. "You're doing everything you can. But I'm going to do more than everything. I'm going to see that Corbett and tell him to pull out. I'll tell him to his face he's a spoiler and to get out of the Senate race."

Jimmy chuckled. "Yeah, and he'll just move over."

"Goddammit, he's a wishy-washy son of a bitch, that's all he is. And do you realize what he's doing, that meaningless piece of shit? He's standing *in my way.*"

Jimmy did not have the nerve to remind the overwrought man that Corbett was, after all, the incumbent Senator, no minor impediment, and certainly no Johnny-come-lately spoiler. Simmons was rubbing his eyes furiously.

It was almost midnight when the doorbell rang. Lou Rabin, in his bathrobe, peered through the door viewer and saw that it was Ron Corbett. He fumbled for the latch. "Senator, come in. How wonderful to see you."

Corbett was apologetic. "I happened to be in town. I'm at the Morrisania Hotel. We're going to be all over the city tomorrow, and there'll be a party for me at night that Wilkerson's coming to. I need all the rest I can get, but who can sleep? I just wanted to talk to you."

"I'm honored, I'm honored. Come in the kitchen. Lottie's making me a glass of tea. You'll have one too. It soothes the nerves . . ."

"Tea in a glass?" asked Corbett, shaking hands with Lottie Rabin.

"That's the European way," she explained. "The reason is that the poor people had so little heat, so they warmed their hands while they drank their tea." She brought the steaming glasses to the table. "Now you men can talk and drink your tea. Me, I'm going to bed."

When she'd gone, Corbett stirred the lemon with a spoon hypnotically and then said, "Lou, it looks like I've lost it."

"No, you can't say that, Ron. You never know until Election Day, and you've got more than a week to go. We've agreed not to lean too much on the polls. In an emotional kind of thing like what's going on between you and the Vice-President, the public attitudes can leap to extremes from one day to the next."

"That's the point, Lou, it's an emotional matter. That's where I've lost it. Dammit, I was so positive it was going to play into my hands, make me the martyr, make me the symbol of the strong, sane voice speaking out even when they're trying to muzzle me in Washington . . ."

"Now, Senator, I don't know what you're despairing about. I believe that's just the way people are thinking of you."

"No," Corbett insisted. "They're beginning to see me as a loser. Believe it or not, even though the administration's actions toward me border on tyranny, the public can't get rid of that American revulsion toward a loser."

The old man's voice scolded him. "How can you say that? On what evidence? This is purely a subjective conclusion on your part. You simply have no objectivity in this matter. You're letting feelings and hunches get the best of you."

"The polls, Lou. I'd love to forget them, but one look at the numbers and I can feel people deserting me. And all the liberal writers are saying they should switch to Simmons so that Buzz Taylor doesn't get it."

Lou sipped his tea. "Well, just don't allow yourself to become defeatist, no matter how you *think* public opinion is moving."

"I don't *think*, I *know*. I'm seriously considering throwing in the towel and getting behind Simmons."

Rabin made a rasping sound of disgust. "That mama's boy isn't half the man you are. Believe me, you'd be doing the state a disservice. Drink, drink, relax."

The Senator followed his prescription. His tone was more subdued as he asked, "Lou, you can't honestly say you think I have a chance of winning, can you?"

"Damn right, I say it."

"Well then, give me your opinion on this. My staff thinks I should go on TV, buy a half hour, bring my case to the public."

"I don't know. If you're going to project the defeatist attitude you've got right now you're better off staying out of sight as far as I'm concerned." Suddenly the old man's voice became angry. "Listen here, Senator, let me tell you something you seem to have forgotten. You are one of the most fantastic and productive Senators this state or any state has ever had in the halls of Congress. Jesus Christ, for a freshman Senator you turned out more original bills than any man I can think of. You're a whiz, you're a phenomenon. What the hell is the matter with you—wanting to hand over that job to that Simmons creep? You fight, do you hear me? How often do you think we get a man like you?" The older man sighed. "I'm sorry, Senator. I shouldn't talk to you like you need a pep talk."

"No, don't apologize. I do need a pep talk. I need something, that's for sure. I've always been a hardworking Senator, as you said; I've produced. I'm the one who developed some of the best and earliest legislation for community health clinics, subsidized housing for low-income families, home ownership for welfare recipients . . . bills for cutting down on weapons spending and the Pentagon budget, First Amendment rights for servicemen, the rights of homosexuals, students' rights, the right to dissent . . . stronger busing laws for integration, the right to strike down suburban zoning laws . . . I've produced, I've produced."

"Ron, what's the matter with you? Please don't upset yourself."

"I'm just not sure about what I believe any more. I'm not even sure that I know what I was producing while I worked so hard in the Senate. Perhaps I was doing all the wrong things for the people of this country."

"It's no time to doubt yourself, Ron. I assure you, the liberals of this country know you for a true champion. Do you really doubt the value of the social legislation you fought so hard for?"

"Let me put it this way," Corbett rushed in. "I've been asking myself this question lately: Ten or fifteen years from now, will I discover that I made mistakes, that just because it's somehow supposed to be 'good' to hand out the taxpayers' money to anyone who wants it and to be a liberal in general—by doing that, did I help to lead the country into a position of weakness? And I mean militarily and in every other way."

"Ron, you mustn't talk in this manner. I think you're just going through a period of self-doubt that will—"

"Yes, self-doubt," said the young man in an emotionless tone. "I think that describes it pretty well, Lou."

"And who can blame you? You've been reviled. Few men can stand up under the kind of pressure you've had to undergo. You've been personally attacked. I mean, very personally, and by so many people. You'd be quite remarkable if you didn't begin to wonder whether you weren't some kind of pariah, whether all these other people couldn't be just a little correct."

"I don't know Lou . . ."

"How does your wife feel about all this?"

The Senator brightened perceptibly. "Ah, she's a dear. She cheers me up just by being there. But she always did. What I need is to have you and Debbie with me all the time . . . *inside* me, in fact. Then maybe I'd stop having these doubts . . ."

"Now I've got a helluva busy day today ahead of me," said the Governor, fresh from a satisfying night's rest, a few strokes across the indoor pool and a tasty breakfast. "I'm flying into the city to receive some endorsements and attend a dinner later. And do you know who a few of the endorsers are today?"

The seven well-dressed men seated in the Green Room of the Governor's mansion nodded sheepishly.

"Well, I'll tell you." Wilkerson spread out his hands. "Your brethren, that's who. The almost two-hundred-thousand-member Construction Trades Union Council. They're going to go before those TV cameras and newspaper people and say I'm their boy." His eyes widened as he raised his brows. "Because I *am* their boy. Just like I'm your boy. Now tell me, fellas, why are your locals holding out on me?"

"We're not holding out," one of them said. "We just haven't succeeded in convincing the rank and file to endorse you. We've got meetings coming up this week and we hope to swing the majority vote . . ."

The Governor pointed vigorously. "I'll tell you what you do, men. You tell your rank and file that because of a guy like me in the State House they've been doing pretty well for themselves these past dozen years or so."

"We tell them that, Governor. But some of them still have that old feeling for the Democratic Party. You know how it is."

He winced. "Let me ask you something, men. Do they know what color your unions would be now if it was the Democrats in the driver's seat? Pepper and salt, that's what. Have you spoken to your men kind of private-like about the economic threat that hangs over every one of them? Do they know that every time the blacks tried to hold up construction on state projects until you boys put more minority group people on the jobs and in your unions—are you and your members aware that I'm the fella who talked them out of it with all sorts of promises? I'm the one who kept the building going on in this beautiful state, and you still have the same number of black men in your union, isn't that so, boys? And we'll keep it that way. But I need your support. I don't have to tell you what's going to happen if that other crowd gets into office, esppecially with that black Lieutenant-Governor. Use your imaginations, men!

"For the good of our state my reelection is essential. It's a must if we're going to keep the standards of union membership up to par and not just let people in because of some un-American quota system or anything. My opponents are advocates of racial discord and unrest, I want you to remember that."

When they left, the governor dressed and began what was just about an ordinary campaign day, starting with a copter flight to the city. At the Press Club, Tony Giachetti and the newsmen and television people were waiting. Soon after he arrived the lights went on and Tony began his hearty nasal spiel.

"You all know me," he said, stretching to top the microphones, which had been poorly adjusted for a short man. "I'm a Democrat. I was my party's candidate for Mayor only last year. And I'm sure you realize how difficult it is for me to have to go against my own party's choice for Governor. But go against it I must, because I must go against the kind of liberalism that scoffs at all our true American values . . .

". . . Ornstein, all he can do is criticize and make promises . . . He gives sermons on morality while Wilkerson gives us more universities and more prosperity . . .

". . . and those of us who see the danger of the liberal-left have to get together behind the only man who can win for the side of moderation and good sense. Some of us, because of what the liberal-left have brought us to, are tempted to vote for the gubernatorial candidate of the Freedom Party, also a fine man who sees the danger from the left. But we all know that a vote for him means taking a vote away from Governor Wilkerson. So we can't afford to waste our votes. We want to reelect a man who knows how to get things done in our state, a man who doesn't roil up one ethnic group against another or scoff at the principles we all hold dear . . ."

When he was finished, Wilkerson pounded him on the back before the cameras and gave him several hugs.

"Welcome to the team, Tony. You're a fine man, Tony, and I'm glad to have you on my side."

Still hugging and grinning into the lights, the Governor said from the side of his mouth, "Tony-boy, we haven't had a chance to iron things out. Can I do something for you? How's about a judgeship, like on the Court of Claims? It's about thirty-five grand a year."

"Forget it," Giachetti said.

"Well, you tell *me*. What've you got in mind?"

Tony smiled his famous election-losing smile. "Warren, this bear hug you're giving me will keep me warm enough through the whole winter."

"You don't want *anything*?"

"Governor, I'm not hungry; I've got a good law practice. Believe it or not, I think you should be elected."

Wilkerson was dumbstruck. He left the building in a pensive frame of mind, newsmen and camera crews following dutifully.

The stopover at the site of a major office building under construction in midtown was not an unplanned adventure, although it was made to look that way for the newspeople. The Governor ordered his car halted and chatted with the friendly construction crew while the cameras moved in.

"Hey, fella, get me one of those hats, will you?" he shouted in his gravelly voice, waving to the husky foreman. A moment later the Governor was grinning for the photographers with a canary-yellow construction helmet perched on his head.

To the applauding workers he spoke with great earnestness.

"Those of us who love this country are willing to fight for the values we believe in, and that means taking a hard and careful look at what some of the extreme revolutionaries are trying to do to this country.

". . . and if the Democratic Party wants to embrace the New Left revolutionaries, then we know where we stand, and it isn't with the Democratic Party . . ."

The next stop, after he and the newspeople went their separate ways for lunch, was at the Governor's city campaign headquarters, a morale-boosting visit, always a good idea when in town. There he entered the private back room unobtrusively and listened as the bright aide and sometime speechwriter finished dialing the telephone and held up his hand in greeting.

"Hello, this is Drug Referral Service," he said into the mouthpiece. "Is this the Methadone Agency office? Listen, we've got an application from Fred O'Brian. Yeah, O'Brian, the man who's managing the Ornstein campaign, you know, Cameron's brother-in-law. He wants to be put on methadone. Yes, yes, he's on heroin. Now our question is—would he be eligible? I mean, he's from out of state, one of the New England states. And wouldn't he have to wait just like anybody else to get on the list? Yes, please, check it out. My number here is 467–5538. Al's the name. Just Al. If I'm not here, ask for Sid Rifkin. Good, good. Thank you."

Wilkerson waited for him to hang up, then said, "First question: What if he calls and asks for Al?"

"There are a couple of Al's in Drug Referral. Eventually he'll get to Sid Rifkin—and there is a Sid Rifkin there. By that time he'll have explained the story to a couple of more people." The young man swiveled in his chair as he spoke. "Look, Governor, I could just call up the newspapers or various people and tell them the straight facts. But that wouldn't spread the story. They'd suspect political hatchetry and they'd be noble anyway. The newsmen have been holding it back as it is, out of some kind of perverted nobility. But this way— if I tell everybody—including the newspapers and A.P. and U.P.I.— that he's applied for the Methadone Program, they've got to make calls and check it out. Me and Sam—we've been making a couple of calls between us every day. The story's beginning to get around. It's what you call a propulsive beginning."

"Okay, speechwriter, but remember to disguise your voice."

The young man shrugged. "Who knows my voice?"

From there the Governor and his entourage went to meet the television crews and newsmen at the headquarters of the 19,000-member Construction Trades Union Council. The union men had nice things to tell the world about Warren Wilkerson.

"Our Governor is an internationally known and wealthy man," intoned the jowly union chief, "but his home has always been open to me and other labor leaders . . .

". . . The Democrats can no longer count on the labor vote, not in this state, not when we have a Governor who's done more for us than they could do or would do . . .

". . . Governor Wilkerson is a builder and his investments in new universities, highways, airports and dams have kept my men working. The earnings of the construction worker in this state have gone up at least forty per cent in the last five years because of the overtime we get on state construction projects . . .

". . . So we're behind this Governor, because he's the buildingest Governor we ever had in this state. We're behind him all the way.

I'm certain all our members will be out there voting for him on Election Day. Yesterday at our statewide union meeting our membership endorsed him unanimously . . ."

When they left union headquarters, the press and the Governor's aides were exhausted, but not Wilkerson. There was one more stop to make and he was in no rush to get there. He was due to put in an appearance that evening at Ron Corbett's fund-raising party at the Eastern Squire Inn. As he told his aide in the car, "I'm glad to go to the Senator's party and show how much I'm behind him. But let's make sure we get there a little late for the story to be on the eleven o'clock news . . ."

At the restaurant he was cheered and photographed from dozens of angles with his arm draped over the beaming Senator's shoulders.

"Of *course* we're in this together, Ron and me," he told reporters who asked. "It's all the way with Ron and me. Does he really have my support? Listen here, there's not an ounce of non-support. Ron and I disagree on a few things, but the strength of our party, as you all know, is that it combines a cross-section of opinion."

"That's right boys," said Corbett.

Still smiling, the Governor hugged him and remarked from the side of his mouth, "I told you to move to the right, you idiot."

TWENTY

▬▬▬▬▬▬▬▬▬▬▬▬▬▬▬▬▬▬▬▬

MIKE Eberly, young campaign manager for Ron Corbett, peered through the amber liquid in his glass, squinting at his boss, who was seated across the booth in the plush seaside bar. Outside could be heard the rush of long slow waves. It was not yet dusk and they had been drinking silently for some time.

"Senator" he said, "I see you through a glass darkly. It's the first time we've gotten even a little drunk together."

"We approach the wire," Corbett said. He gulped his drink and signaled the waiter for refills. "I'm one of those men who ordinarily doesn't like to get drunk. I like to be in control. Rule with the head, you know."

"You're an intellectual. You were top man in your law class at Yale, weren't you?"

"That I was," The Senator rubbed his mouth energetically. "And I think it's time for me to get back to the practice of law." He observed the younger man's reaction and patted his hand. "Mike, old pal, you've got to help me out of this . . ."

"Get you out? Get you out of the race?" He sat with tight, disapproving lips, waiting while the drinks arrived. "You're not serious, I'm sure. If this is what drinking does to you . . . My job is to keep you in the race until you win." He stopped when the Senator shook his head.

"No, let's forget about winning. The polls show that I can't. Mike, I'll be honest with you. I don't want to go on another minute, not with the whole goddam state, the whole goddam country, the whole goddam Republican party cursing me out. I've had it with vilification. I'm a simple boy from a small town and I want to be loved by all. Now my whole town hates me because I'm such a liberal and because their President and their Vice-President tell them to hate me. I was once the fair-haired boy in that town; they were proud of me. Now I'm ashamed to look them in the eye."

His campaign manager made a rude noise. "They should all burn in hell, from the Vice-President on down," he muttered. "How could you let those characters get to you, Ron? They aren't worth your little finger."

"Mike, I want to confide something to you."

His young friend nodded. "That's what campaign managers are for."

"I'm no good with Debbie."

"What?" Eberly didn't understand. When he grasped what he had been told he was dumbfounded. The Senator had never discussed personal matters.

"All of a sudden," Corbett sighed, "I'm a dud in bed. Do you see what I'm getting at, Mike?"

Mike looked down at his half-empty whiskey and soda. "Well, I don't wonder . . . the strain you've been under lately . . ."

Corbett hit his fist against the table. "It's destroyed my manhood. You don't know how it feels, everyone treating you like a pariah, wondering if your best friends don't think you're some kind of untouchable . . ."

"Forget it, Ron. When the election's over, all this'll be forgotten. Your wife is a wonderful woman and I'm sure she understands—"

"That's not what I want from a wife, understanding. Mike, it's one of the most powerful forces on earth."

"What is?" Mike assumed the Senator meant sex and he had become quite uncomfortable.

"Ridicule, that's what. When the Vice-President and all the other fat cats in the party laugh at me it's like I'm being castrated. I want out."

"Senator, let's just have a good drunk and forget politics for tonight."

"The obvious thing," Ron went on, "is for me to declare myself out of the race in favor of Simmons . . . so that Taylor can't win because Simmons and I are splitting the liberal vote. In that way, at least half the population will stop cursing me."

Mike Eberly, beginning to rise from his seat, said softly and confidentially, "It's the liquor talking. This is no time for you to start getting sensitive to all the name-calling. Jesus Christ, you've only got a few days before Election Day. So plug up your ears and let's fight."

Corbett spoke soberly. "I'm going to take that half-hour of television time we've got reserved for tomorrow night and announce that I'm stepping out of the running."

Eberly sank back. "That's a hell of an expensive way to say goodbye. All you have to do is call a news conference. But of course you're not serious," he said worriedly.

"I am, Mike. And if I'm going to do it at all, I have to explain myself properly, no matter how much a half-hour of prime TV time costs."

"Ron you're kidding about this. Please say you're kidding!"

"I want to see Simmons. I barely know the guy. He's got to promise me he'll support my legislation when it comes up. Can you get him, Mike?"

"You mean tonight?"

"Yes, here. I can't go home. Can you have him meet me here?"

Eberly was near to tears. "Don't ask me to do that, Senator."

"If you don't, I will. And one thing more. It wouldn't be right for me to make this decision and not tell Lou. Call him for me after you speak to Simmons, will you? But I don't want to speak to Rabin myself. I don't want him trying to talk me out of this."

His face pale, Mike went to the telephone booth and tracked down Simmons.

"Is he ready to get out of the race?" Simmons asked excitedly.

"I didn't say that." Mike's voice was tight and hostile. "All I said was he wants you to come here and talk."

"Then I'll be there. Now where the hell is this place . . . ?"

When he finished with Simmons, Mike dialed Lou Rabin's home number and explained the situation.

"Shall I come out there, Mike?" Rabin asked, his voice strangely calm.

"No, that wouldn't be fair to Ron. He only wants to see Simmons."

"Let me talk to him."

Mike sighed. "No, I'm sorry, he doesn't want to . . ."

Lou Rabin stared at his wife as he hung up the telephone receiver.

"Lottie, that was Corbett's campaign manager. Ron wants to quit the race. He's going to go on television tomorrow to announce that people ought to vote for Simmons instead of him."

"Lou, why should he do such a thing?"

"Because he's a thumb-sucking idiot, that's why." His calm was deserting him. "Do you realize what this crazy man is doing to us?"

"No, I hadn't thought . . ."

"Then think! If that big baby tells people not to vote for him then nobody's going to vote on the Progressive Party line. They'll vote for Simmons, who's in the Democratic column, and they'll stay in the Democratic column if they want to vote for Ornstein . . . and you can just forget there is such a thing as the Progressive Party altogether. Even our own party members won't vote for us. We'll have our lowest vote total in history. Lottie, we can't survive a debacle of that sort . . ."

Rabin paced up and down from one room to another.

"Sweetheart," he announced finally, "do me a favor. My hands are shaking because I want to strangle that idiot. So you dial the telephone for me tonight, all right?"

Mrs. Rabin didn't dare hesitate. "Who should I call, Lou?"

"First get me the Mayor. Ron thinks very highly of him, so maybe he'll listen to reason from somebody else. After that I want you to get Addison and then Judge Rosenthal. Larry Rosenthal's an expert on election law. After that you'll get Johnson upstate. He'll put a little pressure on that—"

"Stop already!" She was holding her head. "First let me get the Mayor, then you'll tell me who next . . ."

They walked slowly along the beach, Corbett puffing his pipe, seemingly more interested in the vast breathing ocean at his right than in the man who walked beside him. Simmons was impatient, striving for friendship.

"It makes you feel small, doesn't it Ron? The ocean, I mean."

Corbett was thoughtful. "Not really."

"Well it does that to me. It reminds me that you and I are just ordinary men. I mean, everybody looks at us with awe—you a Senator, me a Congressman. But you and I know, Ron, that we're just the lowest . . ."

"What's that you said?"

Simmons smiled and tried to restrain his impatient steps on the wet sand. "Don't take offense. I'm talking about myself too. No, the important thing is that you and I have to get down to essentials and break down all the barriers between us."

"That's a worthy objective, I suppose. But do you really consider that you're the lowest form of man?"

"Certainly I do," Simmons supplied. "And so should you. Only if leaders can identify with the lowest of the low, only if they have true humility, can they really serve the people. That's my philosophy Ron."

The Senator shook his head wearily. "Well, then I must be something of an elitist, because I—"

"I don't believe you. I think you've got similar qualities to mine." He looked at Corbett but received only a cool response. "Anyway, I have no doubt your heart's in the right place, Ron."

Corbett looked down at his hands.

Simmons said, "The polls show you trailing a distant third, Ron. I think you called me here because you know you lost it."

"Yes, I've probably lost it."

"Ron, if you step out now, it'll be like you're winning with me. Because everybody will know you made the right gesture. The best move for the good of the state. I know the Democratic Party will be extremely grateful. I speak for some of the leaders, by the way, including the State Chairman. Now be truthful, Ron, they're trying to kick you out of the Republican Party—isn't that what the Vice-President is doing?"

Corbett nodded briefly. "You might say that."

"So who knows? You may want to cross parties after all this is over," Simmons went on eagerly. "You may want to run for office as a Democrat in the near future . . ."

"Are you offering me a deal?" asked the disbelieving Senator.

"Sure, I am. Listen, we'll be grateful. We'll owe it to you."

"I see."

"And you need money, don't you?"

"*What?*" The Senator was aghast.

"No, I mean, you must owe a lot of money; you must be getting into a hell of a hole."

"Oh, yes. Yes, a small fortune," Corbett said helplessly. "But I don't see—"

Simmons was frantic. "I'll clear it up. I'll take over the whole goddam thing for you. All your indebtedness . . ."

"Hank, let's just drop this," said the Senator. "Let's walk back."

"No, no, listen. Please. This is the moment that counts. I've got to make it now. All my goddam life hinges on right this minute. If I can convince you to do the right thing. You *know* you can't win and that all you're doing is taking away just enough to throw it in Taylor's lap. That's the extreme right wing we're talking about, Ron—the Vice-President, the Freedom Party. We can't let that happen, Ron . . ."

TWENTY-ONE

IT was incredible, thought Addison, that this could have happened, that he should find himself riding in Shelley Greenfield's car. He had gone to an assembly district club meeting, after work, in Colby County where Earl Eaton spoke on the welfare problem, where Shelley had no business attending but showed up nevertheless. And then, what with the sudden storm outside and a few club members hustling him into a car so that he wouldn't have to walk to the subway in the rain, here he was, seated beside his enemy.

"Let me out," the old man demanded stentoriously, reaching for the door.

"Ad, it's storming out there, raining like crazy," Shelley said, moving the car forward.

"Stop. I don't want to ride with you."

The car leaped ahead. "Take it easy. I just wanted to give you a lift home."

"I told you I don't *want* a lift. You tricked me into entering this car. Drive me back immediately."

"Then I'll drop you off at the nearest subway station, okay, instead of taking you home. What the hell's the matter with you? I'm not going to abduct you."

"Gall! Gall!" the enraged man muttered.

"Come on, don't be such a horse's ass. It would be inconvenient for you to turn back, and if I did you'd probably find that everyone's left, and then you'd really be at a loss. After all, if you don't get home tonight, you won't get to see your boy Corbett on TV. Even I'm going home to see that show tonight. But I wanted to talk to you for a few minutes. I hear lately you've been showing the strain of all that hard work you do."

"I'm not at a loss," said Addison Blum, seeming not to have heard the last few sentences. His mouth was tight in its wrath. "You can stop right here and put me out in the rain and I would not be at a loss."

Shelley laughed. "No, you'd probably get pneumonia. Just a few more minutes now, Ad, and I'll have you at a subway stop."

The old man nodded stiffly. "The sooner the better. Being with you is intolerable."

"Easy . . ." Shelley said, as to a bridling horse.

The eyes flashed. "What the devil do you mean, easy? This is intolerable, intolerable. If Lou found out I was with you, he'd be furious, and rightly so."

Shelley pulled his gaze away from the slick highway to gape at the old man.

"Jesus, Ad, if you knew how funny that sounds . . . Stop worrying, old man, I won't tell your boss . . ."

"Don't you dare use that word, boss! Don't you dare call me "old man." You racist! You hypocrite! I know what you say privately to people about what your real principles are."

"So I despise the blacks, so what?"

"So leave this party, that's what. There's no place for your kind of man—"

"Aw, you're full of shit," Shelley said scornfully. "You don't believe any of that bullshit about the poor black bastards any more than I do."

Blum was pale. For a moment he seemed to have calmed. "You mustn't say those things," he said in a hushed voice.

"Say it yourself!" Greenfield demanded. "Admit you can't stand the dirty blacks."

Blum shook his head sadly, "Oh, this hate in you is a terrible, terrible—"

"Fucking liar!"

"Don't you see what it's doing to you?"

"Ad, you're the laughing stock of the party, did you know that? They say that if a black man kicked you in the face you'd kiss his foot."

"Don't say another word," Blum snapped, disgust wrinkling his features. "You're sick. It's not good. I must get out of this car before I become physically ill. Let me out. Let me out!" The old man's eyes seemed to bulge. Shelley looked at him in wonder. He couldn't refrain from taunting. He made a tsk-tsk sound of disapproval.

"Did I upset you, Ad? I'm sorry, really I am. But I don't know why the hell you hate me so much. After all, we have many things in common. We're both staunch Progressives in the old tradition. Can't we work out some kind of compromise between us?"

"Compromise!" Blum glared ahead.

"Sure, why not?" Shelley asked gently. "After all, I've never done anything to hurt you personally."

The old man was breathing heavily. His voice was hoarse. "You are the lowest," he said.

Shelley smiled and shook his head.

"Yes, yes," Addison Blum went on, his chest heaving. "You are a disgrace to our party, a disgrace to the cause of liberalism, to our great leadership—" When Greenfield chuckled, the old man turned upon him with such intensity in his snarling face that the younger man was taken aback. "You are *evil*," Blum whispered.

Shelley suddenly gripped the bony arm in his powerful hand. He smiled into the pale face. Blum's body trembled as he in turn looked into the narrowed blue eyes. His vision began to blur. It seemed as though red waves were filling his mind and that he had become light and was floating. He was aware of a new source of strength, physical strength . . . It seemed to Blum that he had never felt anything so profound, so Godlike. He wanted to destroy this man beside him, physically destroy him. A hoarse sound was coming from his own lips.

"Easy, old man . . ." said Greenfield, releasing him.

But the trembling did not stop; the passions overwhelmed the old man. His face was deathly white.

When the car came to a halt at the subway station, he stepped out looking like a man of ninety. He watched the car drive off, then turned to glance down the busy midtown street at the flashing neon signs. He was frightened now and needed a drink.

It was the wrong kind of place, but who cared? He sat at the bar and watched the topless go-go dancer wiggle obscenely under the colored spotlight while the rotund bartender stole his money. He just didn't care, and he was too tired to leave. The bartender for the second time withheld some of his change. One could only marvel that a man so clumsy at stealing money could survive from night to night. Evidently, he noticed his customer was old and frail and distracted, and assumed he was drunk or so breast-hypnotized by the dancer that he would fail to notice the cheating. Actually Addison was hypnotized by death. It was terrible. He could not shake off the vision of the face of death.

"My name is Sonya. Buy me a drink?"

Ad stared. "Sonya—that's a very musical name." He smiled. "I once knew a girl—she was a singer . . ."

"A singer, huh? You're a strange one, all right. So, mister, are you buying? I work here. You want me to drink with you, I drink with you. I get two bucks an hour and twenty-five cents for every single drink and fifty cents for every double. But don't let's be talking about singers you once knew, okay? You're a man, I'm a girl. I'm a bar girl, if you know what that means."

"Very pretty girl. You're certainly a very pretty bar girl."

"That's the spirit." She signaled the bartender and murmured to him briefly. She had red-tinted hair and large black-rimmed eyes. She was probably about thirty-five. She was more than passably pretty.

"Come on, let's bring these to a table," she said, taking the drinks from the bartender. Seated in a booth, she held up the swizzle sticks. "See these? Blue sticks for double shots." She slipped them into a thin gold-beaded purse. "I save these until the end of the night and then the boss counts them and pays me. Orange sticks for single drinks and blue for double. This is going to be a blue night for us, right?"

He nodded and offered her a smile. "Nothing but the best."

"Hey, you're a real nice guy. You're old, but you're nice." She patted his hand. "Usually Fridays are lousy. Don't ask me why, but Fridays and Saturdays are always the worst nights in the week. Ask any of the girls. You'd think on weekends . . ."

He stared at the men who sat at the bar and they seemed to be frozen. No one was moving anywhere. He looked from one face to another, and it was as though they were carved on a horizontal frieze. He knew all too well why he saw them through this veil of stillness. Because death was here. Death had arrived by stealth and was wagging a majestic finger.

"What's your name?"

"Addison."

"Oh, that's unusual. You foreign?"

He blinked at her.

"Don't misunderstand me," she said. "I have nothing against foreigners. No, that's not true. I don't usually like anybody who ain't American. I'm prejudiced. We have a girl here who comes from England. Pamela. Son of a bitch. I hate her guts. She cuts in on you and she even steals from the girls she works with. One day I was getting ready for my act—I do a go-go routine, we all do—and I was downstairs dressing. I put about twenty sticks on the top shelf of my locker, and like an idiot I don't even bother locking it. And during the time I was upstairs doing my act all my sticks were stolen. And Pamela who came on after me, was the only one down near the lockers."

"Yes, I see."

She raised her hand for the bartender. "Come on, honey, another drink, okay? Anyway, when Pamela came in on her night off last week she sat next to me at the bar. I was on the cigarette tray that night and I had the tray right on the bar in front of me. Anyway,

Pamela had the blues and started crying to me how broke she was and how she'd had an argument with Eddie, her boyfriend. He plays the trumpet in some lousy combo. So she's crying to me and I'm figuring what the hell, maybe she ain't so bad. Then I get called away a minute by the boss. And when I get back, what do I find but that she's gone and a pack of Marlboro's is missing from my tray. I know because there was only one pack left. How do you like that?"

"The bartender stole some of my change," Addison offered mildly.

"He did?" She looked at him nervously. "Now that's a pretty serious accusation."

"It's all right. I didn't really mind at all."

"Hey, you're really something. And that's how you got that fat lip, pulling at it all the time. I thought someone socked you. Listen, you keep doing that and you'll look like a Ubangi. Yeah, that bartender, that fat bastard, he sure is a crook, isn't he? You don't know the half of it. He steals from the boss, too. He doesn't ring all the drinks he sells on the cash register, you know what I mean? Sometimes he just rings the customer's drink and he puts the money for the girl's drink in his pocket, even though the customer paid for two. But that's his business. Here we all mind our own business. Like there are certain rules that the girls break that the bartenders know about but they don't rat on us.

"Like for instance," she went on, "we're not supposed to take any money—I mean money as presents—from the customers. Do you know why? I'll tell you why. Because you never know when a guy's going to come back the next day and say he got rolled or had his pockets picked or something. So if anyone, like you, for instance, wanted to give me money, I'm supposed to turn it in to the boss, and he'd hold it for a couple of days, and if you didn't come back then I could keep it. My ass! Once I'd turn it in I'd never see a cent of the money again. They'd give me a cock-and-bull story about how you came back for your money the next day while I was off duty. You can't trust anybody."

"That's true."

"Sure. Sometimes we get cops in here trying to find out if any of the girls are making any money on the side, if you know what I mean. Like one guy was trying to proposition me. He offered me a hundred bucks just to spend a half hour in bed with him. But I turned him down flat. Then he tells me he'll give me twenty bucks if I could fix him up with one of the other girls—that's a hundred and twenty bucks he wanted to spend all together. I still wanted nothing to do with it. He just smelled like a cop to me, that's all. So he went to work on Oscar, the doorman out front. He told Oscar the same story, that he'd give him twenty bucks if he could set him up with one of us girls. Oscar came running in here like a damned fool all fired up about it. He begged all the girls to go with the man. He promised to go along to the room and stay right outside to make sure we got paid. What a jerk. Maybe it wasn't a cop, who knows? But a girl's got to be careful. I can tell you're not a cop, honey."

"No, of course I'm not."

"You're too old, honey. No offense, but I never saw a cop your age."

She went on talking about cops and how she'd never been in trouble herself; then about a girl named Karen who always cut in, and how a girl didn't dare leave a man even to go to the bathroom lest Karen move in while she was gone. Addison tried to decide whether he dared to leave now, whether the streets were less strange now, whether they were safe. He didn't know in what way they would be unsafe but he couldn't shake off a vague apprehension. The thought intruded itself. *I don't deserve to live, I don't deserve to live.* He denied it. He refused to hear.

How would it feel to be dead, forgotten? Not to be here? What was he thinking of—some kind of retirement? How about England? He always thought of England as the place where one should go in the later years to reflect. But he wasn't a reflecting man, was he? Oh, no. That was what was so frightening about what was happening to him. Instead of functioning with that sureness and efficiency he was so proud of, he was thinking of, or rather he was aware of, thought processes, emotional processes.

He hated introspection and elaborate attention to self, self-pity, sentimentality. He was a compassionate and sensible man who had decided early in life that he wanted to lead in the crusade for a better world; he was a perfect combination, he liked to believe, of pragmatism and idealism. He had feeling for the sufferings of others. He'd certainly never felt that he wanted to kill; but now the thought was large in his mind, that he mustn't kill Shelley Greenfield or anyone else except himself. He was unable to point rage in an outward direction. He watched helplessly as the rage turned inward, like a knife, pointing clearly to his own death. Yet it fit the pattern of his life, as though all he had done for others less privileged than himself was a way of atoning for his own joy in living, his own talent, his own success. In some way he had been driven to a rage that had molded itself to his habits of thought; sparing the original object, it now dictated a self-inflicted punishment. How utterly strange to see a thought being bent as though it were a piece of soft metal . . .

"Don't you agree?" Sonya was asking.

"Sorry . . . I didn't hear . . ."

"That hundred bucks is really too expensive. For a good time, I mean. I suppose I could get a hundred bucks a night if I asked for it. I mean, I'm pretty enough, ain't I?"

"Oh, more than just pretty enough."

"I'd only ask for fifty. The bar's going to close in about half an hour."

"Oh," he said.

"So what do you say? We'll go to my apartment, okay?"

He looked at her.

"Well?"

He nodded helplessly.

On an impulse Barbara decided to brave the rain and went out that night into the black section. Earl was speaking at a party meeting and would be home very late, and she found it impossible to remain alone in the apartment. She discovered the stores closed at that late hour, fenced with steel, only a few persons afoot, and those few running for shelter from the storm. She wandered the streets with a sense of anticipation and daring, vaguely disappointed as she walked from one strange neighborhood to another that nothing happened to threaten her safety.

She was happily invigorated and stirred by the rain in her face, peacefully stirred. She had always been susceptible to environment, to the ambience, the setting, in which she and her emotions lived. Terror needed a setting—one must run from a physical something—so the opposite must be true, that one could run toward and into love and peace and fulfillment. As a child she had sought places that spoke to her of silence and secret happiness: a forgotten place in the woods, a back yard, a prismatic world in a pure marble held up to the light where one could find shadowy birds or exotic plants. She sought in private places what others sought in persons—the rain-on-window joys, the backyard places, the unpainted-sides-of-houses places, the hum of summer places from which she could hear but not see the revelers or swimmers in the distance, Andrew Wyeth places, dark night places, raining places too . . .

There was a contradiction in her feeling for places. The streets she chose to walk tonight, though unfamiliar, were not strange or terrifying. Only when she became familiar with a street, or a house or room, did she become aware of its strangeness and forbiddingness. It was as though the frightened person within her understood that what had not been seen before must be taken at face value, requiring adrenalin and courage; what was known, on the other hand, had the dreadful potential of becoming suddenly unknown. She was one of those who could not, if taken unawares, describe a landmark she had passed every day for years. Her subjectivity was such that it melted reality; the walls of residence or business were unseen, expanded with neglect; but neglected too long they began to assert their strange closeness; even sidewalks rose and hummed . . .

Life in a familiar world going strange required a balancing act of some virtuosity; the effort had to be made to know streets well, to carry maps about in her mind. Sometimes it was required that a point on the landscape be chosen as a goal, and she had to refrain from running toward it—as she refrained from running now toward the goal she had chosen out of the night—much as a spinning dancer fastens her gaze on some distant point in the theater to counteract the dizziness. In this way, holding to the night goal, she told herself —walking faster now toward where Shelley lived—one could survive even in the streets of great cities . . . When she rang his bell, she prayed, eyes shut tightly, her breath quickening, her legs trembling, that he would be home. He opened the door.

TWENTY-TWO

H<small>E</small> lay beside her, spent from lovemaking. "I'm going to surprise you in about fifteen minutes by turning on television. I hope you're insulted."

Barbara laughed. "No, you can't insult me. Because I know Senator Corbett's coming on and I want to watch it too. Earl was supposed to rush home so we could see it together. Shelley, I'm not going back to him."

"I wouldn't let you," he said earnestly. "Christ, why the hell couldn't you be white?"

She moved against him. "You could help matters just as much by being black. Honey, don't feel bad. You're not expected to marry me, you know."

"I know, I know. One day we'll just say goodbye. That's the way it's going to be, baby."

She shook her head. "I can't imagine doing that."

"No? You're going to want to marry somebody who gives you

something solid in life and I'm going to probably end up marrying some rich babe who's way out of my class and who'll want lots of kids. After all, I'm soon going to be over the marriageable age. Listen here, Barbara, you don't let me screw up your life. Don't let me keep you dangling if I move on to some other dame."

"Let me worry about that."

"Well, then, maybe I'll send you out whoring again. That's one way to get rid of you."

"Oh, no you won't. I can't enjoy anybody else but you, so I'm not much good at that job."

Shelley snapped on the lamp and reached for a cigar. "Barbara, I'm a lucky man."

"Why?" she asked, sighing.

"Because I'm a good lover. Some men have no staying power. Me, I could screw all night."

Barbara chuckled. "You rat. I thought you were going to say you're lucky to have me."

"Oh, that, too, of course." He fondled her possessively. "You know what I am, Barbara—I'm a braggart."

"You don't say!"

"I'm going to start a campaign to change our image. The braggarts of this world have been maligned for too long. Bragging is beautiful. Think for a minute about the typical braggart and you're liable to find that he has some very laudable qualities when compared to the modest man. Even if you suppose that the braggart is only trying to impress people because of his own knowledge of the qualities he's lacking—why, even that can be a very good thing. That's pride, the kind of pride that may have come from a need to fight off pity from others because of his very deficiencies. Now that's not a bad thing, is it?"

"No . . ." Barbara said doubtfully.

Shelley fluffed his pillow and continued on one elbow, his cigar suddenly going furiously. "Now take the modest man. By definition he's a man who's willing to accept any assessment of his worth, even pity for his apparent deficiencies, extra consideration, extra quarter. Of course all modest men aren't like that. But braggarts are *never* like that. So"—he nudged her with his elbow—"we have to give the braggart his due."

Barbara sighed. She understood that he was trying to tell her that at one time he had had to repress his own longing for pity.

"I think," she offered, "that you should be more tactful with people, less rude. Bragging is fine, if you say so. But rudeness—"

"I'm a rebel, that's all." He seemed to believe that was an acceptable and self-justifiable category. "I'm a sizer-upper. I don't like to be told how I'm supposed to react. I don't like to be intimidated by the invincibility or impenetrability or the sanctity of anything or anybody or any group of anybodies. The rules of the game can be brought to bear on me as well as anyone else, but as soon as I get a chance I'm going to tell them where to shove their rules and their cherished protocol and scale of values."

"A little bit of sugar . . ." she said tentatively.

"Hell, no." Shelley stroked her arm and admired its light-brown color. "If you're at all honest with yourself you'll admit that the sweet and nice people are really people who were afraid to grow up. Some of them may have been just too stupid to see the way life really is; but most of them, I'm sure, decided they couldn't stand the hassle of exposing themselves to the real climate and they decided to play the Christian. Lucky for them there are some sweet old lady societies for them to join up with. If there wasn't this whole cult of nice-guyism, what the hell would all those weaklings do? Me, I like a fight." He turned toward her. "I guess I came out of that home with a real thing about authority."

"You mean against authority?" she said.

"Of course. But maybe I'm not being fair to all those weaklings. It doesn't say too much about a man's manhood just because he bends to authority. You know what's sad, beautiful? The average man develops an incredible tolerance for the unbelievable insolence and bungling and cowardice and lack of discipline and character in his superiors. He learns to judge them with good humor. Sometimes, if they see the glint in his eye, they begin to suspect that he's laughing at them. But he's not. He's laughing at the knowledge that he must laugh, that he can't simply squash those vermin into the ground."

She thought: He's ashamed of being unable to fight them when he was a kid. That's what's killing him.

"But hate can destroy you," she said. "I know that from personal experience."

He waved this thought away. "Not hate—contempt. Sure, I'll admit to that. And I know that with just a little more thought and study and a little more of looking into the reasons and the backgrounds and the problems of the very people I despise . . . if I were willing to do that, I'd probably have some feeling for them or be able to identify with them." He made a noise like a laugh. "But that's the very difference betwixt thee and me. I simply refuse to give it a little more thought and a little more study. You go right ahead, you bleeding heart you, and study your way into passivity . . ."

"I'll do that," she said, rolling toward him.

He slapped her behind. "Don't be a bleeding heart. It's much wiser to build your strength on contempt rather than sympathy. Then it becomes impossible that they can ever surprise you or disappoint you."

"Shelley, darling, don't be so defensive."

"I'm not. That's not a defense. It's a lucky fact of my constitution. I'm hard; I've got strength and I've got character. Not always good character, but it's real stuff. Rabin knows it. He saw it when he first met me. He's got some pretty remarkable qualities himself and he's been nervous about me right from the start. He doesn't want anyone else around him who's a real man, understand? He likes the idea that everyone he has to deal with is carrying around inside him a great big yawning vacuum, like Blum for example. The last thing he wants is a guy with real stuff, who'll stand up to him. A man like me just won't fall into line."

"It's true, you don't like authority. That's what you're all about."

"Maybe," he said. "Or maybe I'm much more than that, or much worse than that. You know, when I got out of the home, I looked at the city, I looked at the whole skyline, and I felt I had nothing to do with it. I was *outside* . . . but yet I knew it. I was sixteen then, but I figured out that there was some kind of structure or some kind of grouping or some kinds of loopholes . . . No, no, I was like a surgeon. There was this big mass out there and I was going to probe into it.

It was vulnerable, I was sure of that. I was going to probe into it here and there and lift the skin a little with a scalpel and I'd find my opening." He looked at her. "Does that sound familiar to you?"

She was puzzled. "I don't know what you mean."

"Don't you get the picture, honey? That's the way a confidence man looks at life. Exactly the way I do. Which reminds me, let's switch on Corbett and listen to his con job . . ."

Before entering Studio B where the cameras awaited him, Corbett turned to Lou Rabin with the most ghastly look on his face.

"I'm scared," he said, as though surprised.

"Of course," said Lou heartily. "Everybody's scared at a time like this, especially a live, extemporaneous—"

"I'm scared I'm going to cry."

The older man was flabbergasted. "Don't be ridiculous. You won't cry."

"If I cry, I'll kill myself."

"This is all nonsense. I'll call it off."

"No, we've barely got a minute."

Rabin gave him a hard look. "You've got no right to dramatize yourself. You go out there and you do a job and you stop dramatizing yourself, do you understand?"

"Is that it? Is that what I'm doing?"

"You're thinking too much of yourself." Rabin gripped him tightly by the arm. "You go in front of that camera and you do nothing except represent the Republican Party and the Progressive Party as a candidate. You are not to act out a private drama of your own. If you have your mental breakdown here and now, tonight, young man, you'll disgrace your family and every friend you ever had. You're right to be scared. I want you to be so scared that you're numb." He shook the man. "The very second you feel an emotion coming up inside of you, switch over to one of your stock speeches. Bore the hell out of them. This is a job you have to do, that's all it is."

Corbett was still nodding as he entered the studio.

Watching from the control booth, Lou was gratified to note that the Senator's television consultant had smartly imposed a structure on the show by starting with film clips of the Vice-President criticizing Corbett. This exploited the theme Corbett would have to use to appeal for the liberal vote. Still, once those segments were over, the Senator was on his own, with no prepared speech. But he was good.

"I'm speaking to you live tonight without a prepared speech," he said, "because I want you to feel you're with me right now, experiencing what I'm experiencing, going through the anguish of a decision that I have made tonight and that I want you to share with me.

"First of all, I want you to know who I am, that I'm an unpopular man. At least in some quarters I'm unpopular. Am I ashamed of that? Well, I tell myself that popular men are all too often those who are afraid to fight for what they believe in, to change the status quo, to fight the establishment or even to fight the leaders of their own parties.

"Though I don't like being unpopular—especially with some people in my own party—I think that a United States Senator has to speak up and provide leadership on the issues, even if some people begin to hate him for it. They hate him because he reminds them again and again of the country's weaknesses. But a Senator can't back down because people don't want to hear the truth. He's got to be strong and he's got to speak up, even if those in power vilify him and want to purge him from their ranks.

"I ask myself—what is my duty to my state and my country? Would it help my country if I throw up my hands in defeat because the Vice-President has chosen me as his target? Our country is in deep trouble, deep internal trouble, and I have been speaking out on the issues. That's why certain forces in the government for whom the Vice-President speaks have called for my destruction. Shall I let them destroy me . . . ?"

Lou rabin nodded, eyes closed, listening with approval as the Senator continued his extemporaneous talk to the public, delivered without pause or doubt, expressing the true brilliance and clarity of thought that had led Corbett to the Senate in the first place.

"I can tell you," Ron was saying, "that Henry Simmons has been in the House of Representatives for almost five years now, and the record shows that in that period he has given leadership to only one piece of legislation, so minor that nobody remembers what it was. In the Senate, on the other hand, my name is attached to or is on top of forty-five pieces of legislation. You tell me which of us, which of the two of us, has been working harder to solve the problems of our country . . ."

At the end, Ron Corbett said, looking directly into the camera:

"I say to you that I have anguished over what I should do, what is the best thing to do for my country, and I have concluded that it would be wrong for me to buckle under, wrong for me to yield to pressures from the right and from Washington. They want to destroy me. Well, I am not going to be destroyed—I'm going to fight. I'm asking you to fight with me. I have tried to represent the Republican Party—the real Republican Party—in the United States Senate and I shall continue to represent you and the people of this state in the United States Senate . . ."

TWENTY-THREE

AS they entered her hotel apartment she said coyly, "You don't have to pay me anything in advance. I know you're an honest man." She snapped on a lamp in the bedroom. "Wait here. Take your things off, make yourself comfortable. I'll get myself fixed up."

She was in the bathroom quite some time. Just as she was patting herself with talcum powder she heard a loud crash of furniture in the other room. "What happened?" she screamed and ran naked into the bedroom to see the old man lying on the floor with the orange curtain tassels around his neck, her upholstered chair knocked over and a hole in the ceiling where the overhead light fixture had been. The crazy son of a bitch had pulled down half the ceiling trying to hang himself. He was moaning and mumbling incoherently.

Cursing him, she sped to the telephone on the other side of the bed and dialed the nearby precinct.

"Detective Calhoun," she said. When the detective got on, she said directly, "Cal, it's Sonya. Can you come up to my place quick? I got a problem."

"Want a squad car?" he asked.

"No, no. Look, it's nothing too serious, but I want you to take care of it. Make it fast, will you?"

When the detective arrived, broad-shouldered, mustachioed, Addison Blum was seated on the bed speaking in a surprisingly powerful and sonorous voice.

". . . the upstate counties have five petition forms. Canvassers will have to take out four or five of these different petition forms . . . one for the Congressional candidate, two for the State Senatorial candidate, three for the State Assembly candidate when the Assembly District is in and within the county . . . this will also include two State Committee candidates from the Assembly District, two County Committeemen for a particular Election District in the A.D. and delegates and alternates to the district judicial convention if such is to be held . . . these petitions are filed with the County Board of Elections . . . for the State Assembly candidate when the A.D. covers more than one county or parts of more than one county . . . this will include two State Committee candidates for that A.D. and delegates and alternates from that A.D. to the district judicial convention . . ."

"Jesus Christ," the detective intoned, listening to the man and surveying the room with a glance. "What kind of trade you picking up these days?" Sonya and he moved away from the reciting man so that they could hear each other. She said defensively, "He wasn't acting like that when I met him. He came to the bar."

"What the hell happened to the ceiling?"

"That's why I called you. I was in the bathroom and he tried to hang himself with my drapery cords."

"Well, then, shit, let's get the looney boys down here."

She made a face. "Must you, Cal? I don't want him reported here in my place. I don't want to have to explain . . ."

The detective stopped her. "Don't worry about that. I can say that someone reported his roaming around the halls of the building. You'll be out of it."

"With that hole in my ceiling? And anyway . . . look, I don't want him put away. He's such a nice old guy. Let's see if we can get him home to his family. Will you drive him there if we can find out where he lives?"

"But he tried to kill himself."

"Please, honey."

"Well, let's see if we can find out who he is. Did you get his wallet?"

"His wallet?" She was indignant. "No, he's got his wallet."

Detective Calhoun smiled and hugged her with one hand. "Sonya, when are you going to learn? If you're going to be a big city hustler you gotta learn how to lift wallets."

"Up yours," she said.

They went back to the other room and listened to the old man for a few minutes of shared amazement.

". . . law requires signatures of five percent of the party enrollees living in the political subdivision where a public office or party position is to be filled . . . for example, five percent of the Progressive enrollees in an Assembly District where delegates to a judicial convention are to be nominated . . . for safety sake, based on the experience of past years, we must get at least ten percent . . . the latter must be considered a minimum figure . . ."

"This guy's unbelievable," said the detective. "What the hell does he do, memorize all that. . .?" He smoothed down his mustache as though to clear a path for his voice. "Hey, old man! Hey!"

"Yes," said Addison, pausing before falling back into his recitation.

"Hey, I'm Detective Calhoun. Let's see your identification."

The old man's voice trailed off as he reached into his jacket pocket and handed his wallet to the officer. The detective frowned, then raised his brows over the cards and papers in the wallet.

"Mr. Blum," he said with great gentleness to the now silent man, "who do you want me to call?"

Addison nodded wearily. "Lou. Lou Rabin . . ."

When the party chairman arrived a half-hour afterwards, he strode directly to his friend, who was still seated on the bed, and put his hand on the man's shoulder. He listened incredulously to the detective's explanation, shook the woman's hand and Calhoun's, then said to the detective, "You've been very kind. I'm grateful. It's lucky I was home for your call; I've been at a television studio and I just came in the door when you called. I have a taxi waiting downstairs. I'll take my friend home with me. Do you mind, Mr. Calhoun, if I mention your kindness to certain people?"

The officer understood him. "I don't mind at all, Mr. Rabin."

In the taxi, seated beside his friend, Lou asked, "What is it Ad? Please tell me."

The little man looked at him blankly. "All the people who have suffered."

"Yes, I see."

"But always, Lou, there's always been the starvation and the torture and meannesses and women crying over dead babies . . ."

Lou reached out to touch him. "Come on, it's not good for you to think about all the depressing things."

"But did you ever think, did you ever realize the degree of suffering behind every door?"

"God forbid. Who should want to know all that? Now come on. You know what I think, I think you're having a crying jag. Only you're not crying."

"I want to murder."

Rabin moved back reflexively. The driver, too, stiffened.

"You? Now who are you going to murder?"

"I don't know . . ."

After a pause, Rabin said softly, "The policeman told me you really wanted to kill yourself. Ad, why would you do such a thing when we need you so much?" He sat up straight, removing his hand, taking command. "You're going to stay at my place a few days. I told Lottie to phone your wife and tell her both of us got a little drunk and you're staying with me tonight. I told her to call the doctor, too, and he'll be there later to give you something to help you sleep. I'll sit with you while you sleep. You're in my care."

"It's very black," said Blum.

"Yes, it is. Then we'll make it bright. For the weekend and for the next few days you're going to stay with me. No work for either of us. I won't even talk to anyone on the telephone."

Addison lifted his head and shook it from side to side, "There's so much work . . ."

"Our secretaries can do it better than we can."

Later when Addison was in bed, Lou Rabin said to his wife, "It's a shock, a horror, to see this happen to the oldest friend you have in the world."

She shrugged sadly. "Age. He's becoming senile, that's what it is."

"But he's coming out of it. I could tell before he fell asleep. He's becoming lucid again. I'll put him back to work in a day or two."

"It'll be a matter of time."

He chuckled grimly. "It'll be a matter of time for all of us. If you ever leave me, Lottie, I don't believe I'd want any more time for myself."

She held his hand. "It's silly to talk about such things like that. A lifetime of loving each other, that maybe we should talk about. That a woman enjoys talking about."

"No." He withdrew his hand gently. "I'm not so old that I want to dwell on the past. Believe it or not about your husband, but I have a future. Call it my swan song, but before they bury me I'm going to see that man in the White House . . ."

"Casey? We'll see, we'll see . . ."

"I feel for him sometimes like a son."

"You think that's a big secret in this town?"

"You know something, Lottie, about Casey. Never once has he been disrespectful to me."

"He wouldn't dare!" She was indignant. "Nobody has ever dared showed disrespect to you."

The party leader smiled. "Oh, there have been a few. You haven't personally met Shelley Greenfield, have you? Casey's capable of it, don't fool yourself. He's an arrogant man. But he's always deferred to me or he's at least been tactful." Rabin nodded decisively. "You know something—I like a man who's respectful to me and good to his wife."

They heard a low moan from the bedroom.

"I'll go in now and sit with him a while," Lou said softly. "You'll see, he's going to be fine."

TWENTY-FOUR

〜〜〜〜〜〜〜〜〜〜〜〜〜〜〜〜〜〜〜

O N the morning of Election Day, Bernardo Rodriguez and fifteen of his friends, male and female, entered Grover Cleveland Hospital in the Puerto Rican section of the city. Bernardo did not have to ask directions at the reception desk. He had visited and mapped the hospital on previous days. Though the young woman receptionist tried to stop him, he and his friends hurried past, up the stairs to the third floor, and stopped in the Pediatrics Division, where they barged into the administrator's office.

"Dr. Morris Cohen?" Rodriguez asked the chubby man seated at the desk.

"Yes. What are you people doing in here?"

"We're taking over," said Bernardo with a smile. "We are the Young People's Army and we are dismissing you from your post and replacing you with a Puerto Rican doctor."

"What are you talking about, you crazy man?"

"Do you have a woman doctor who is Puerto Rican on your staff, Doctor Cohen?"

"Yes, yes."

"We know about her." Rodriguez waved his group into the room and shut the door. "She's going to be moved up to your position. You —you are going out."

The doctor reached for the telephone. "We'll see what the police have to say about this."

Rodriguez pointed at him. "Think twice, old man. You want a big fuss and all the newspapers and television stations here? You see this man behind me?" He gestured toward Bill Sokolov, who hovered in the background. "He's a newspaper reporter who's very interested in the treatment given to us community people. We are not going to leave your office until this hospital replaces you, initiates door-to-door preventive health care in the community and grants all Puerto Rican orderlies a minimum wage of a hundred and forty dollars a week. I think you'd better talk this over first with the man who's in charge of the hospital before you call the police."

Dr. Cohen looked at him with visible trembling anger, then rose from his desk and made his way out of the room past the unfriendly visitors. When he was gone, Rodriguez sat in the doctor's chair and put his feet up on the desk.

"Hey, man," one of his cohorts asked, "how'd you know he wouldn't call the police?"

Bernardo twisted his face into an elaborately pained expression. "They don't like to make a fuss. Those people just don't like to make a fuss. Settle in, boys and girls. We're here for a long stay . . ."

His mother had insisted on being present at his headquarters tonight to listen to the election returns. She sat like a lump and frowned disapprovingly at almost everything he said and did. Considering the way the numbers seemed to be going in favor of Buzz

Taylor, she was the last person he needed with him. He looked away from her with disgust as Jimmy came in with election figures in his hand. Simmons glanced at him. "The same?"

Jimmy shook his head dolefully. "Any next of kin you want me to notify?"

He was startled by Simmons' flaring anger. "What the hell are you joking about?"

"I'm sorry, Hank. Christ, I didn't mean—"

"I'm going to get that son of a bitch," Simmons hissed between his teeth.

"Who?" the young aide asked timidly.

"Bohland. I'm going to mess up that bastard's Presidential ambitions and cabinet ambitions and state ambitions if it's the last thing I do. He killed me. He went out in the streets and told them to stick with Corbett—"

"Blame Lou Rabin for that."

"Rabin, too, that lousy bastard."

"Hank, how about a drink or something?"

"Leave me alone. Get the hell out. Come on, leave me alone."

His mother, tight-lipped, was staring at him and he scowled back at her. Suddenly she was out of her chair. Sometimes Mrs. Simmons was able to remind her son that she was a woman of some grace, some breeding, notwithstanding his conviction that she was monumentally stupid. The way she got up from a chair, as she did now, almost effortlessly, which was startling, considering her bulk, created an entirely new picture of the woman. The oddness registered in his consciousness only for a few seconds; then he told himself it was probably a trick they taught her in the defunct finishing school she'd attended God-knows-when. Yet her technique of rising from a chair and a few other inconsequential acts invariably served to disconcert him long enough for her to say or do something that flanked his defenses and caused him anguish. She seemed to know that there was an advantage in speaking and moving at the same moment. This time she said a terrible thing, getting past his defenses with a real wallop.

"Henry, dear," she said, halfway through her fluid ballet, "I wish you didn't have to boss people and force yourself on them.

You always seem to be forcing yourself on everybody. Not only buying them, but insisting that they listen to you and like you."

"*What?*" He turned crimson and she thought he was going to cry. "Do you know something?" he finally blurted out. "You're *crazy.* You're absolutely *insane.*"

Now she, too, was furious. "Don't you dare talk to me that way!"

"No, no, no, no!" he raged. "Don't *you* dare. How could you say that I force myself on people? People voted for me, don't you realize that? They did it willingly. I'm an elected official, don't you know that?"

"Oh, Henry, you bought that seat in the House and you know it as well as I do." The stout woman stood adamantly, with her legs somewhat farther apart than usual, as if braced for attack. "Yes, I do object to the whole concept of *buying* an election, buying up everybody who can help you get the nomination, like your own party leaders, then saturating the neighborhood with posters and paying off the newsmen, and all those spot commercials on the television just like toothpaste advertising."

He walked about the room, shaking his head. "Mother, you don't know what the hell you're talking about! You just don't understand politics. You've got to fight if you want to get elected. Money's the best weapon you can have. Christ, Mother, don't be so goddam naive. People have to be conditioned—yes, just like dogs. You've got to pound your name into their heads and pound it and pound it, until they begin to think they really know you and you've done great things for them. I don't give a shit if they like me, as long as they vote for me. You think I care about people liking me? Mother, I want you to go home. Now. This is going to be one of the worst nights of my life and I don't need any more aggravation . . ."

On the day after the election, Governor Wilkerson, who had won handily in his bid for an additional term, telephoned Casey Bohland

and arranged for a private meeting that day at the Mayor's residence. They sat facing each other in the oak-beamed study of the Mayor's mansion. Wilkerson seemed grim and tired and rather sad.

"We'll probably never have a chance to talk again like this," he said. "At least I don't think I'll ever have the impulse to do this again. But before we stop communicating with each other altogether, Casey, I want to know once and for all what it is that makes you tick."

Bohland was mildly surprised at the Governor's earnestness. He shrugged and looked at him calmly. "Do you think I'm so complicated, Warren?"

"I want to know what happened, why you became such an ingrate. No, that's too gentle a word for it. When you consider that the first time you ran for mayor I offered you not only the hand of Republican friendship and support but also considerable money—which you were glad to take—then I think your behavior toward me over the past few years and your endorsement of Ornstein—"

"Did that upset you very much, Warren?"

Wilkerson wagged his head. "See, it's beyond understanding how you can treat a broken promise so lightly. You did promise me you wouldn't endorse Ornstein, don't you remember?"

"Vaguely." Casey leaned forward. "Are you saying that because you once gave me money you have the right to expect loyalty for life?"

"Just one second, Casey. I said friendship and money and support. My support was crucial, I would say. All I'm asking you is whether in most human relationships past favors are so easily shrugged off and forgotten. I never said you have to belong to me just because I gave you some money. I never made that kind of claim on you. What I want to know is what caused you to think of me as your enemy."

Casey blinked. "You're my natural enemy, Warren."

"Apparently. But why?"

"You're the Governor. I'm the Mayor. And as the Mayor, I have to line up every year and beg you for favors for my city. That makes you my enemy."

"Your real enemy or your public-image enemy? Do you mean it or are you just using me as a foil in order to throw your name into the public eye?"

Casey gave the question a moment's thought. "Both."

"Is that why you've denied that I ever gave you any money?"

The barest smile etched itself around the handsome lips. "No, let me ask you a question, Warren. Why did you give me the money—so that I would admit it afterwards?"

"What difference? The thing is you deny it and you know your denial is false."

"I deny the strings that came with it," Bohland said flatly.

"There were no strings. I didn't set any conditions."

Casey's eyes widened. "Public gratitude, that's a condition. The implied role of protégé, that's a condition."

"All right, all right, what's wrong with those things? Hell, there's nothing immoral in gratitude or even the idea that you're something of a protégé." The famous eyebrow quirked. "Now I never said anything about gratitude and protégé; you did. But even if these things are implied, what the hell's wrong with them?"

Bohland rubbed his eyes and folded his hands under his chin. "If I had allowed that relationship to exist, then it would have become impossible for me publicly to kick you in the teeth."

"That's my question. Why did you have to kick me in the teeth?"

"Because I couldn't afford to owe you anything or be your friend or your protégé or your son or your second fiddle or anything like that, Warren. That just couldn't be. Now that I've endorsed Ornstein I'll never have a chance to do or be anything in the Republican Party . . ."

"You can say that again!" the Governor expostulated.

The younger man nodded. "I was dead in the Republican Party anyway and you know it. But I didn't think that way a year ago and before that. I thought I could go to the White House riding an elephant. And I always figured that when the time came for me to ride past you on the way to Washington, I didn't want the public and our own party leaders telling me, 'Oh, no, Casey, it's not your turn to move up; it's Wilkerson's turn. After all, he's been like a father to you; and you're so young, after all, so you can move up *after* he's served his two terms in the presidency.' " The Mayor shook his head. "If you and I seemed to be in the same family, Warren, like father and son, then you were in the way."

The Governor spoke sourly in a gravelly voice. "I have no more ambitions for the presidency. Three times out is enough."

Bohland declined to respond to the remark. "Warren," he went on, "let's face it: you are, as I said, my natural enemy. Even though I'll probably leave the party, I can't afford to love you publicly or be indebted to you. You're the Governor—"

"I know, I know, and you're the Mayor. In one thing I agree, there'll be no public love between us, or private love either. But you have in the past exaggerated the differences between us on the professional level." Wilkerson sighed. He seemed to have access today to a reservoir of reasonableness. "I understand that to an extent some mayors may feel a little oppressed and resentful of their governors. It's true you always have to come around asking for what you need, you have to petition for it. But in a way I do the same thing with regard to the Washington boys; I have to petition them for what the state needs. But I don't hate the President just because he's holding the purse strings. I do what I can do."

"You don't do enough," Bohland said blandly. "And if you did hate the President perhaps you'd be able to do more for the state. You've got to personalize things. The administration in Washington isn't the villain, the President's the villain."

"That's just my point—"

"No, that's my point, Warren. I personalize everything. That's my style. And some years ago I elected you as my nearest villain."

Wilkerson stared at him with amazement. "You're an incredible person. How can you just sit there so calmly and say such an offensive thing?"

"I just said it. It's easy."

"I see." The Governor scratched his ear. "And all this time you expected me to lay back and take it. You expected me always to be Mr. Nice Guy, while you behaved in the rudest and most boorish—"

"No, I don't expect you to be Mr. Nice Guy. Certainly not now. Before you leave here today you're going to threaten to ruin me. I've heard something about your plans to show me up as a poor administrator and that kind of stuff. I expect you to start acting like the villain I always portrayed you to be."

Wilkerson looked down at his hands. "It's with some reluctance,

Casey, that I accept such a role. But you're right. This city is a mess, and I can't allow you to separate yourself from all the things that are wrong with it. They're going to be hung around your neck for all the country to see . . ."

The Mayor smiled. "Warren, you subscribe to that old theory that once someone gets bogged down or identified with the problems of this city he can never go anywhere else up the ladder, that this town historically eats up politicians like the proverbial dragon."

"Is that what I think?" Warren asked mildly, no longer earnest.

"Yes, I think that's what you think—because you're an unimaginative man who depends on polls, and I'm sure you depend just as rigidly on history as well."

"Oh, I'm unimaginative."

"Certainly, Warren. You must know that about yourself by this time."

Wilkerson chuckled. "Well, by this time I know you're capable of saying anything. That much I've learned. But please go on, fella. How are you going to defeat the dragon? How are you going to get out of the city alive?"

"Wrong question," said Casey. "The question is how am I going to keep the city alive. It's the city that's dying, you know."

"Yes, indeed I know it. And what I'm going to have to do—reluctantly, mind you, very reluctantly—is show the country that you have something to do with the process. In fact I may have to spend the next few years doing that kind of thing, Casey."

"Warren, I always expected you to react in this way."

"Then I won't disappoint you," said the Governor. "I'm going to destroy the image of urban leadership you've been trying to build for yourself nationally. I'm going to show you to be an inept administrator, I'm going to expose corruption within your city government, I'm going to set up commissions and study groups to look into every aspect of city administration and turn over every rock—"

Casey held up his hand. "I get the picture."

"Fine. But you haven't answered the question you posed. How *are* you going to keep the city alive?"

"I probably won't," said the Mayor blandly. "All the big cities are dying, so I can't really be blamed. I'm not even going to worry about it. The death of all the cities in this country is going to become my greatest asset. It's an old adage in the advertising business, Warren: make a liability into an asset. I'm going to talk about the plight of the cities and talk about it and talk about it. A dying city is going to be my showpiece for the nation."

"Don't be silly, Casey. You're just as worried about the city's condition as any one of us."

"True. I don't want it to die. Certainly not yet. Not while I'm Mayor. But I don't lose any sleep, because it's dying anyway. In a few years it's going to be another Newark. You know it and I know it. And *you're* the one who loses sleep over it, Warren."

"What do you mean?"

Bohland smiled. "You know what I mean. You're the one who owns blocks and blocks of real estate in this town. Your brother's the one who owns a couple of banks in this town. Me—I'm free and clear. The city is your problem, Governor, not mine. Haven't you heard? I'm moving to Washington or the State House, one or the other."

TWENTY-FIVE

"LATELY I've read some damaging publicity about you Progressives," said the wealthy man who did not know whether to contribute to the party's fund-raising committee and had asked for a private audience here at the union office. "Do you think the party is really as democratic as it should be?"

"Yes, I do," said Lou Rabin.

The smooth-faced man smiled. He was in his fifties, but somehow no lines marked his countenance. "That was a stupid way for me to phrase the question. What I mean is whether the party is truly as democratic as the reformers, like Assemblyman Greenfield, say it should be."

"Then the answer is no," said Rabin. "There has got to be some control. Otherwise you haven't got a party. Especially with a small organization, you can't afford to let it go wild."

"Wild means democratic."

"Everything is a matter of degree. Look what happened to the

Democratic Party. Idiocy. They're doing everything by primaries, they stifle all leadership, and what have they got? They had the most unbalanced ticket any party has ever run in political history."

"Jews and a black and all from the city, you mean."

"Sure. That's pure idiocy, isn't it? But that's the kind of thing the Democrats are proud of, and look at the condition of their forces. They're the most disarrayed, fractionated, broke—"

"So you are what they say you are. A party boss."

Rabin stiffened. "Don't call me that word, please. I give leadership; I never boss. We have as much democracy in our State Committee and our Advisory Commitee as the members want to have. They can vote any way they want on any issue. They choose to respect and rely on their leaders, or at least on our recommendations. If we failed them, they wouldn't rely on us for long. We serve them, we don't fail them."

The questioner made a gesture of appreciation.

"You are certainly to be credited," he said, "with political instinct and acumen. You're probably one of the best political minds in the country. Or maybe you've just been lucky."

"There is certainly an element of luck," Rabin admitted.

"Yes, I don't buy this genius stuff."

"I assure you, I don't either."

"But you must have perpetuated the idea."

"Wrong," said Lou. "I think it's terrible that people think you always have to be right, that *I* always have to be right. That would inhibit me too much. I should have as much opportunity to make mistakes as the next man."

The wealthy man digested this, then smiled again.

"No, I don't believe you," he said. "You think you're right most of the time or all of the time. Else you wouldn't have the nerve to lead so strongly. But you've done very well. Still, you're only a small party . . ."

"We never said we wanted to be a big party."

"Then it is true that you've actually discouraged enrollment. You don't throw out a net for new enrollees, you don't recruit, you don't proselytize, the way other parties do."

"Why should we?"

"To grow."

The chairman's face showed his disinterest in such an end. "We want new enrollees, but we're selective. We need young smart people, but we don't like the New Left types at all . . ."

"What about blacks?"

"Not too many. They're not a loyal people, they're not smart, they're not good party workers. All they'd want to do, if they came into the party in any number, would be to take it over. The same thing with the Puerto Ricans. They'd form a dissident group along with the blacks and the commies, they'd establish voting blocs, they'd fight the establishment, which means the leaders . . . bah, who needs all that?" Suddenly he pointed his finger at the man. "Now don't get me wrong. We serve the blacks and the Spanish-speaking people and we have great compassion for them. You know how we work on their behalf. Everyone knows our position on these matters. But party organization and morale are entirely different from platforms. We want to keep a certain class of membership."

The wealthy man looked at the party leader. "I like your answers," he said. "You're an honest man. I suppose that's why so many people have decided to trust you with leadership. And I like the way you don't pretend to love everyone. Who do I make out the check to . . .?"

"Look here, Rodriguez, you've been here three days already and you're putting us all in a very awkward position. I want you to clear out your people so we can resolve this problem behind the scenes, out of the public view."

Bernardo Rodriguez shook his head and grinned at the tall and rather attractive black woman who bore the impressive title of the city's Commissioner of Human Affairs and the impressive salary that went with it. Naida Slaughter was impervious to his charm. "Out," she said, pointing to the open door of the doctor's office. "You're violating Dr. Cohen's rights."

"No, he's violating our rights! This is a Puerto Rican community. We want that Jew doctor out and we want a Puerto Rican doctor put in charge of the Pediatrics Division."

The Commissioner glared at him and the members of the Young People's Army. "You can't talk that way. A Jew has as much right—"

"And so do we." Rodriguez stepped forward arrogantly. "We're throwing him out whether you approve or not."

Naida Slaughter spoke with a pained expression. "Don't you see that you're causing a polarization problem? The Mayor wants to avoid this kind of conflict."

"That's fine. But we're not moving. Look, Miss Slaughter—Commissioner—you can ease the old Jew out and you can make sure there's no polarization or any crap like that."

She sighed. "That's easier said than done. There are a lot of groups complaining about your actions here. They point out that Dr. Cohen has his human rights just as well as anybody else." She blew out her breath. "Oh, damn, here come the reporters. Rodriguez, please, you're putting the Mayor on the spot. He doesn't want to refuse the Puerto Rican community some representation—"

"He'd better not," said Bernardo.

Bill Sokolov, along with a black reporter from the major black weekly and a reporter from the Spanish-language daily, greeted them. Sokolov spoke to her directly.

"Commissioner, we understand the city is asking the pediatrics chief of this hospital to step down to be replaced by a doctor who speaks the language of this community."

Naida Slaughter was startled by the directness of the question and the implied point of view the reporter intended to pursue.

"The city is looking into the situation," she said carefully.

"What about the accusation that there are political aspects to Dr. Cohen's removal and an ethnic bias in your decision?" Sokolov asked.

Repressing her anger at the reporter's handling the ouster as a *fait accompli* and his insistence on driving her into a corner, she replied snappishly.

"We're not sure how this problem will be resolved. But we have come to the conclusion that the possible removal of Dr. Morris Cohen has nothing whatever to do with political or ethnic considerations. As you know, the doctors in this hospital are supplied by the Zion Medical College, which has shown itself to be sloppy in its administration of the hospital's personnel needs. A situation has been created by the poor service to the community that, in turn, has resulted in community resentment and ultimately in increasingly deteriorating care for the patients who depend upon this medical facility. Health service has suffered in this hospital as a direct result of poor supervision by the college and a growing callousness toward the needs of the community. The doctor may have to go, but ethnic considerations have nothing—"

"Then there is definitely no ethnic motivation in the proposed changeover?" asked the Puerto Rican newsman.

"Definitely not," said the Commissioner, closing her eyes.

After the reporters left, Bernardo smiled at the woman who stood with a grim frown on her face.

"Hey, you're good," he said. "You told it in just the right way. Now I know why you're a Commissioner."

Henry Simmons lay back against his pillow and pushed aside the breakfast tray.

"You just don't understand." He glared at his mother who sat beside his bed. "Rabin didn't just want me to lose so that Corbett could win. He knew Corbett couldn't win. He wanted me to lose because he didn't want me to be the leader of the Democratic Party in this state."

"You would have been the leader of the party?"

"If I won, of course! I'd be the highest public official in the state. But he didn't want me to be. That's why he and Bohland were so strong behind Corbett at the end, the bastards."

Lucille Simmons shook her head patiently. "I don't know if that's true, Henry. As Mr. Rabin himself said in the newspapers just the other day, how could he not support his own candidate?"

"Mother, what's the matter with you? Do you believe what that man says?" Simmons did not conceal his disgust at such naivete. "Let me explain. He and Casey Bohland want to take over the Democratic Party, do you understand? I mean, the party's leaderless in this state, it's a wreck. The public doesn't even know how feeble we are right now. And that's just the way they want it. Because Casey Bohland now thinks he can offer what the party needs, a strong leader."

"But he's a Republican."

"He's going to change parties. Mother, listen, if this is too complicated and Machiavellian for you, I assure you it's not too complicated for Lou Rabin. That son of a bitch!"

"Now, dear, please don't get agitated. And I don't want you to forget you're still in the House of Representatives," she consoled. "After all, it's not as though you're completely out—"

"I'm *lost* in the House!" He rubbed his eyes vigorously. "I'm lost in a cast of thousands!"

"You won't be there forever. Didn't you say you might run for governor next time?"

"That's four years away."

"Well, you said it about running, not me."

"I know, I know. But I have no patience. I think I'm going out of my mind. And that's what those sons of bitches Bohland and Rabin are after—the governorship. I'll never be rid of them. I'm telling you, Mother, they're going to haunt me the rest of my life. You can bet your eyeteeth that I'll be up against them four years from now."

"I thought Mr. Bohland is interested in the Presidency."

Simmons made a face. "He'll try for it, but he won't get near it. He's going to leave the Republicans and then follow me to my grave. Picture it, mother. I'm going to be up against him in the gubernatorial primary—*of my own party.* Can you imagine that? I feel like crying all over again. I tell you, I'll never be rid of those bastards, both of them . . ."

It was an excellent stage musical, and as they emerged from the theater on Saturday afternoon, Shelley boasted of his prowess in obtaining the tickets.

"In other words, you're fantastic," said Barbara.

"That's the idea." He stretched his arm around her and hugged her as they walked in the thin autumn sunlight. "Do you realize that this is a red-letter day?"

"I sure do. You finally let me out of the bed."

He nodded vigorously. "That's right, that's right. And here I am walking with you. In public."

"Wow."

"Question," he said. "Should a superior white man be out walking and theater-going with an inferior black girl?"

"Conclusion," she said. "Drop dead."

"Barbara, you must be honest. You've got to admit that my appeal to you is that I'm white and superior. That's part of the whole picture of sexual submission. You would have been happy as a slave, you know that?"

She chuckled and skipped a step to match her cadence to his. "Oh, boy, and would you have loved being master of the old plantation!"

"That's true. How come you and I never tried the whipping scene? It's a natural, for us."

"No, thank you, Mr. Assemblyman."

"No, really . . ."

"I said 'No, thank you.' Just whip me with that thing you got, that's good enough for me."

"You can tell, huh?" He threw back his head to laugh. "Then you know I'm using it to hurt you?"

"You do, man. And you sure like to talk about this stuff."

He tightened his hold. "I want us to understand each other."

"Okay. You be master, I be slave."

"Maybe you're all I deserve," he mused. "After all, what am I? A Jew, a lawyer, an orphan, a great Assemblyman . . . Maybe I deserve a lesser being like you."

"You are despicable!" she said.

"But on your part," he went on, "the act of fornication is an elevating experience. You're in love with a superior white being. You've reached the heights."

"Jesus, you are unbelievable!"

"I certainly am," he said in a lower octave, "because I've got feelings for you I didn't think I could have for anybody. But don't get any big ideas. You're not going to destroy me. I'm going to destroy you before you can do it to me. *Nobody* destroys me."

"I don't know what you're talking about, Shelley."

He looked up at the clear sky showing between the skyscrapers and nodded sagely. "I think God has finally figured out what my punishment's going to be."

Lou Rabin called an evening meeting of the party staff in the conference room a week after the election to review the outcome and to impart organizational plans.

"We didn't win," he said, "but unlike the Democrats, we don't always lose; sometimes we do win. The Democrats didn't do a thing for their statewide candidates; we did all the work. They're a very divided party.

"In the beginning we had trouble, we had doubts about David Ornstein. As the campaign developed, however, our respect for Ornstein increased.

"In Corbett we nominated a good man. It didn't take us long to realize his own party had deserted him. We were there to support him, but without his own people behind him there was no chance for him." He looked about the room. "Have any of you been getting calls blaming us for having split the vote and electing Buzz Taylor?"

One of the new organizers said he had received such calls.

"And you explain," asked Rabin, "that it would have been immoral for us to have deserted our candidate?"

"Yes, I explain all that to them."

"Good." The chairman stroked his chin. "I realize that some people are disturbed and blame us in part for having put a conservative into the Senate. But in all honesty. I must say, in the immortal words of Jack Valenti, that I sleep better at night knowing Simmons is in the House of Representatives.

"All in all, it was a very difficult election year as we anticipated, but we avoided calamity. Addison and I will review the figures that have finally come down from the Commissioner of State and we'll give you the breakdowns county by county later in the week. What we have to concern ourselves with now is the future.

"In the next year or two," he said energetically, "we'll be building a progressive movement. This won't be along assembly district lines. We'll build little branches, neighborhood branches . . . in homes. These are not going to be political clubs, and this will have nothing to do with the legal structure of the party." His expression showed second thought. "Of course if you build up strength in a neighborhood, that helps when it comes to getting people for petition-signing work . . .

"A Speakers Bureau!" he continued enthusiastically. "We'll have people come to homes to hear speakers on given subjects."

"But, Lou, where are these speakers going to come from?" asked Milt Holloway. "Will you and Ad be available?"

"Certainly," said the chairman. "I don't care if there are only five or six people in a group . . . we'll make ourselves available. The party has a whole list of good speakers. Don't forget, Milt, we've got lots of men in city government who are experts in what their departments take care of. We have a top man in Corrections to talk about prisons; we have judges to discuss crime; we have experts in consumer problems."

"Sounds good," said Milt, "as long as these people really make themselves available."

Lou Rabin held up his hand in assurance. "Leave that to me. You'll be given a copy of the speakers list. We want to build about a hundred small clubs like this around the city. These are not to be clubhouses in any political sense. I want us to think of this as a social-intellectual movement . . ."

Milt Holloway smiled to himself as Rabin went on. A hundred clubs! A hundred flowers will blossom! What the hell was the old man talking about? He'd be lucky if he could keep five or six clubs active in the whole state. Did he think this was the old days before television, and perhaps even before radio, when Jews from the Old Country met in each other's homes and in schools to hear what they used to fondly call "lectures," followed by tea and sponge cake? Didn't he realize that all those old people who made up the rank and file, even those still enrolled, had deserted the party and the ideas of liberalism long, long ago? He looked at the old warhorse and he knew that Rabin knew and wanted the knowledge hidden. Milt was relieved when the telephone on the desk outside the conference room rang, demanding attention; he went to answer it. The call was for Lou— Sylvia Lazarus. The chairman rose and proceeded in a sprightly, soldierly walk out of the room to pick up the telephone receiver.

"Hey, Rabin," she said, "I wanted to call you to tell you to go screw yourself."

He let out his breath. "Mrs. Lazarus, let me first congratulate you on your victory, a victory you unfortunately had to win without our help. And as for our endorsement, I want to assure you I did everything I could—"

"Rabin."

"Mrs. Lazarus, please believe me—"

"Rabin. Screw you, Rabin."

Whereupon the Congresswoman-elect hung up.

Later in the evening Lou and Addison sat alone in the executive secretary's office and analyzed the election figures the Commissioner of State had mailed to them. They sat side by side at Blum's wide desk and clucked and groaned over the numbers.

"Ad, when you put all the facts together, we didn't do badly," said Lou Rabin finally. "We survived."

"Not badly at all, Lou; I think you're right about that." Addison Blum shifted the long printed sheets and the handwritten pages on his desk. "See, here's our total for our gubernatorial entry, about two hundred and thirty thousand. Now that's just about our usual. We can't compare this with the campaign four years ago, because we ran an independent then, and the enormous vote we got for Casey last year was a freak. So this is our usual number."

Rabin was sour. "Well, yes, it's respectable. But we didn't get back Line C. We're still fourth on the ballot."

"Oh, we knew that was going to happen. In a conservative year we did fine."

Lou smiled reluctantly. "All right, let's remember that for everybody we talk to—we did fine. You know" —playfully he punched his old friend on the shoulder— "we could have really rolled up a good vote if it had't been for all that switch-to-Simmons business that cost us so many last-minute people."

"Yes, but that's part of the picture," Blum said pedantically, peering at his notes; very much his old self, Lou was happy to observe. "When we say 'all things considered,' we mean that, too. All in all, we came out with our scalps intact."

"And with our honor," Lou offered, glancing aside at Addison, wondering how long their secret would remain between the two of them, whether there would be relapses . . . He would have to keep a vigilant eye on his old friend, he noted to himself. Then he had an odd thought. Who, he mused, was there to keep an eye on Lou Rabin?